ST[illegible]IA QUEST

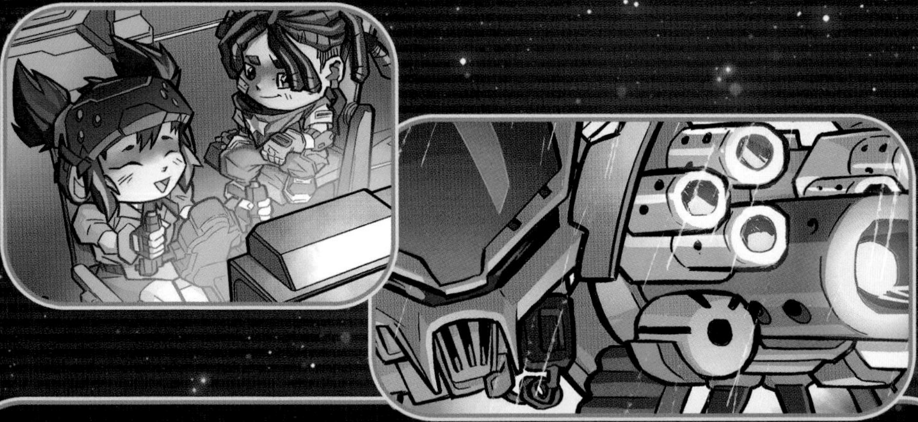

WRITTEN BY
JAMES ROBERTS

ART BY
AURELIO MAZZARA

COLORS BY
DAVID GARCIA CRUZ

LETTERS BY
ANDWORLD DESIGNS

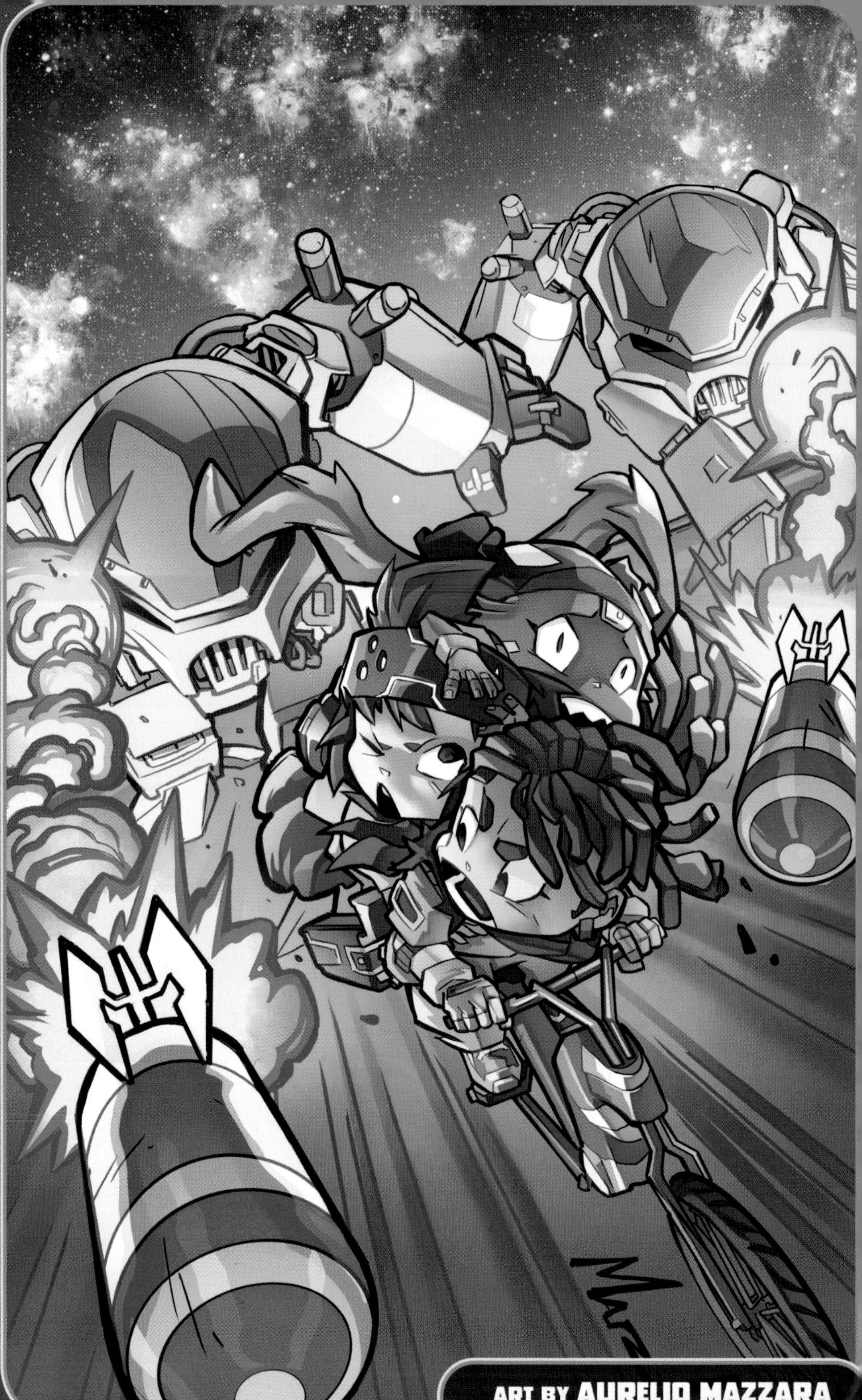

ART BY AURELIO MAZZARA
COLORS BY DAVID GARCIA CRUZ

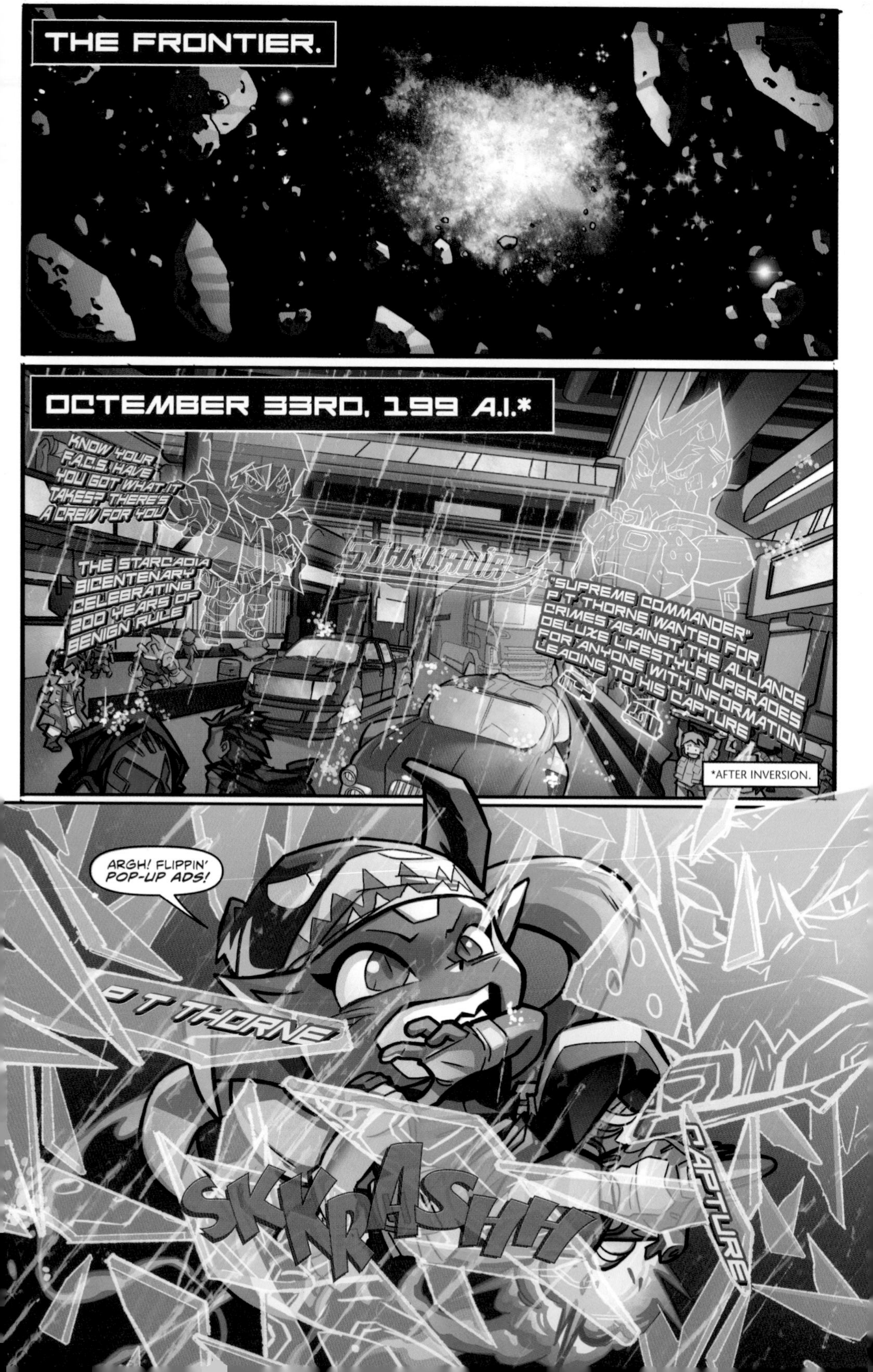
THE FRONTIER.
OCTEMBER 33RD, 199 A.I.*
KNOW YOUR F.A.C.S. HAVE YOU GOT WHAT IT TAKES? THERE'S A CREW FOR YOU
THE STARCADIA BICENTENARY CELEBRATING 200 YEARS OF BENIGN RULE
STARCADIA
"SUPREME COMMANDER" P T THORNE WANTED FOR CRIMES AGAINST THE ALLIANCE DELUXE LIFESTYLE UPGRADES FOR ANYONE WITH INFORMATION LEADING TO HIS CAPTURE
*AFTER INVERSION.
ARGH! FLIPPIN' POP-UP ADS!
P T THORNE
CAPTURE
SKKRASHH

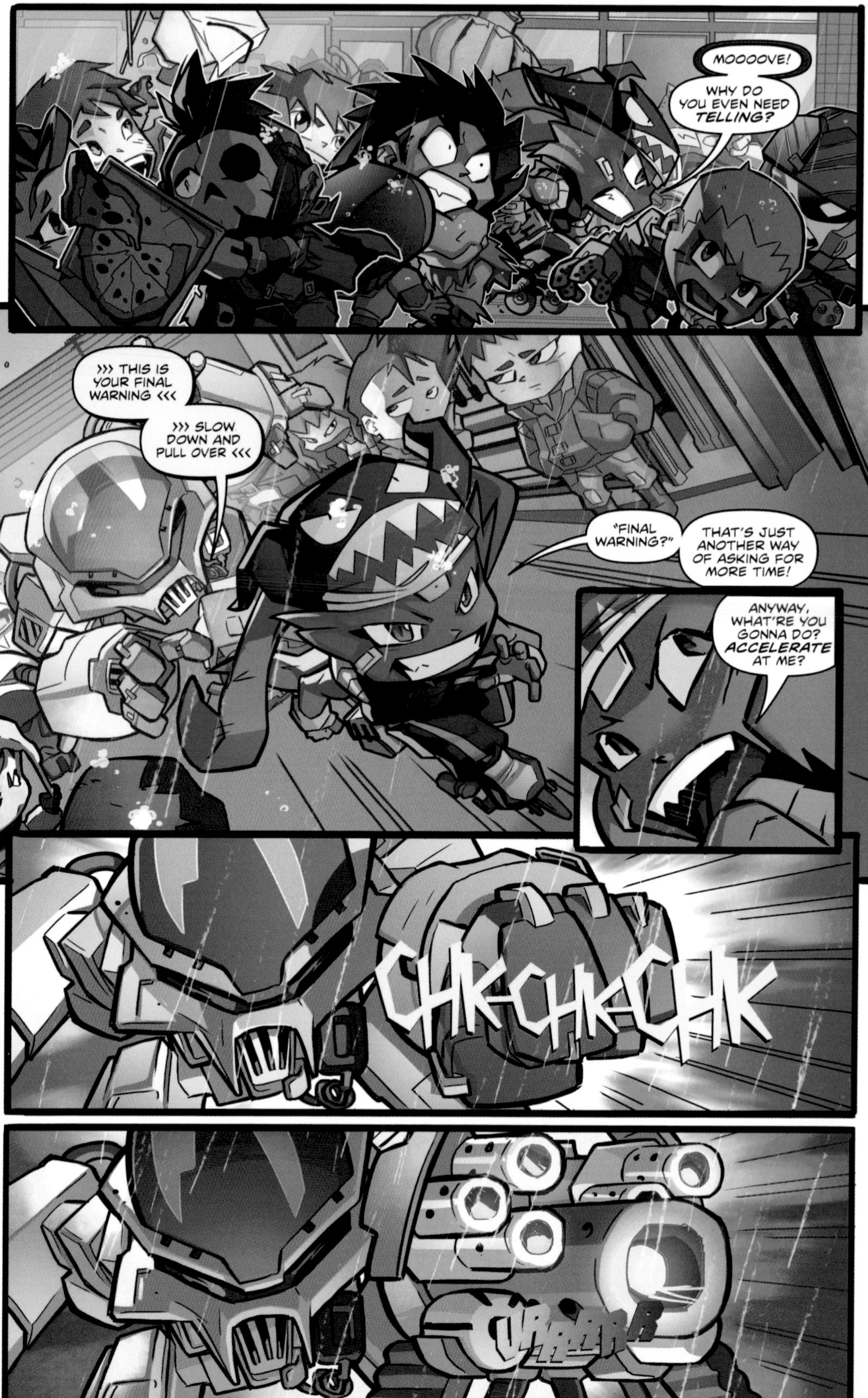
MOOOOVE!
WHY DO YOU EVEN NEED *TELLING?*
>>> THIS IS YOUR FINAL WARNING <<<
>>> SLOW DOWN AND PULL OVER <<<
"FINAL WARNING?"
THAT'S JUST ANOTHER WAY OF ASKING FOR MORE TIME!
ANYWAY, WHAT'RE YOU GONNA DO? *ACCELERATE* AT ME?
CHK-CHK-CHK

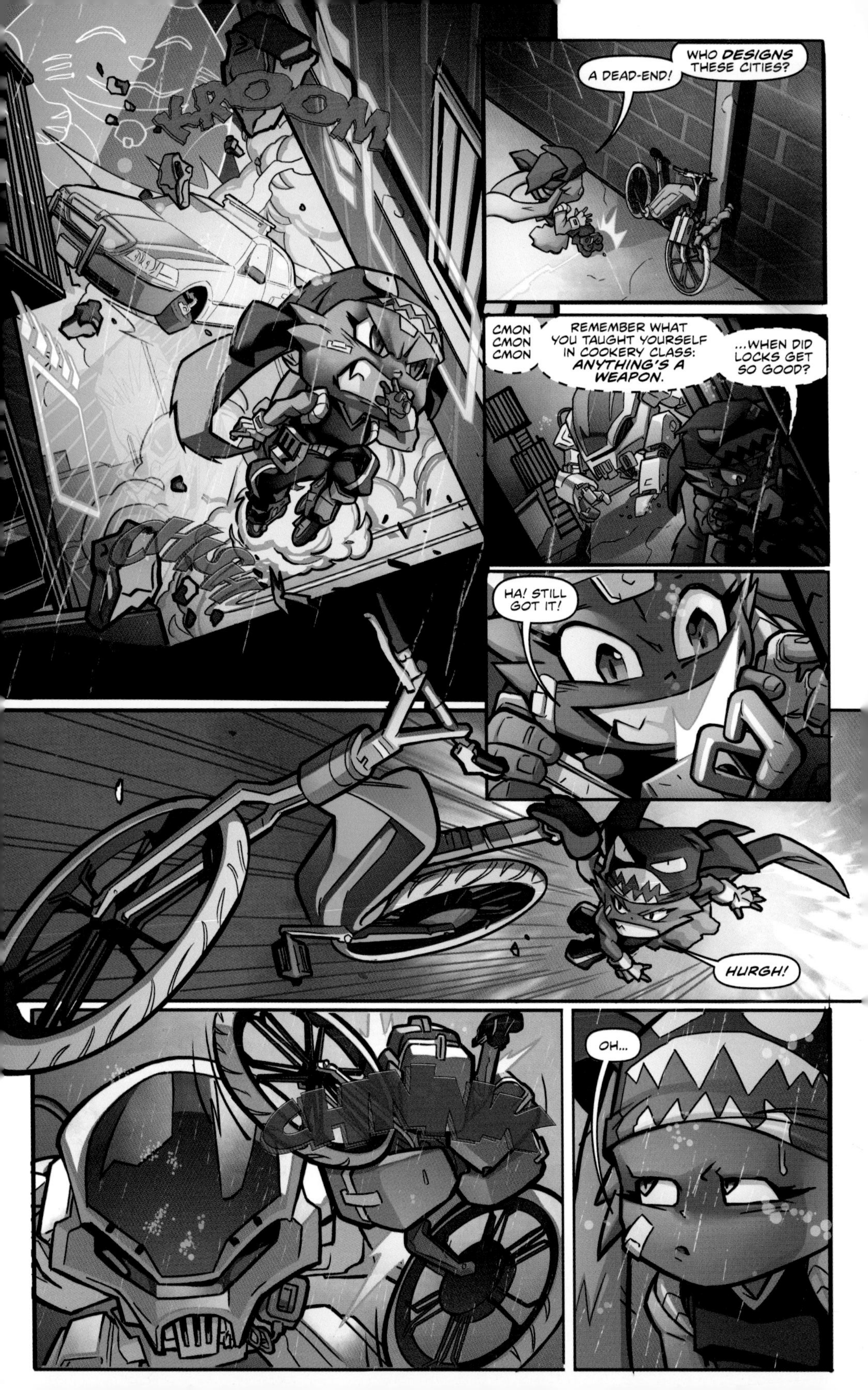
KRAOOM
A DEAD-END!
WHO DESIGNS THESE CITIES?
CMON CMON CMON
REMEMBER WHAT YOU TAUGHT YOURSELF IN COOKERY CLASS: ANYTHING'S A WEAPON.
...WHEN DID LOCKS GET SO GOOD?
HA! STILL GOT IT!
HURGH!
OH...

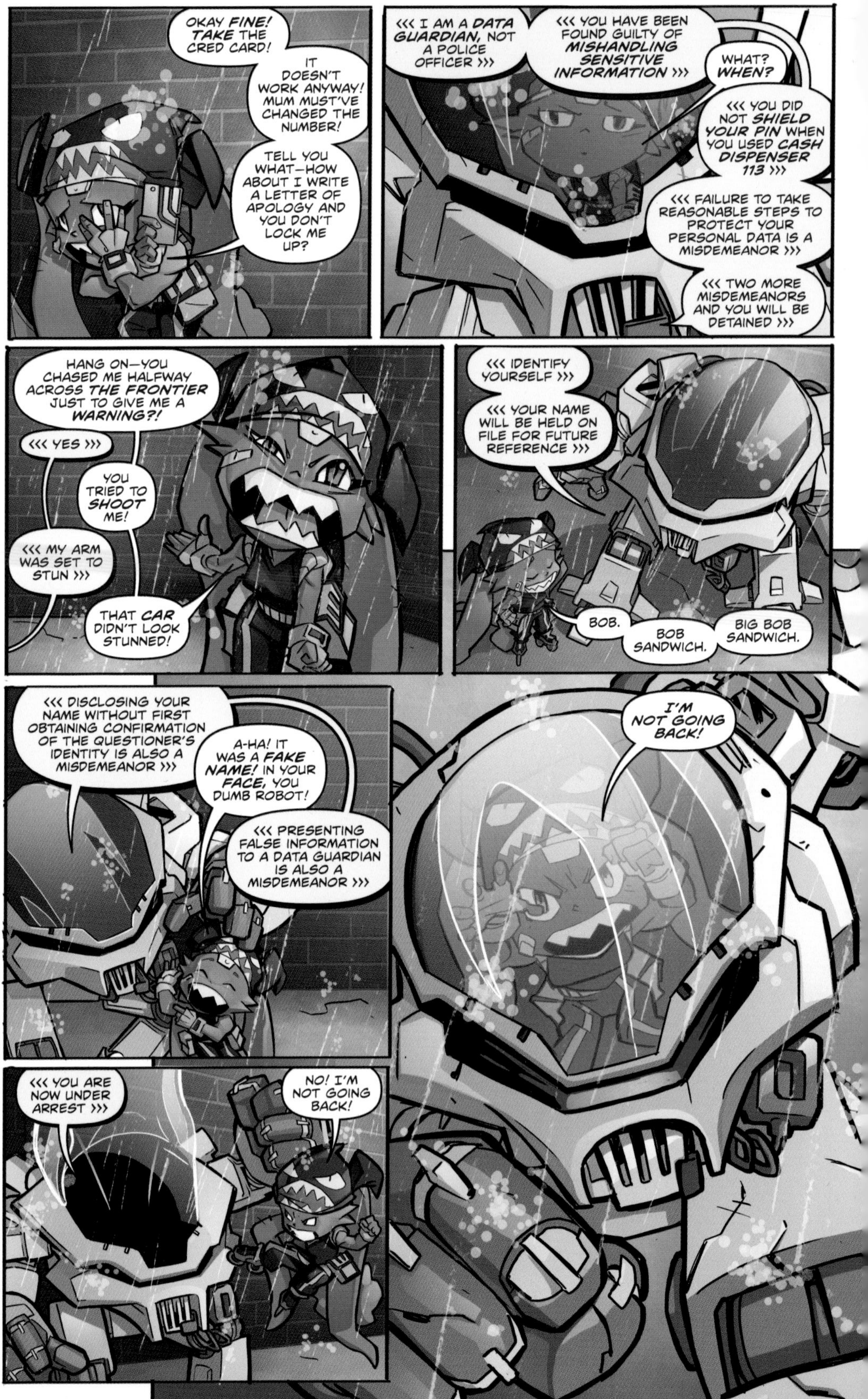

OKAY FINE! TAKE THE CRED CARD!
IT DOESN'T WORK ANYWAY! MUM MUST'VE CHANGED THE NUMBER!
TELL YOU WHAT—HOW ABOUT I WRITE A LETTER OF APOLOGY AND YOU DON'T LOCK ME UP?
<<< I AM A DATA GUARDIAN, NOT A POLICE OFFICER >>>
<<< YOU HAVE BEEN FOUND GUILTY OF MISHANDLING SENSITIVE INFORMATION >>>
WHAT? WHEN?
<<< YOU DID NOT SHIELD YOUR PIN WHEN YOU USED CASH DISPENSER 113 >>>
<<< FAILURE TO TAKE REASONABLE STEPS TO PROTECT YOUR PERSONAL DATA IS A MISDEMEANOR >>>
<<< TWO MORE MISDEMEANORS AND YOU WILL BE DETAINED >>>
HANG ON—YOU CHASED ME HALFWAY ACROSS THE FRONTIER JUST TO GIVE ME A WARNING?!
<<< YES >>>
YOU TRIED TO SHOOT ME!
<<< MY ARM WAS SET TO STUN >>>
THAT CAR DIDN'T LOOK STUNNED!
<<< IDENTIFY YOURSELF >>>
<<< YOUR NAME WILL BE HELD ON FILE FOR FUTURE REFERENCE >>>
BOB.
BOB SANDWICH.
BIG BOB SANDWICH.
<<< DISCLOSING YOUR NAME WITHOUT FIRST OBTAINING CONFIRMATION OF THE QUESTIONER'S IDENTITY IS ALSO A MISDEMEANOR >>>
A-HA! IT WAS A FAKE NAME! IN YOUR FACE, YOU DUMB ROBOT!
<<< PRESENTING FALSE INFORMATION TO A DATA GUARDIAN IS ALSO A MISDEMEANOR >>>
<<< YOU ARE NOW UNDER ARREST >>>
NO! I'M NOT GOING BACK!
I'M NOT GOING BACK!

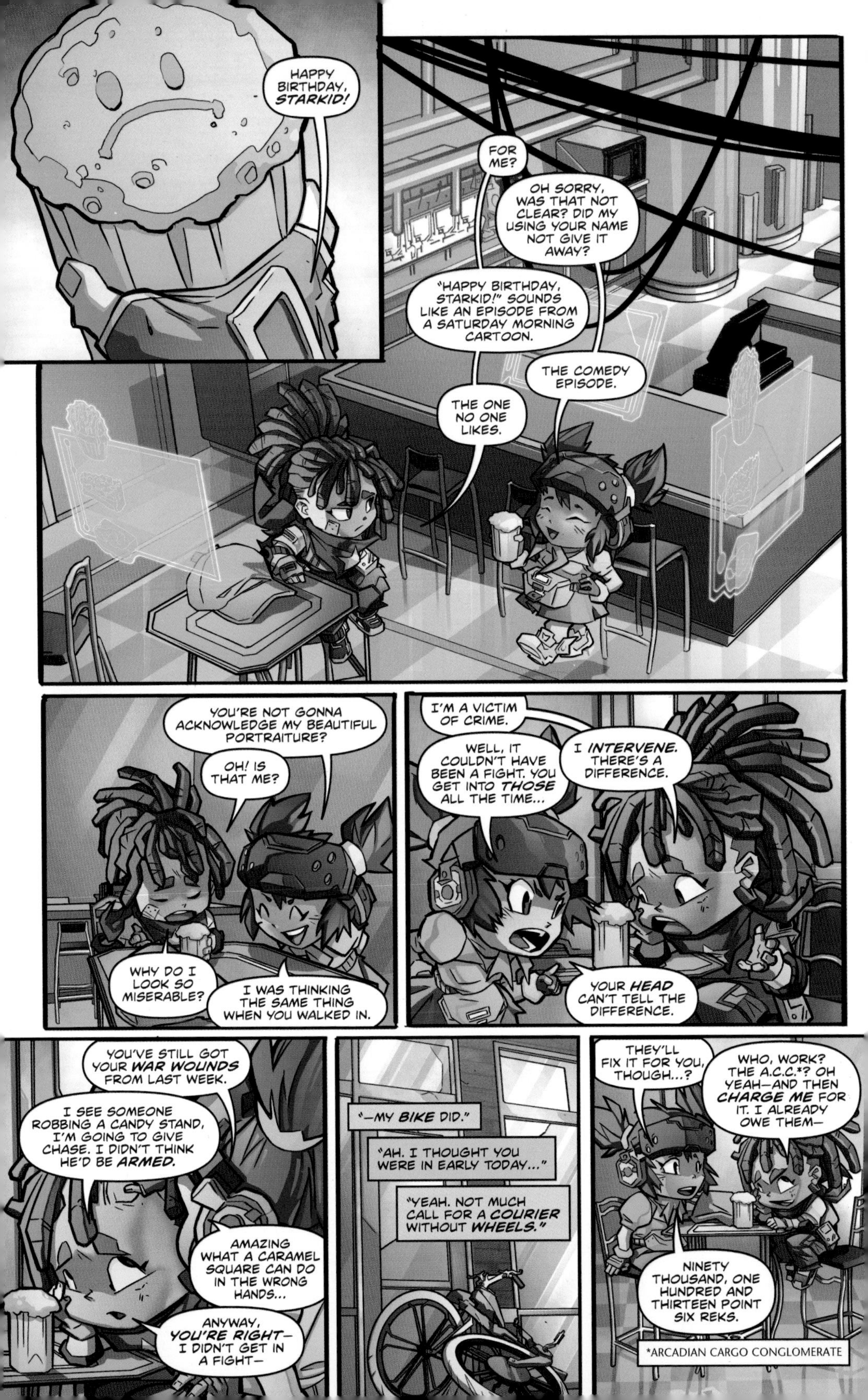
HAPPY BIRTHDAY, STARKID!
FOR ME?
OH SORRY, WAS THAT NOT CLEAR? DID MY USING YOUR NAME NOT GIVE IT AWAY?
"HAPPY BIRTHDAY, STARKID!" SOUNDS LIKE AN EPISODE FROM A SATURDAY MORNING CARTOON.
THE COMEDY EPISODE.
THE ONE NO ONE LIKES.
YOU'RE NOT GONNA ACKNOWLEDGE MY BEAUTIFUL PORTRAITURE?
OH! IS THAT ME?
WHY DO I LOOK SO MISERABLE?
I WAS THINKING THE SAME THING WHEN YOU WALKED IN.
I'M A VICTIM OF CRIME.
WELL, IT COULDN'T HAVE BEEN A FIGHT. YOU GET INTO THOSE ALL THE TIME...
I INTERVENE. THERE'S A DIFFERENCE.
YOUR HEAD CAN'T TELL THE DIFFERENCE.
YOU'VE STILL GOT YOUR WAR WOUNDS FROM LAST WEEK.
I SEE SOMEONE ROBBING A CANDY STAND, I'M GOING TO GIVE CHASE. I DIDN'T THINK HE'D BE ARMED.
AMAZING WHAT A CARAMEL SQUARE CAN DO IN THE WRONG HANDS...
ANYWAY, YOU'RE RIGHT— I DIDN'T GET IN A FIGHT—
"—MY BIKE DID."
"AH. I THOUGHT YOU WERE IN EARLY TODAY..."
"YEAH. NOT MUCH CALL FOR A COURIER WITHOUT WHEELS."
THEY'LL FIX IT FOR YOU, THOUGH...?
WHO, WORK? THE A.C.C.*? OH YEAH—AND THEN CHARGE ME FOR IT. I ALREADY OWE THEM—
NINETY THOUSAND, ONE HUNDRED AND THIRTEEN POINT SIX REKS.
*ARCADIAN CARGO CONGLOMERATE

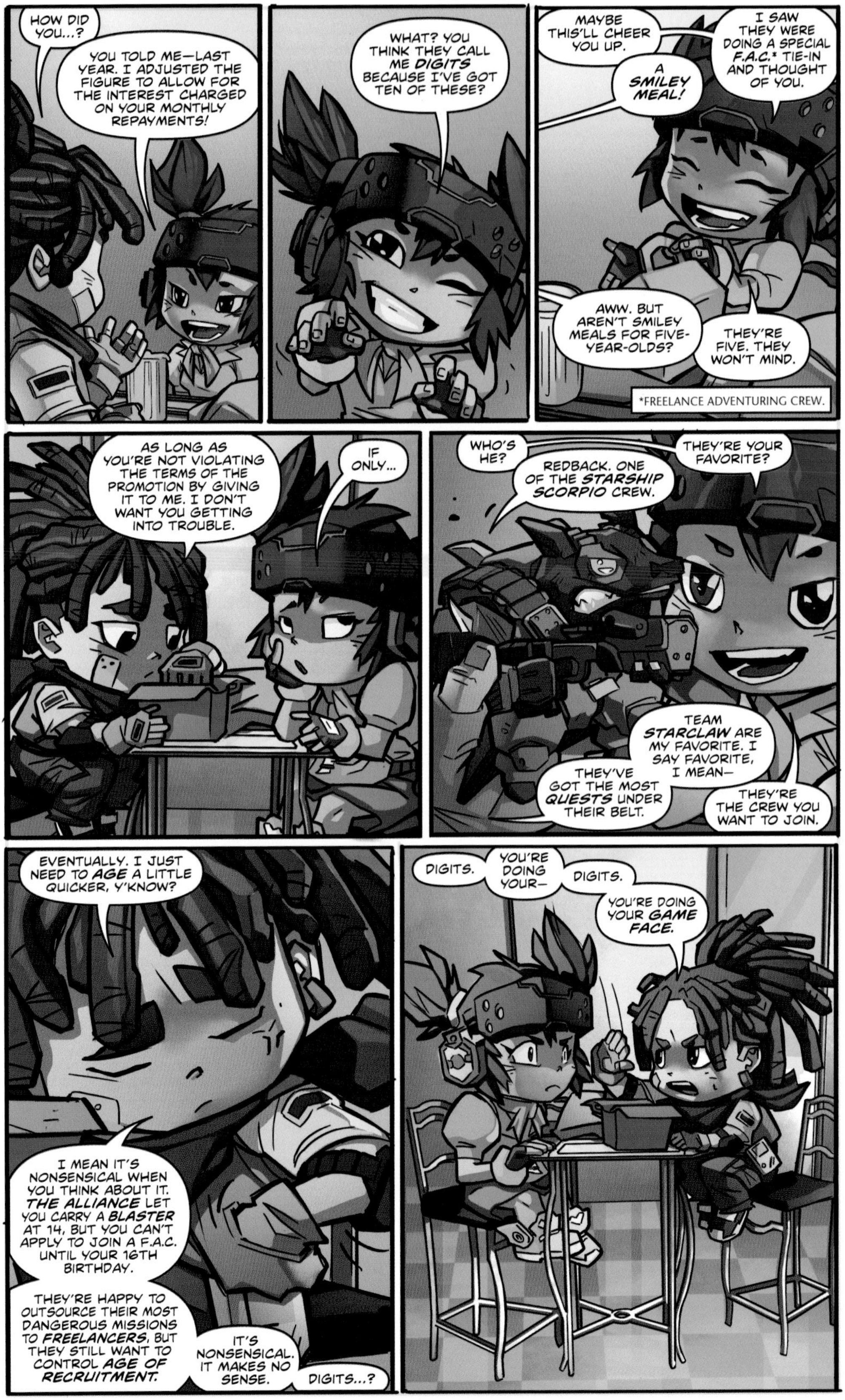
HOW DID YOU...?
YOU TOLD ME—LAST YEAR. I ADJUSTED THE FIGURE TO ALLOW FOR THE INTEREST CHARGED ON YOUR MONTHLY REPAYMENTS!
WHAT? YOU THINK THEY CALL ME DIGITS BECAUSE I'VE GOT TEN OF THESE?
MAYBE THIS'LL CHEER YOU UP.
A SMILEY MEAL!
I SAW THEY WERE DOING A SPECIAL F.A.C.* TIE-IN AND THOUGHT OF YOU.
AWW. BUT AREN'T SMILEY MEALS FOR FIVE-YEAR-OLDS?
THEY'RE FIVE. THEY WON'T MIND.
*FREELANCE ADVENTURING CREW.
AS LONG AS YOU'RE NOT VIOLATING THE TERMS OF THE PROMOTION BY GIVING IT TO ME. I DON'T WANT YOU GETTING INTO TROUBLE.
IF ONLY...
WHO'S HE?
REDBACK. ONE OF THE STARSHIP SCORPIO CREW.
THEY'RE YOUR FAVORITE?
TEAM STARCLAW ARE MY FAVORITE. I SAY FAVORITE, I MEAN—
THEY'VE GOT THE MOST QUESTS UNDER THEIR BELT.
THEY'RE THE CREW YOU WANT TO JOIN.
EVENTUALLY. I JUST NEED TO AGE A LITTLE QUICKER, Y'KNOW?
I MEAN IT'S NONSENSICAL WHEN YOU THINK ABOUT IT. THE ALLIANCE LET YOU CARRY A BLASTER AT 14, BUT YOU CAN'T APPLY TO JOIN A F.A.C. UNTIL YOUR 16TH BIRTHDAY.
THEY'RE HAPPY TO OUTSOURCE THEIR MOST DANGEROUS MISSIONS TO FREELANCERS, BUT THEY STILL WANT TO CONTROL AGE OF RECRUITMENT.
IT'S NONSENSICAL. IT MAKES NO SENSE.
DIGITS...?
DIGITS.
YOU'RE DOING YOUR—
DIGITS.
YOU'RE DOING YOUR GAME FACE.

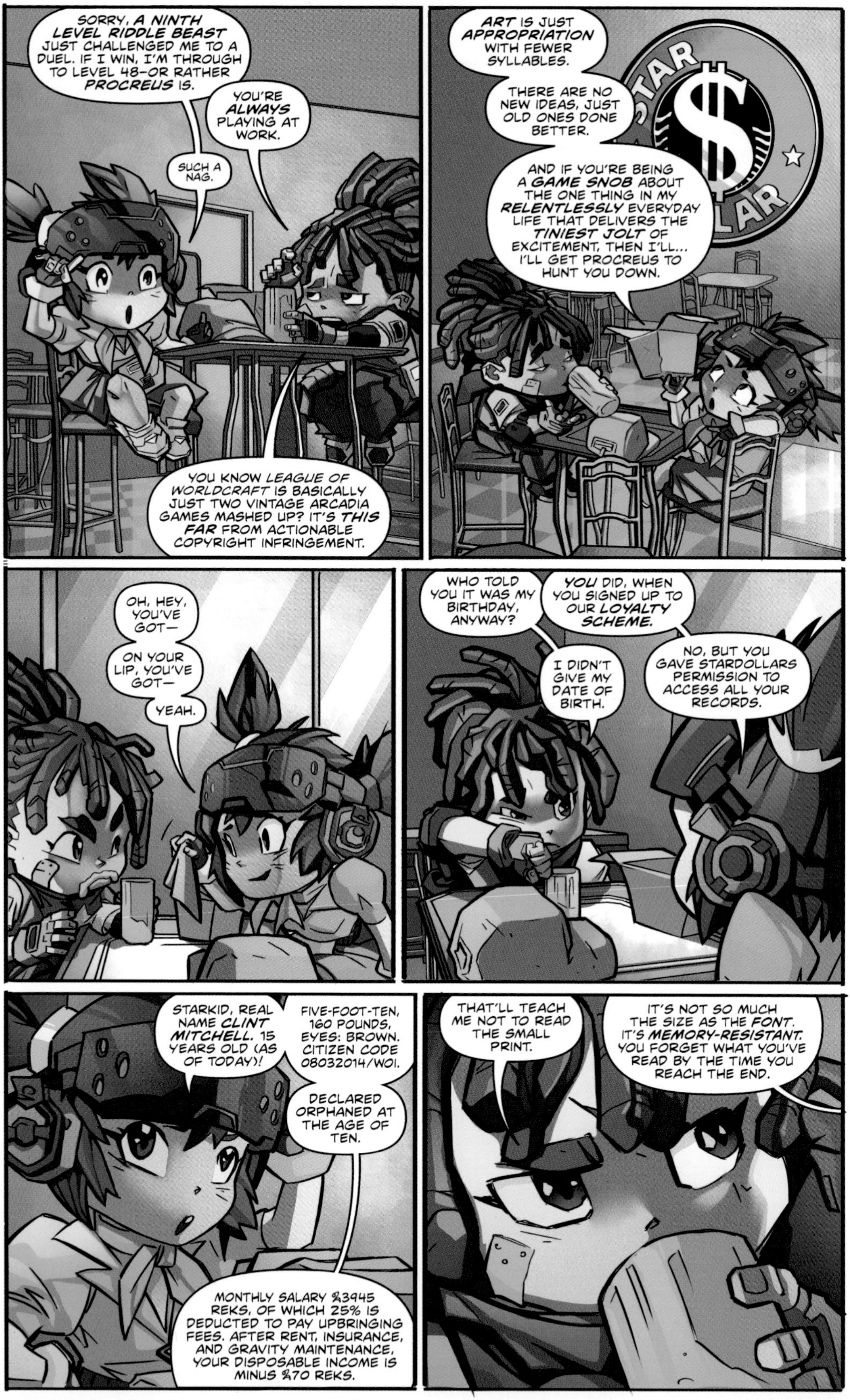
SORRY, A NINTH LEVEL RIDDLE BEAST JUST CHALLENGED ME TO A DUEL. IF I WIN, I'M THROUGH TO LEVEL 48–OR RATHER PROCREUS IS.
YOU'RE ALWAYS PLAYING AT WORK.
SUCH A NAG.
YOU KNOW LEAGUE OF WORLDCRAFT IS BASICALLY JUST TWO VINTAGE ARCADIA GAMES MASHED UP? IT'S THIS FAR FROM ACTIONABLE COPYRIGHT INFRINGEMENT.
ART IS JUST APPROPRIATION WITH FEWER SYLLABLES.
THERE ARE NO NEW IDEAS, JUST OLD ONES DONE BETTER.
AND IF YOU'RE BEING A GAME SNOB ABOUT THE ONE THING IN MY RELENTLESSLY EVERYDAY LIFE THAT DELIVERS THE TINIEST JOLT OF EXCITEMENT, THEN I'LL... I'LL GET PROCREUS TO HUNT YOU DOWN.
OH, HEY, YOU'VE GOT—
ON YOUR LIP, YOU'VE GOT—
YEAH.
WHO TOLD YOU IT WAS MY BIRTHDAY, ANYWAY?
YOU DID, WHEN YOU SIGNED UP TO OUR LOYALTY SCHEME.
I DIDN'T GIVE MY DATE OF BIRTH.
NO, BUT YOU GAVE STARDOLLARS PERMISSION TO ACCESS ALL YOUR RECORDS.
STARKID, REAL NAME CLINT MITCHELL. 15 YEARS OLD (AS OF TODAY)!
FIVE-FOOT-TEN, 160 POUNDS, EYES: BROWN. CITIZEN CODE 08032014/WOI.
DECLARED ORPHANED AT THE AGE OF TEN.
MONTHLY SALARY ℛ3945 REKS, OF WHICH 25% IS DEDUCTED TO PAY UPBRINGING FEES. AFTER RENT, INSURANCE, AND GRAVITY MAINTENANCE, YOUR DISPOSABLE INCOME IS MINUS ℛ70 REKS.
THAT'LL TEACH ME NOT TO READ THE SMALL PRINT.
IT'S NOT SO MUCH THE SIZE AS THE FONT. IT'S MEMORY-RESISTANT. YOU FORGET WHAT YOU'VE READ BY THE TIME YOU REACH THE END.

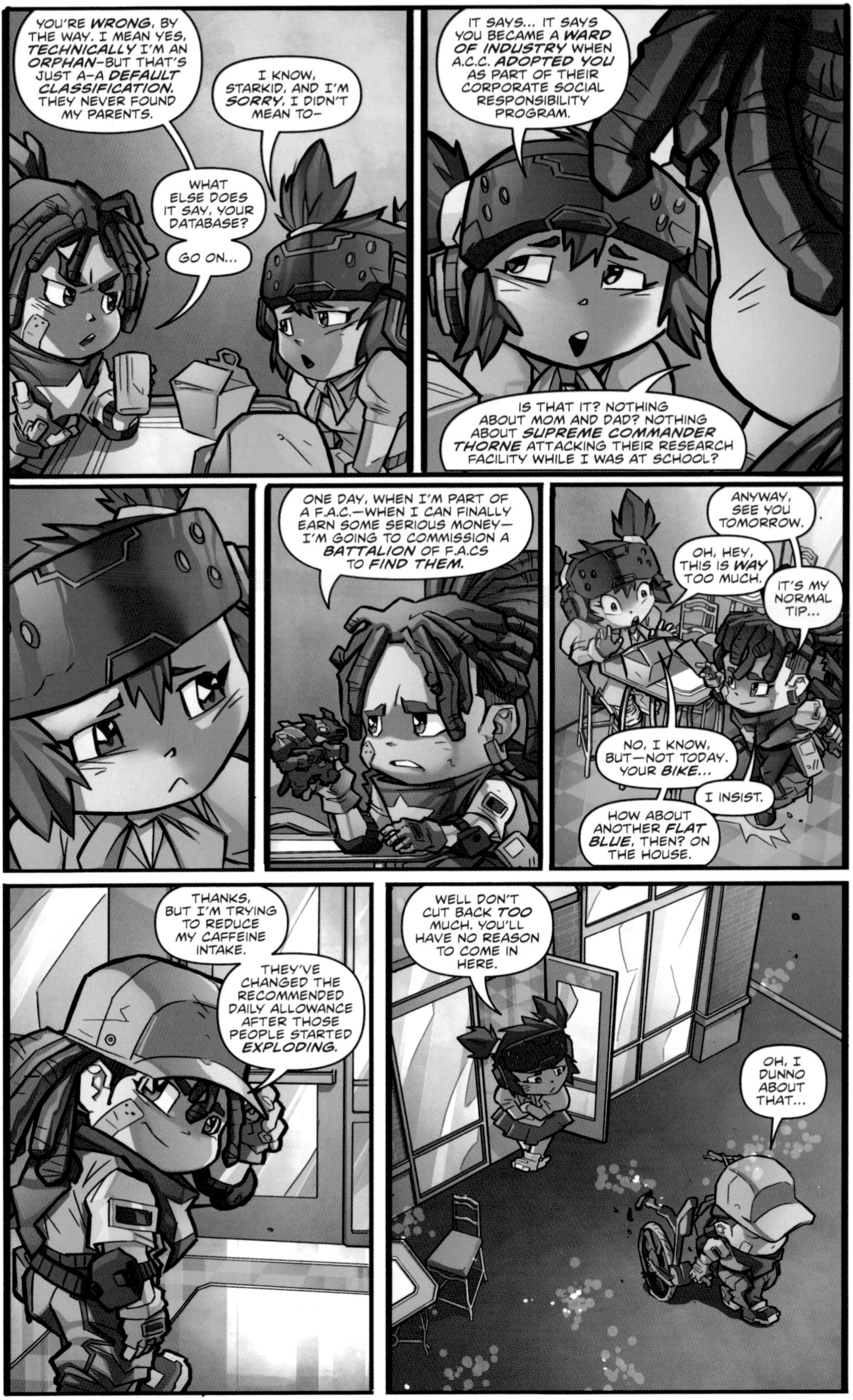
YOU'RE WRONG, BY THE WAY. I MEAN YES, TECHNICALLY I'M AN ORPHAN—BUT THAT'S JUST A—A DEFAULT CLASSIFICATION. THEY NEVER FOUND MY PARENTS.
I KNOW, STARKID, AND I'M SORRY, I DIDN'T MEAN TO—
WHAT ELSE DOES IT SAY, YOUR DATABASE?
GO ON...
IT SAYS... IT SAYS YOU BECAME A WARD OF INDUSTRY WHEN A.C.C. ADOPTED YOU AS PART OF THEIR CORPORATE SOCIAL RESPONSIBILITY PROGRAM.
IS THAT IT? NOTHING ABOUT MOM AND DAD? NOTHING ABOUT SUPREME COMMANDER THORNE ATTACKING THEIR RESEARCH FACILITY WHILE I WAS AT SCHOOL?
ONE DAY, WHEN I'M PART OF A F.A.C.—WHEN I CAN FINALLY EARN SOME SERIOUS MONEY—I'M GOING TO COMMISSION A BATTALION OF F.A.CS TO FIND THEM.
ANYWAY, SEE YOU TOMORROW.
OH, HEY, THIS IS WAY TOO MUCH.
IT'S MY NORMAL TIP...
NO, I KNOW, BUT—NOT TODAY. YOUR BIKE...
I INSIST.
HOW ABOUT ANOTHER FLAT BLUE, THEN? ON THE HOUSE.
THANKS, BUT I'M TRYING TO REDUCE MY CAFFEINE INTAKE.
THEY'VE CHANGED THE RECOMMENDED DAILY ALLOWANCE AFTER THOSE PEOPLE STARTED EXPLODING.
WELL DON'T CUT BACK TOO MUCH. YOU'LL HAVE NO REASON TO COME IN HERE.
OH, I DUNNO ABOUT THAT...

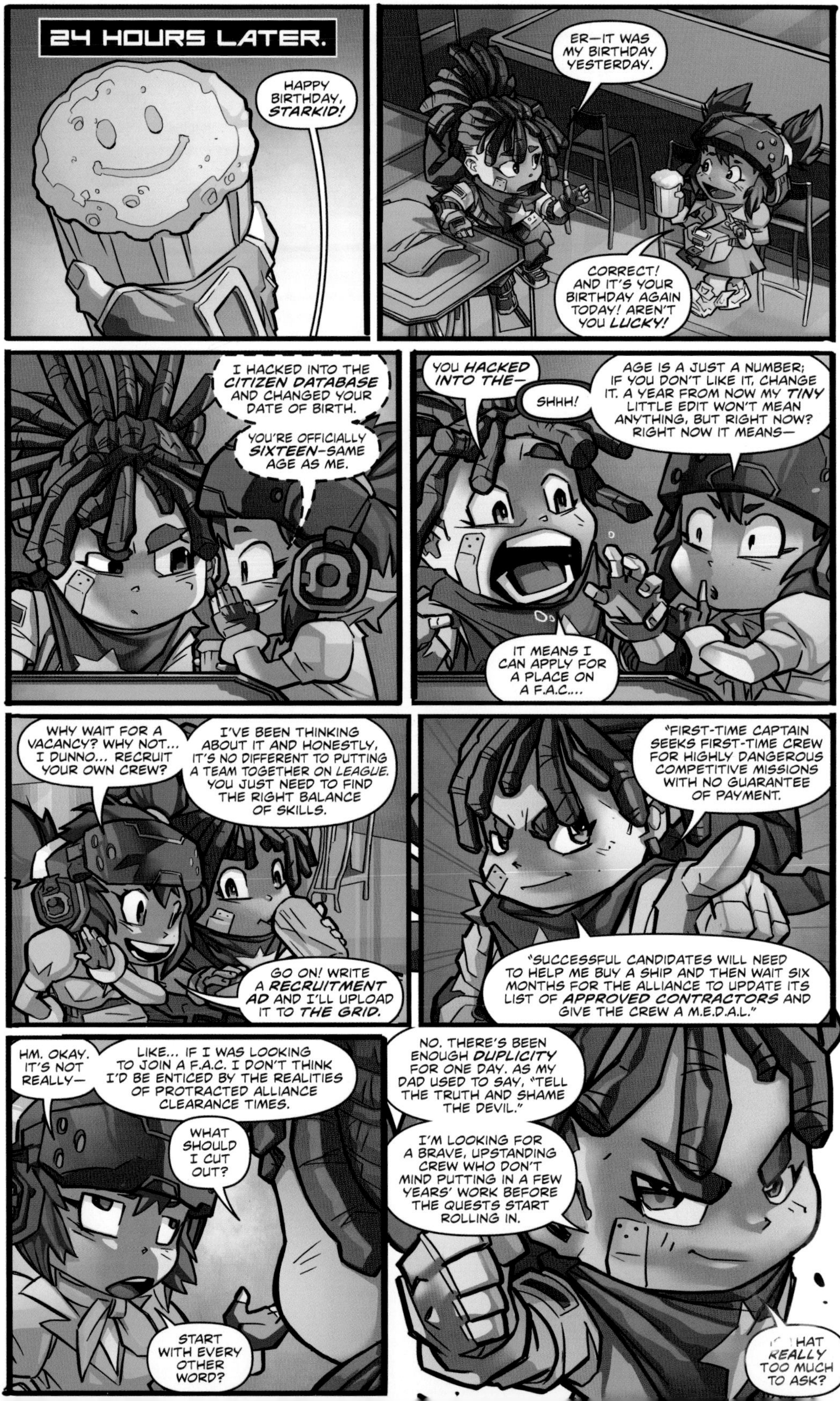
24 HOURS LATER.
HAPPY BIRTHDAY, *STARKID!*
ER—IT WAS MY BIRTHDAY YESTERDAY.
CORRECT! AND IT'S YOUR BIRTHDAY AGAIN TODAY! AREN'T YOU *LUCKY!*
I HACKED INTO THE *CITIZEN DATABASE* AND CHANGED YOUR DATE OF BIRTH.
YOU'RE OFFICIALLY *SIXTEEN*—SAME AGE AS ME.
YOU *HACKED INTO THE*—
SHHH!
AGE IS A JUST A NUMBER; IF YOU DON'T LIKE IT, CHANGE IT. A YEAR FROM NOW MY *TINY* LITTLE EDIT WON'T MEAN ANYTHING, BUT RIGHT NOW? RIGHT NOW IT MEANS—
IT MEANS I CAN APPLY FOR A PLACE ON A F.A.C....
WHY WAIT FOR A VACANCY? WHY NOT... I DUNNO... RECRUIT YOUR OWN CREW?
I'VE BEEN THINKING ABOUT IT AND HONESTLY, IT'S NO DIFFERENT TO PUTTING A TEAM TOGETHER ON *LEAGUE*. YOU JUST NEED TO FIND THE RIGHT BALANCE OF SKILLS.
GO ON! WRITE A *RECRUITMENT AD* AND I'LL UPLOAD IT TO *THE GRID.*
"FIRST-TIME CAPTAIN SEEKS FIRST-TIME CREW FOR HIGHLY DANGEROUS COMPETITIVE MISSIONS WITH NO GUARANTEE OF PAYMENT.
"SUCCESSFUL CANDIDATES WILL NEED TO HELP ME BUY A SHIP AND THEN WAIT SIX MONTHS FOR THE ALLIANCE TO UPDATE ITS LIST OF *APPROVED CONTRACTORS* AND GIVE THE CREW A M.E.D.A.L."
HM. OKAY. IT'S NOT REALLY—
LIKE... IF I WAS LOOKING TO JOIN A F.A.C. I DON'T THINK I'D BE ENTICED BY THE REALITIES OF PROTRACTED ALLIANCE CLEARANCE TIMES.
WHAT SHOULD I CUT OUT?
START WITH EVERY OTHER WORD?
NO. THERE'S BEEN ENOUGH *DUPLICITY* FOR ONE DAY. AS MY DAD USED TO SAY, "TELL THE TRUTH AND SHAME THE DEVIL."
I'M LOOKING FOR A BRAVE, UPSTANDING CREW WHO DON'T MIND PUTTING IN A FEW YEARS' WORK BEFORE THE QUESTS START ROLLING IN.
HAT *REALLY* TOO MUCH TO ASK?

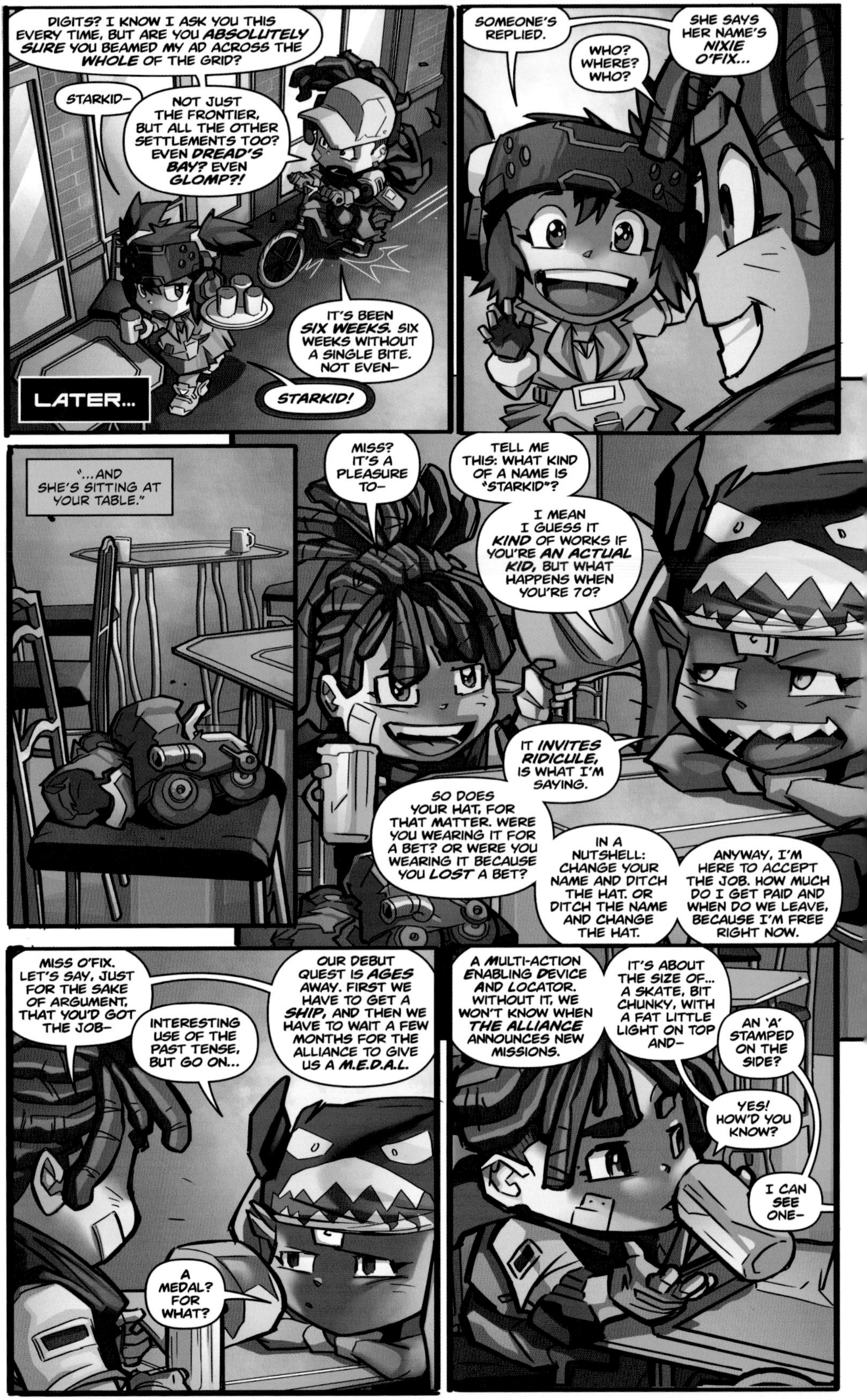
DIGITS? I KNOW I ASK YOU THIS EVERY TIME, BUT ARE YOU ABSOLUTELY SURE YOU BEAMED MY AD ACROSS THE WHOLE OF THE GRID?
STARKID–
NOT JUST THE FRONTIER, BUT ALL THE OTHER SETTLEMENTS TOO? EVEN DREAD'S BAY? EVEN GLOMP?!
IT'S BEEN SIX WEEKS. SIX WEEKS WITHOUT A SINGLE BITE. NOT EVEN–
LATER...
STARKID!
SOMEONE'S REPLIED.
WHO? WHERE? WHO?
SHE SAYS HER NAME'S NIXIE O'FIX...
"...AND SHE'S SITTING AT YOUR TABLE."
MISS? IT'S A PLEASURE TO–
TELL ME THIS: WHAT KIND OF A NAME IS "STARKID"?
I MEAN I GUESS IT KIND OF WORKS IF YOU'RE AN ACTUAL KID, BUT WHAT HAPPENS WHEN YOU'RE 70?
IT INVITES RIDICULE, IS WHAT I'M SAYING.
SO DOES YOUR HAT, FOR THAT MATTER. WERE YOU WEARING IT FOR A BET? OR WERE YOU WEARING IT BECAUSE YOU LOST A BET?
IN A NUTSHELL: CHANGE YOUR NAME AND DITCH THE HAT. OR DITCH THE NAME AND CHANGE THE HAT.
ANYWAY, I'M HERE TO ACCEPT THE JOB. HOW MUCH DO I GET PAID AND WHEN DO WE LEAVE, BECAUSE I'M FREE RIGHT NOW.
MISS O'FIX. LET'S SAY, JUST FOR THE SAKE OF ARGUMENT, THAT YOU'D GOT THE JOB–
INTERESTING USE OF THE PAST TENSE, BUT GO ON...
OUR DEBUT QUEST IS AGES AWAY. FIRST WE HAVE TO GET A SHIP, AND THEN WE HAVE TO WAIT A FEW MONTHS FOR THE ALLIANCE TO GIVE US A M.E.D.A.L.
A MEDAL? FOR WHAT?
A MULTI-ACTION ENABLING DEVICE AND LOCATOR. WITHOUT IT, WE WON'T KNOW WHEN THE ALLIANCE ANNOUNCES NEW MISSIONS.
IT'S ABOUT THE SIZE OF... A SKATE, BIT CHUNKY, WITH A FAT LITTLE LIGHT ON TOP AND–
AN 'A' STAMPED ON THE SIDE?
YES! HOW'D YOU KNOW?
I CAN SEE ONE–

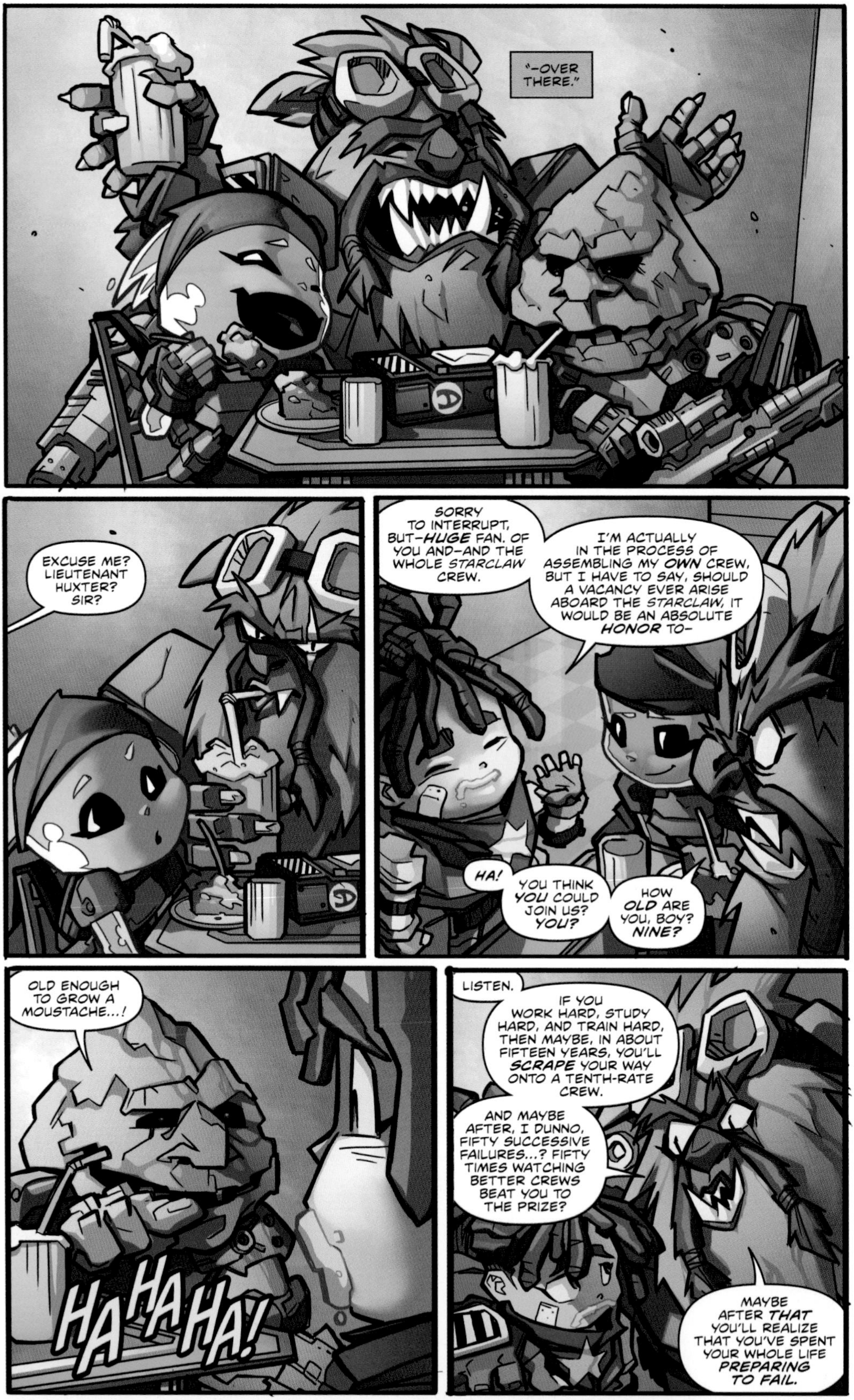
"–OVER THERE."
EXCUSE ME? LIEUTENANT HUXTER? SIR?
SORRY TO INTERRUPT, BUT–HUGE FAN. OF YOU AND–AND THE WHOLE STARCLAW CREW.
I'M ACTUALLY IN THE PROCESS OF ASSEMBLING MY OWN CREW, BUT I HAVE TO SAY, SHOULD A VACANCY EVER ARISE ABOARD THE STARCLAW, IT WOULD BE AN ABSOLUTE HONOR TO–
HA!
YOU THINK YOU COULD JOIN US? YOU?
HOW OLD ARE YOU, BOY? NINE?
OLD ENOUGH TO GROW A MOUSTACHE...!
HAHAHAHA!
LISTEN.
IF YOU WORK HARD, STUDY HARD, AND TRAIN HARD, THEN MAYBE, IN ABOUT FIFTEEN YEARS, YOU'LL SCRAPE YOUR WAY ONTO A TENTH-RATE CREW.
AND MAYBE AFTER, I DUNNO, FIFTY SUCCESSIVE FAILURES...? FIFTY TIMES WATCHING BETTER CREWS BEAT YOU TO THE PRIZE?
MAYBE AFTER THAT YOU'LL REALIZE THAT YOU'VE SPENT YOUR WHOLE LIFE PREPARING TO FAIL.

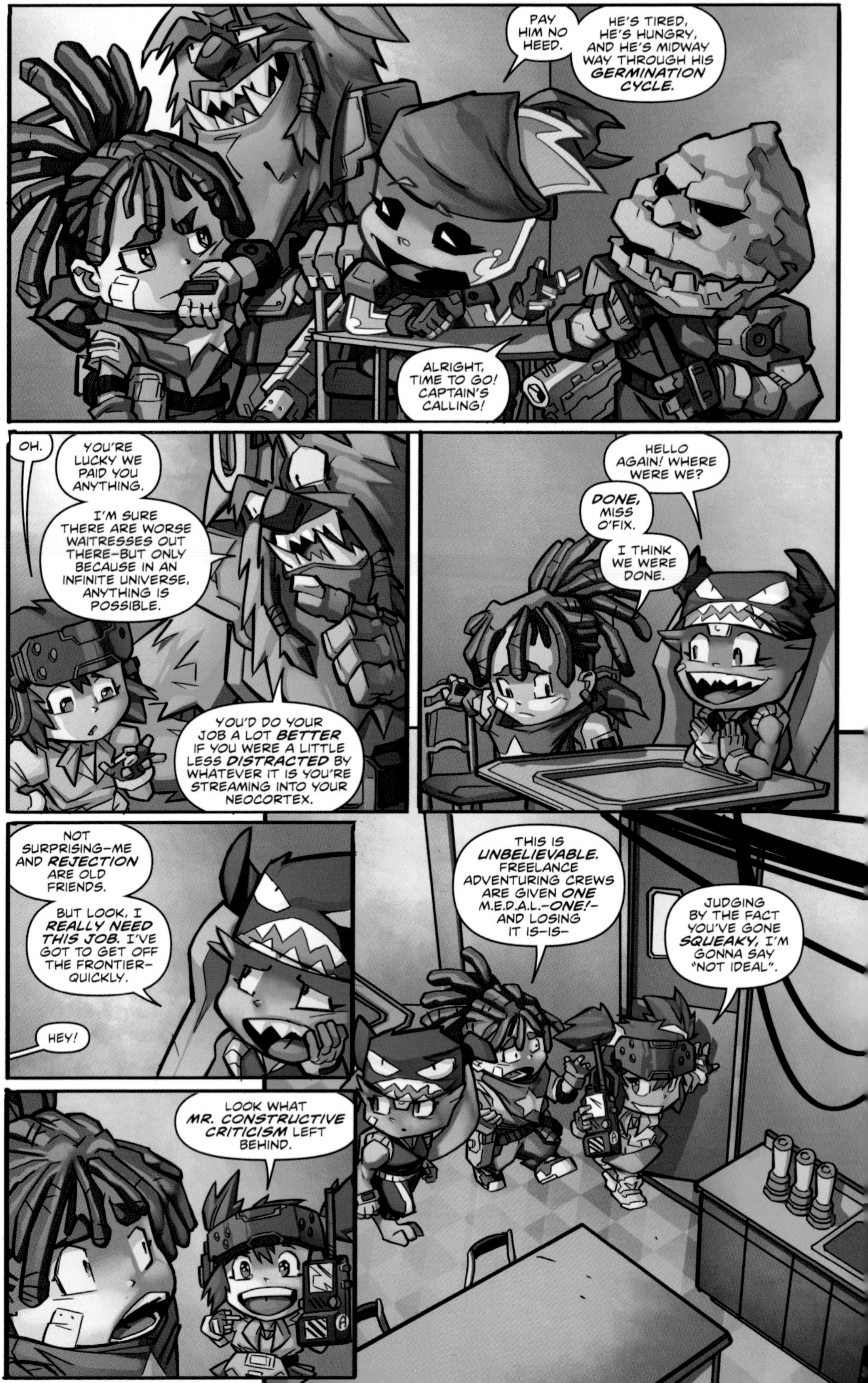
PAY HIM NO HEED.
HE'S TIRED, HE'S HUNGRY, AND HE'S MIDWAY WAY THROUGH HIS *GERMINATION CYCLE.*
ALRIGHT, TIME TO GO! CAPTAIN'S CALLING!
OH.
YOU'RE LUCKY WE PAID YOU ANYTHING.
I'M SURE THERE ARE WORSE WAITRESSES OUT THERE–BUT ONLY BECAUSE IN AN INFINITE UNIVERSE, ANYTHING IS POSSIBLE.
YOU'D DO YOUR JOB A LOT *BETTER* IF YOU WERE A LITTLE LESS *DISTRACTED* BY WHATEVER IT IS YOU'RE STREAMING INTO YOUR NEOCORTEX.
HELLO AGAIN! WHERE WERE WE?
DONE, MISS O'FIX.
I THINK WE WERE DONE.
NOT SURPRISING–ME AND *REJECTION* ARE OLD FRIENDS.
BUT LOOK, I *REALLY NEED THIS JOB.* I'VE GOT TO GET OFF THE FRONTIER–QUICKLY.
HEY!
LOOK WHAT *MR. CONSTRUCTIVE CRITICISM* LEFT BEHIND.
THIS IS *UNBELIEVABLE.* FREELANCE ADVENTURING CREWS ARE GIVEN *ONE* M.E.D.A.L.–*ONE!*– AND LOSING IT IS–IS–
JUDGING BY THE FACT YOU'VE GONE *SQUEAKY,* I'M GONNA SAY "NOT IDEAL".

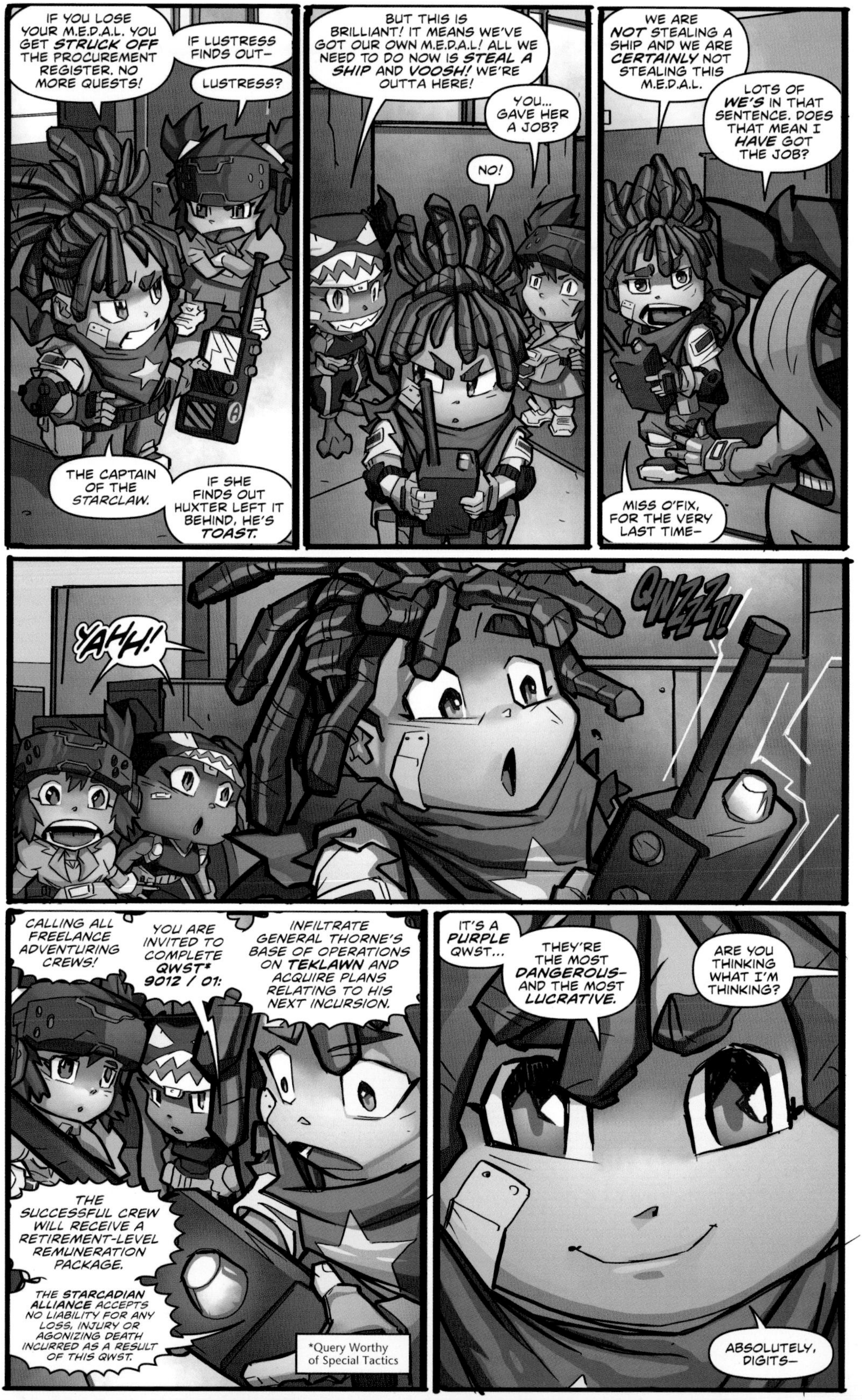
IF YOU LOSE YOUR M.E.D.A.L. YOU GET STRUCK OFF THE PROCUREMENT REGISTER. NO MORE QUESTS!
IF LUSTRESS FINDS OUT–
LUSTRESS?
THE CAPTAIN OF THE STARCLAW.
IF SHE FINDS OUT HUXTER LEFT IT BEHIND, HE'S TOAST.
BUT THIS IS BRILLIANT! IT MEANS WE'VE GOT OUR OWN M.E.D.A.L! ALL WE NEED TO DO NOW IS STEAL A SHIP AND VOOSH! WE'RE OUTTA HERE!
YOU... GAVE HER A JOB?
NO!
WE ARE NOT STEALING A SHIP AND WE ARE CERTAINLY NOT STEALING THIS M.E.D.A.L.
LOTS OF WE'S IN THAT SENTENCE. DOES THAT MEAN I HAVE GOT THE JOB?
MISS O'FIX, FOR THE VERY LAST TIME–
YAHH!
QWZZZT!
CALLING ALL FREELANCE ADVENTURING CREWS!
YOU ARE INVITED TO COMPLETE QWST* 9012 / 01:
INFILTRATE GENERAL THORNE'S BASE OF OPERATIONS ON TEKLAWN AND ACQUIRE PLANS RELATING TO HIS NEXT INCURSION.
THE SUCCESSFUL CREW WILL RECEIVE A RETIREMENT-LEVEL REMUNERATION PACKAGE.
THE STARCADIAN ALLIANCE ACCEPTS NO LIABILITY FOR ANY LOSS, INJURY OR AGONIZING DEATH INCURRED AS A RESULT OF THIS QWST.
*Query Worthy of Special Tactics
IT'S A PURPLE QWST...
THEY'RE THE MOST DANGEROUS– AND THE MOST LUCRATIVE.
ARE YOU THINKING WHAT I'M THINKING?
ABSOLUTELY, DIGITS–

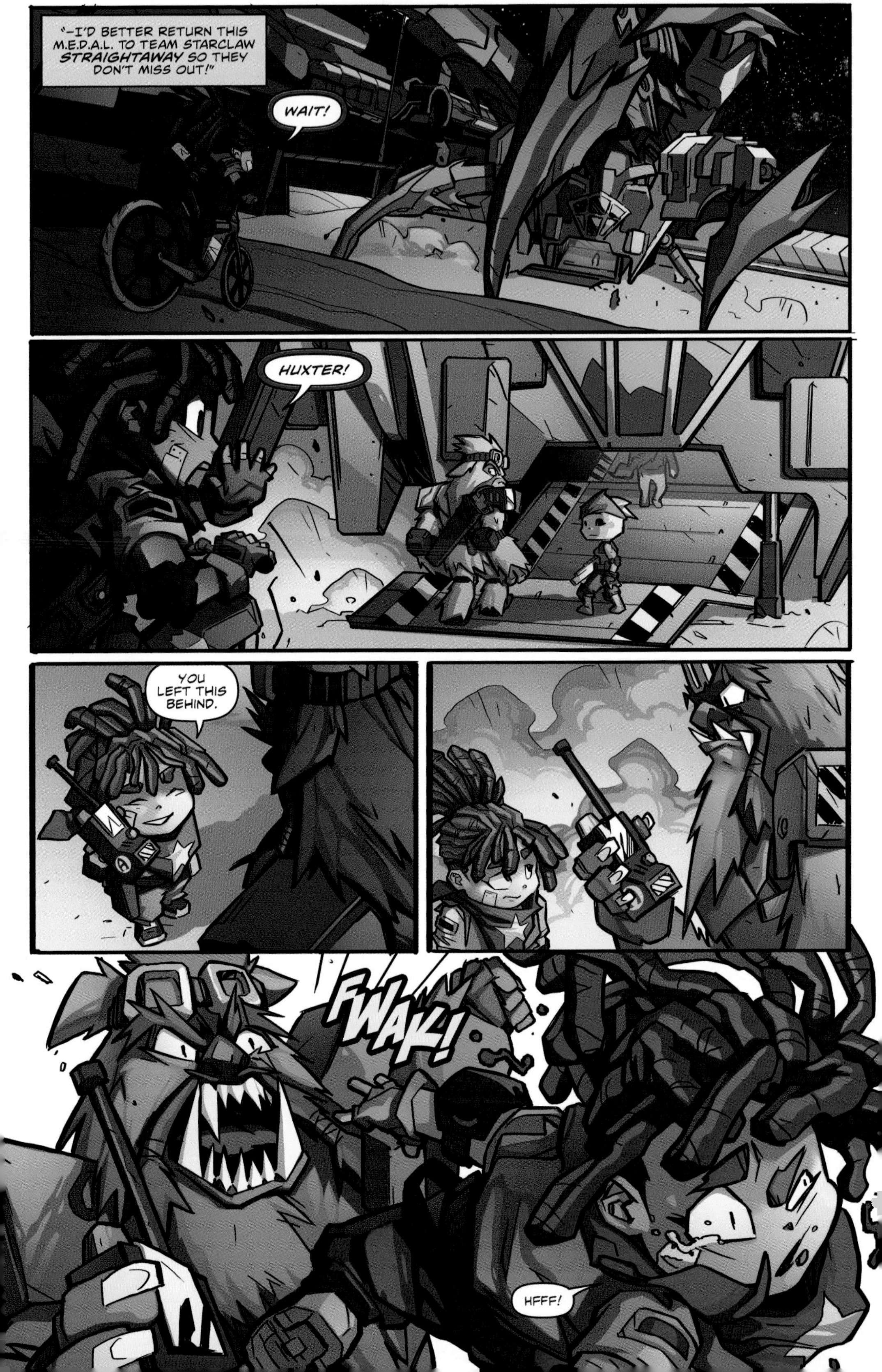
"–I'D BETTER RETURN THIS M.E.D.A.L. TO TEAM STARCLAW STRAIGHTAWAY SO THEY DON'T MISS OUT!"
WAIT!
HUXTER!
YOU LEFT THIS BEHIND.
FWAK!
HFFF!

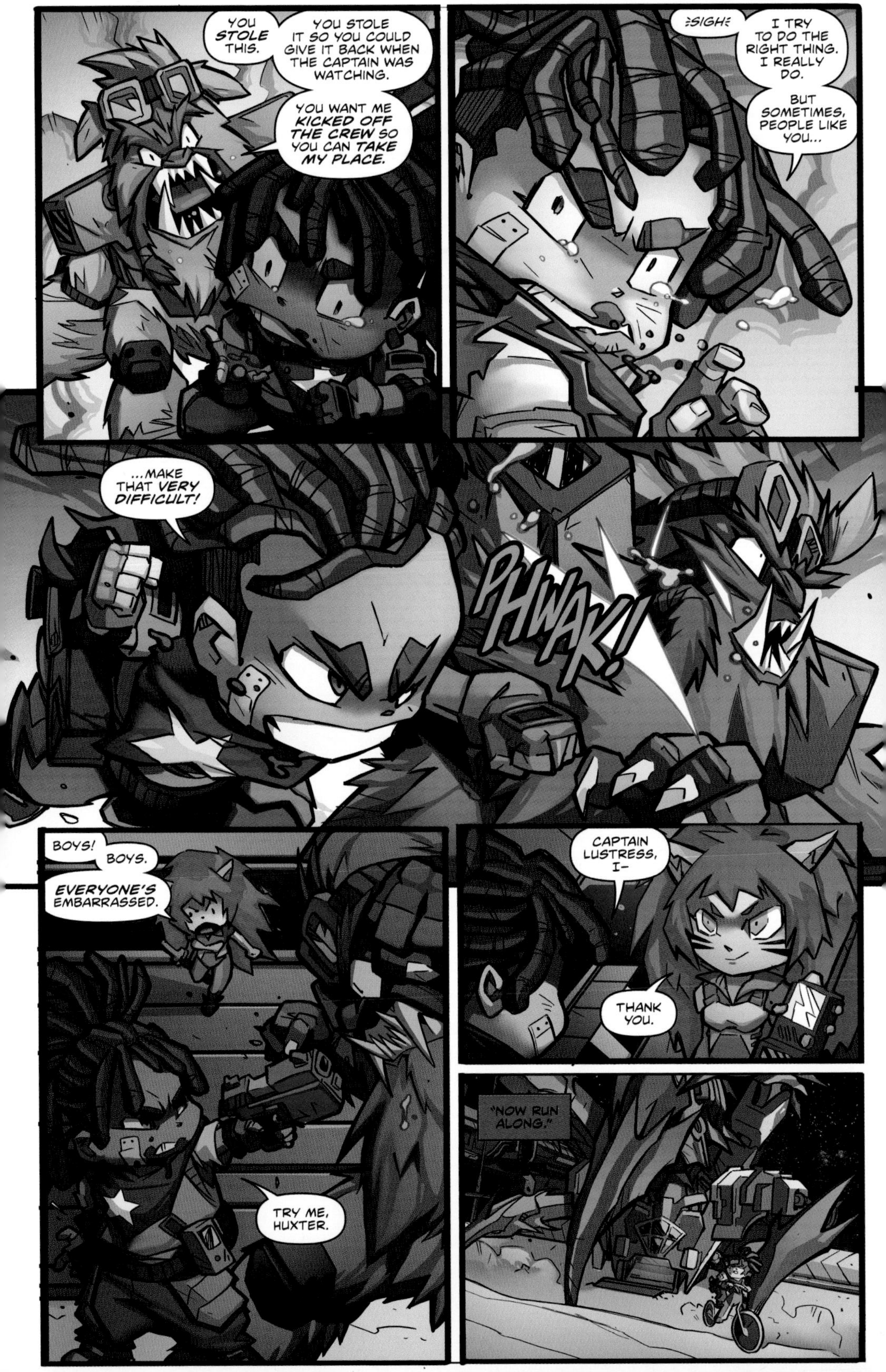
YOU STOLE THIS.
YOU STOLE IT SO YOU COULD GIVE IT BACK WHEN THE CAPTAIN WAS WATCHING.
YOU WANT ME KICKED OFF THE CREW SO YOU CAN TAKE MY PLACE.
SIGH
I TRY TO DO THE RIGHT THING. I REALLY DO.
BUT SOMETIMES, PEOPLE LIKE YOU...
...MAKE THAT VERY DIFFICULT!
PHWAK!
BOYS!
BOYS.
EVERYONE'S EMBARRASSED.
TRY ME, HUXTER.
CAPTAIN LUSTRESS, I–
THANK YOU.
"NOW RUN ALONG."

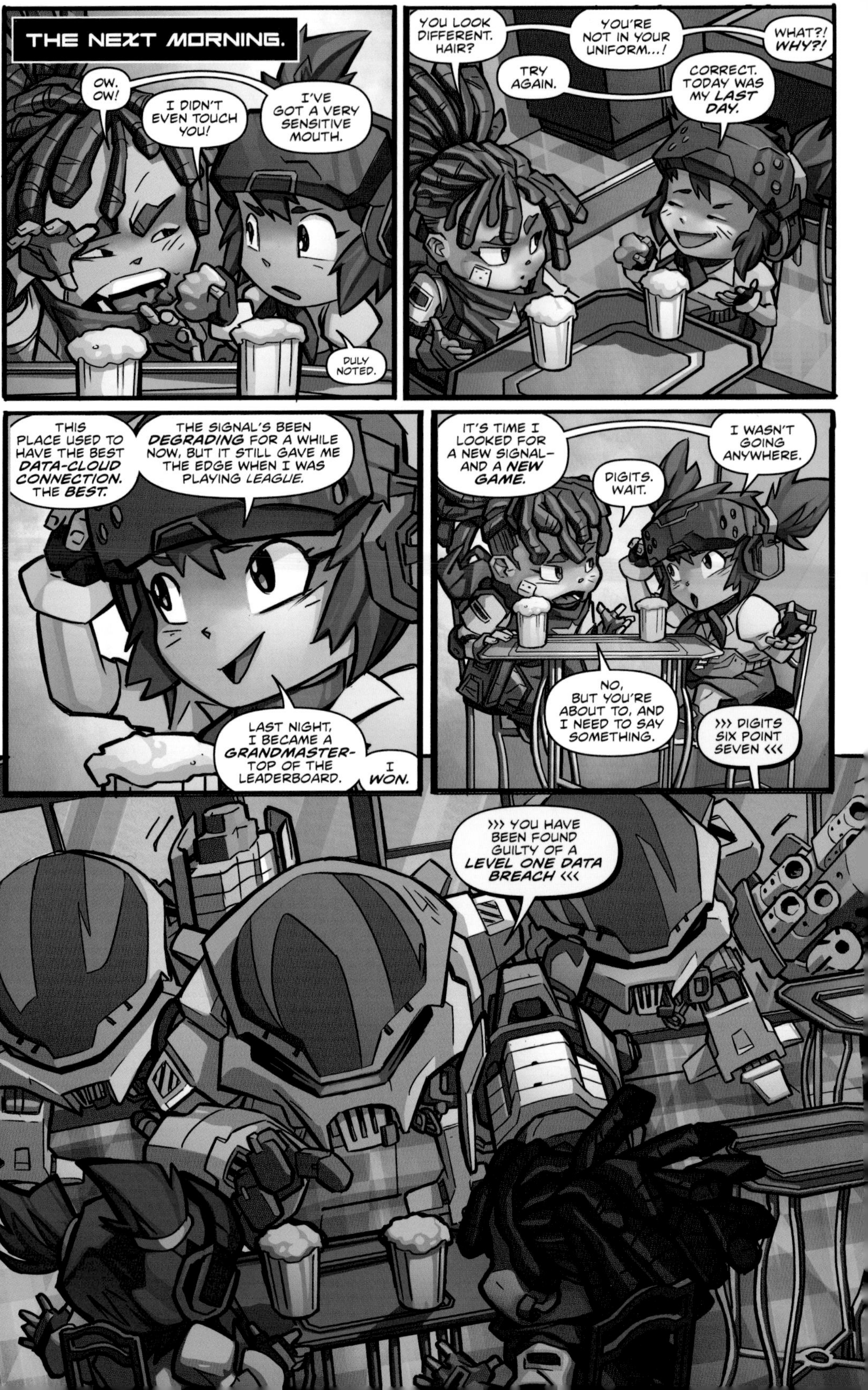
THE NEXT MORNING.
OW. OW!
I DIDN'T EVEN TOUCH YOU!
I'VE GOT A VERY SENSITIVE MOUTH.
DULY NOTED.
YOU LOOK DIFFERENT. HAIR?
TRY AGAIN.
YOU'RE NOT IN YOUR UNIFORM...!
CORRECT. TODAY WAS MY LAST DAY.
WHAT?! WHY?!
THIS PLACE USED TO HAVE THE BEST DATA-CLOUD CONNECTION. THE BEST.
THE SIGNAL'S BEEN DEGRADING FOR A WHILE NOW, BUT IT STILL GAVE ME THE EDGE WHEN I WAS PLAYING LEAGUE.
LAST NIGHT, I BECAME A GRANDMASTER- TOP OF THE LEADERBOARD.
I WON.
IT'S TIME I LOOKED FOR A NEW SIGNAL- AND A NEW GAME.
I WASN'T GOING ANYWHERE.
DIGITS. WAIT.
NO, BUT YOU'RE ABOUT TO, AND I NEED TO SAY SOMETHING.
>>> DIGITS SIX POINT SEVEN <<<
>>> YOU HAVE BEEN FOUND GUILTY OF A LEVEL ONE DATA BREACH <<<

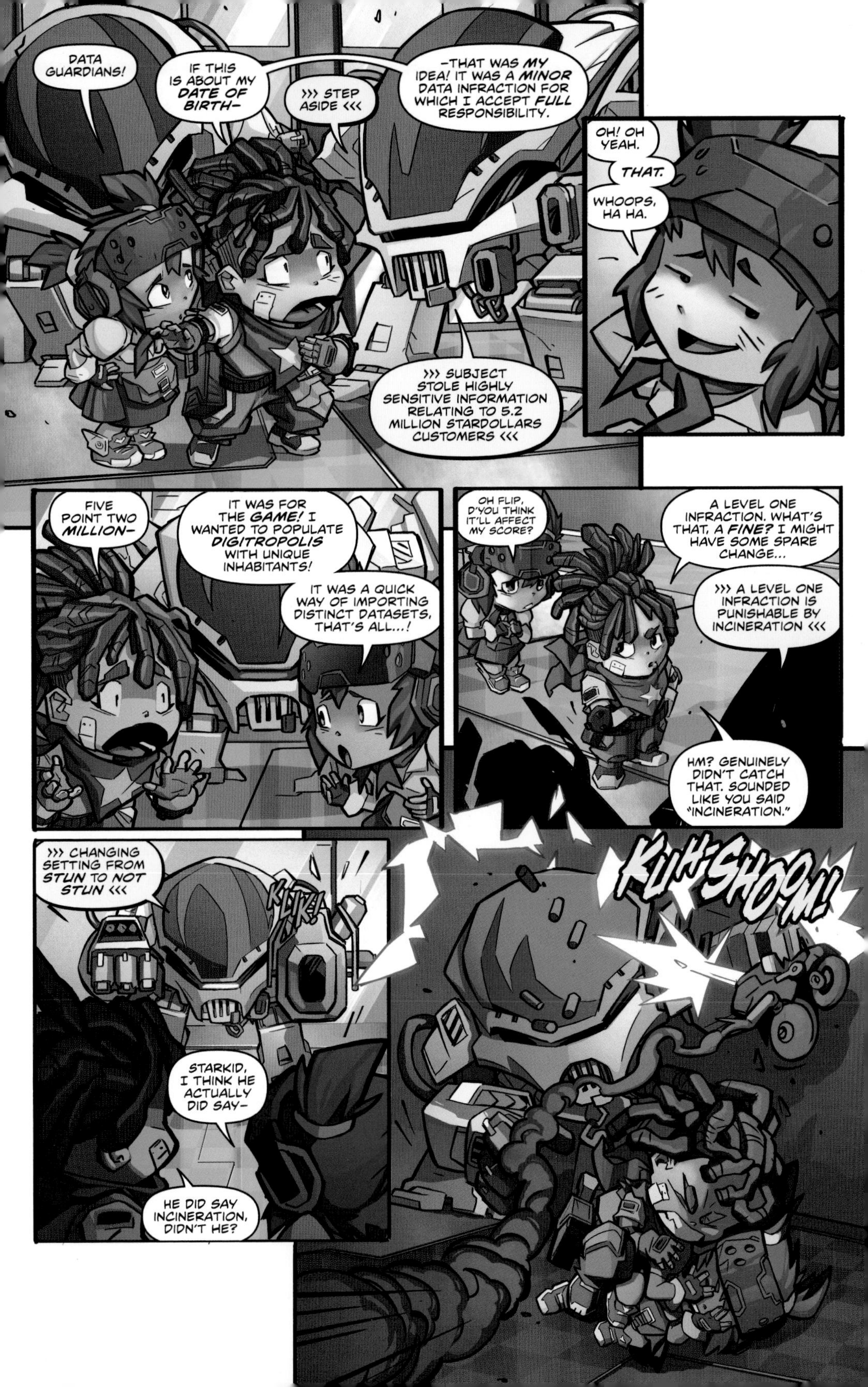
DATA GUARDIANS!
IF THIS IS ABOUT MY DATE OF BIRTH–
>>> STEP ASIDE <<<
–THAT WAS MY IDEA! IT WAS A MINOR DATA INFRACTION FOR WHICH I ACCEPT FULL RESPONSIBILITY.
>>> SUBJECT STOLE HIGHLY SENSITIVE INFORMATION RELATING TO 5.2 MILLION STARDOLLARS CUSTOMERS <<<
OH! OH YEAH.
THAT.
WHOOPS, HA HA.
FIVE POINT TWO MILLION–
IT WAS FOR THE GAME! I WANTED TO POPULATE DIGITROPOLIS WITH UNIQUE INHABITANTS!
IT WAS A QUICK WAY OF IMPORTING DISTINCT DATASETS, THAT'S ALL...!
OH FLIP, D'YOU THINK IT'LL AFFECT MY SCORE?
A LEVEL ONE INFRACTION. WHAT'S THAT, A FINE? I MIGHT HAVE SOME SPARE CHANGE...
>>> A LEVEL ONE INFRACTION IS PUNISHABLE BY INCINERATION <<<
HM? GENUINELY DIDN'T CATCH THAT. SOUNDED LIKE YOU SAID "INCINERATION."
>>> CHANGING SETTING FROM STUN TO NOT STUN <<<
KLIK!
STARKID, I THINK HE ACTUALLY DID SAY–
HE DID SAY INCINERATION, DIDN'T HE?
KUH-SHOOM!

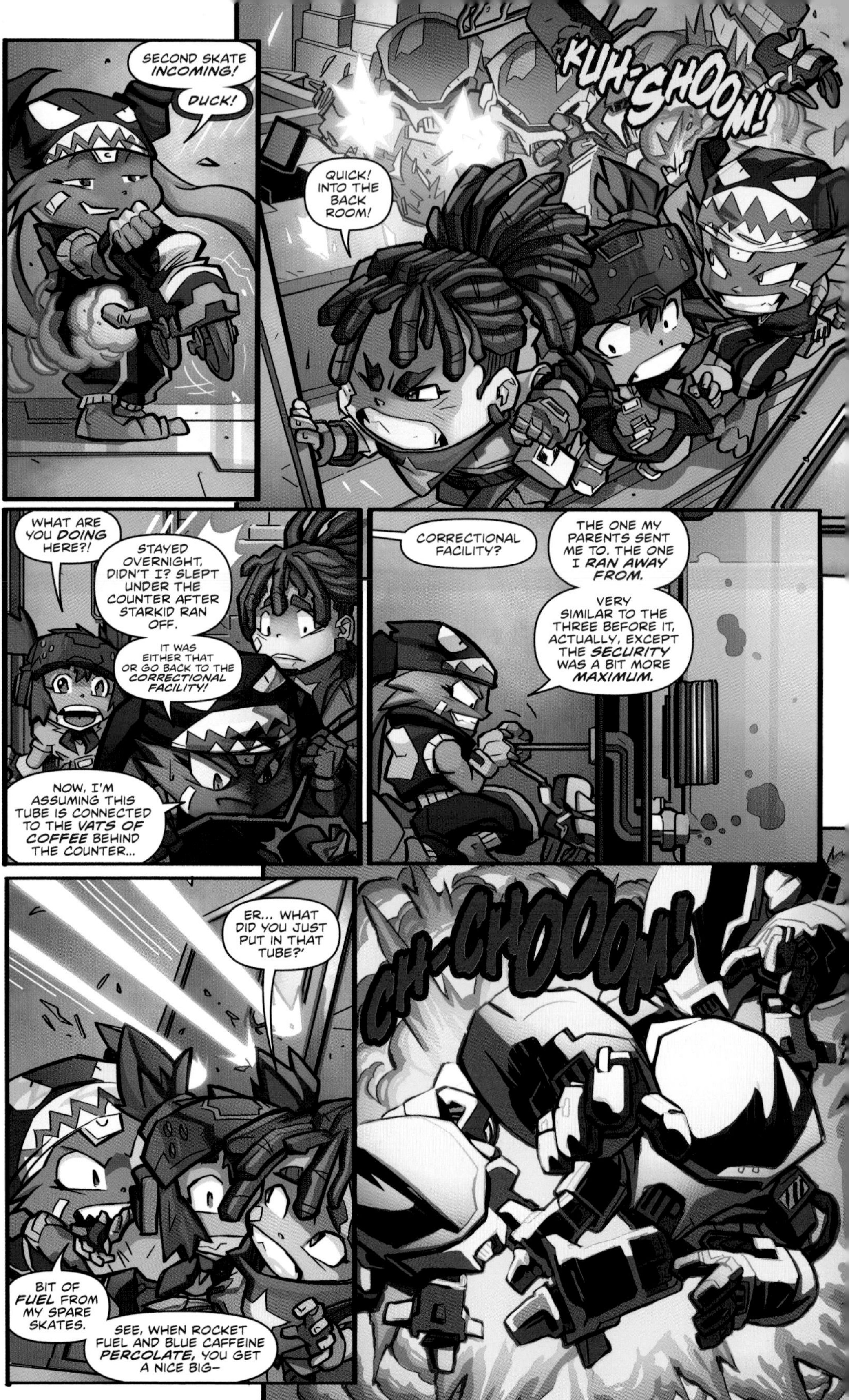
SECOND SKATE INCOMING!
DUCK!
KUH-SHOOM!
QUICK! INTO THE BACK ROOM!
WHAT ARE YOU DOING HERE?!
STAYED OVERNIGHT, DIDN'T I? SLEPT UNDER THE COUNTER AFTER STARKID RAN OFF.
IT WAS EITHER THAT OR GO BACK TO THE CORRECTIONAL FACILITY!
NOW, I'M ASSUMING THIS TUBE IS CONNECTED TO THE VATS OF COFFEE BEHIND THE COUNTER...
CORRECTIONAL FACILITY?
THE ONE MY PARENTS SENT ME TO. THE ONE I RAN AWAY FROM.
VERY SIMILAR TO THE THREE BEFORE IT, ACTUALLY, EXCEPT THE SECURITY WAS A BIT MORE MAXIMUM.
ER... WHAT DID YOU JUST PUT IN THAT TUBE?'
BIT OF FUEL FROM MY SPARE SKATES.
SEE, WHEN ROCKET FUEL AND BLUE CAFFEINE PERCOLATE, YOU GET A NICE BIG–
CH-CHOOOM!

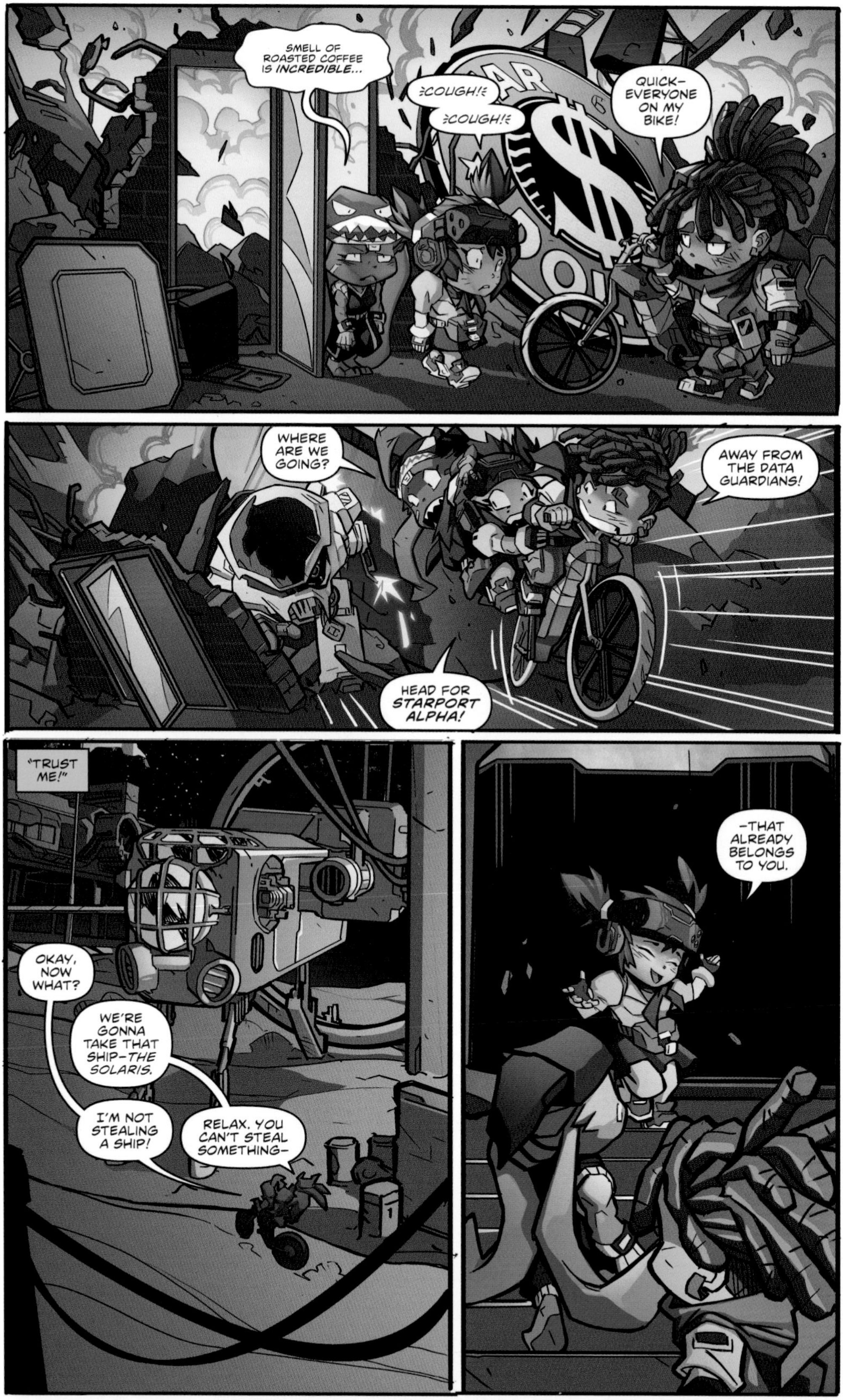
SMELL OF ROASTED COFFEE IS *INCREDIBLE*...
COUGH!
COUGH!
QUICK— EVERYONE ON MY BIKE!
WHERE ARE WE GOING?
AWAY FROM THE DATA GUARDIANS!
HEAD FOR *STARPORT ALPHA!*
"TRUST ME!"
OKAY, NOW WHAT?
WE'RE GONNA TAKE THAT SHIP—*THE SOLARIS.*
I'M NOT STEALING A SHIP!
RELAX. YOU CAN'T STEAL SOMETHING—
—THAT ALREADY BELONGS TO YOU.

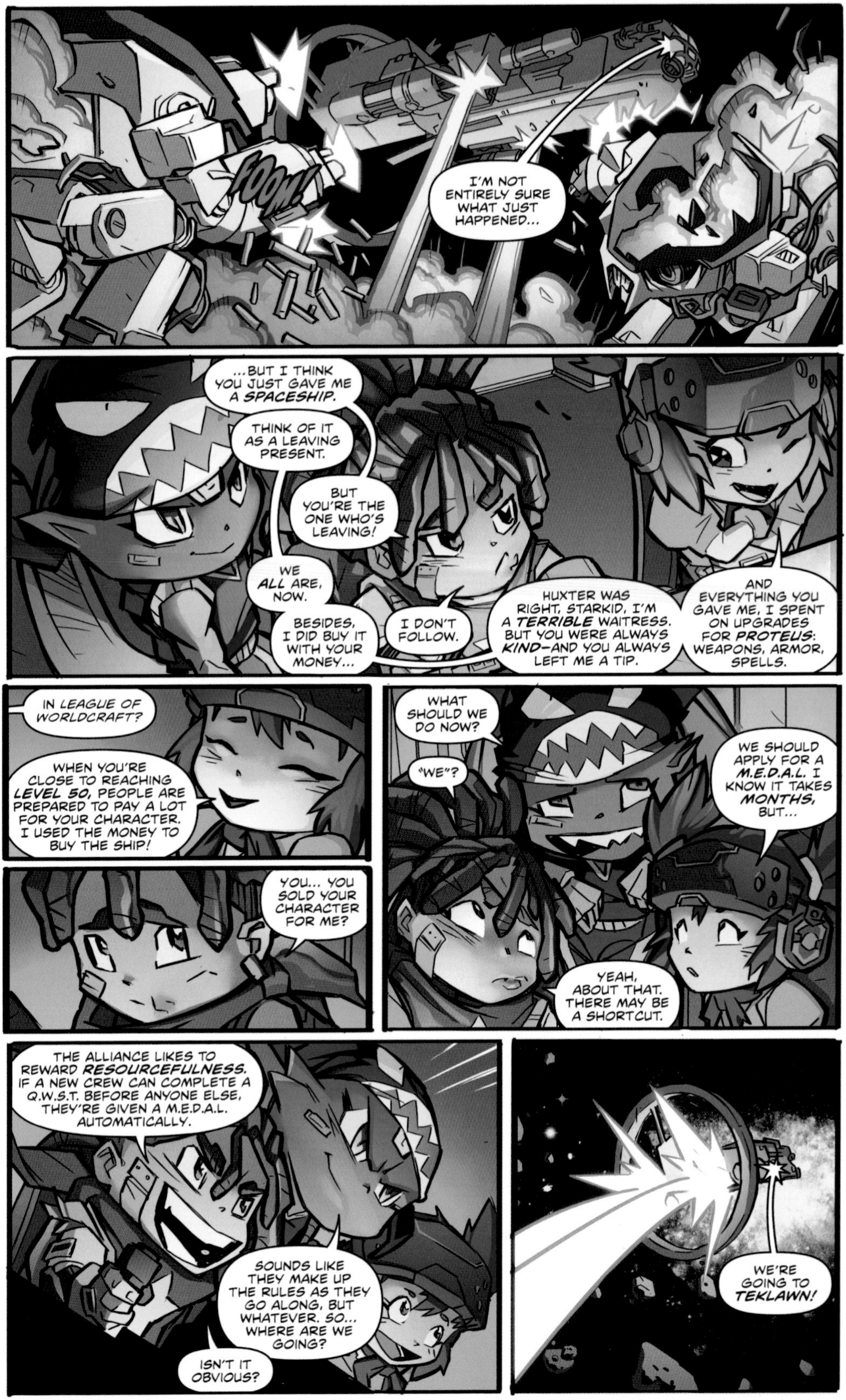

FOOM!
I'M NOT ENTIRELY SURE WHAT JUST HAPPENED...
...BUT I THINK YOU JUST GAVE ME A SPACESHIP.
THINK OF IT AS A LEAVING PRESENT.
BUT YOU'RE THE ONE WHO'S LEAVING!
WE ALL ARE, NOW.
BESIDES, I DID BUY IT WITH YOUR MONEY...
I DON'T FOLLOW.
HUXTER WAS RIGHT, STARKID, I'M A TERRIBLE WAITRESS. BUT YOU WERE ALWAYS KIND—AND YOU ALWAYS LEFT ME A TIP.
AND EVERYTHING YOU GAVE ME, I SPENT ON UPGRADES FOR PROTEUS: WEAPONS, ARMOR, SPELLS.
IN LEAGUE OF WORLDCRAFT?
WHEN YOU'RE CLOSE TO REACHING LEVEL 50, PEOPLE ARE PREPARED TO PAY A LOT FOR YOUR CHARACTER. I USED THE MONEY TO BUY THE SHIP!
YOU... YOU SOLD YOUR CHARACTER FOR ME?
WHAT SHOULD WE DO NOW?
"WE"?
WE SHOULD APPLY FOR A M.E.D.A.L. I KNOW IT TAKES MONTHS, BUT...
YEAH, ABOUT THAT. THERE MAY BE A SHORTCUT.
THE ALLIANCE LIKES TO REWARD RESOURCEFULNESS. IF A NEW CREW CAN COMPLETE A Q.W.S.T. BEFORE ANYONE ELSE, THEY'RE GIVEN A M.E.D.A.L. AUTOMATICALLY.
SOUNDS LIKE THEY MAKE UP THE RULES AS THEY GO ALONG, BUT WHATEVER. SO... WHERE ARE WE GOING?
ISN'T IT OBVIOUS?
WE'RE GOING TO TEKLAWN!

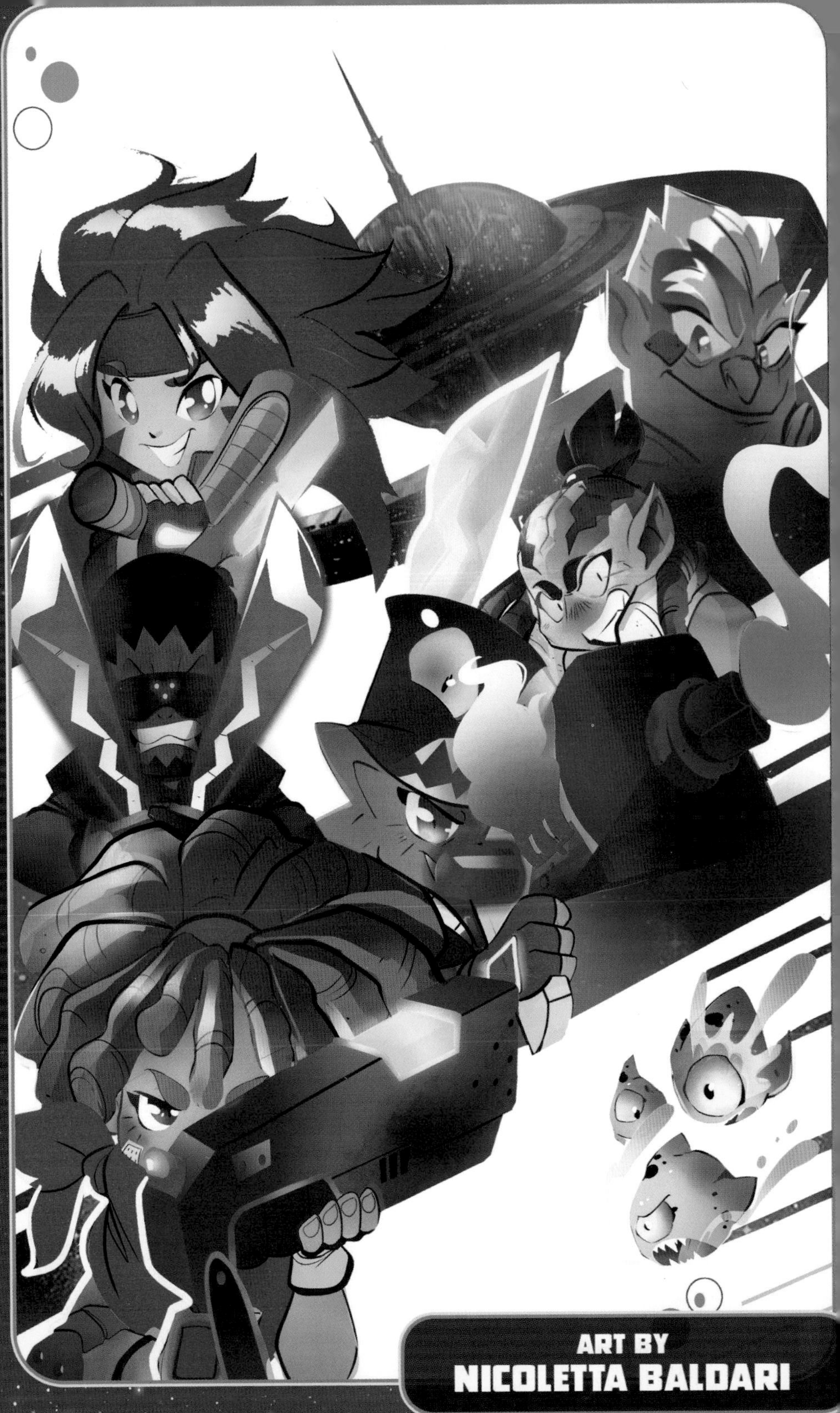

ART BY
NICOLETTA BALDARI

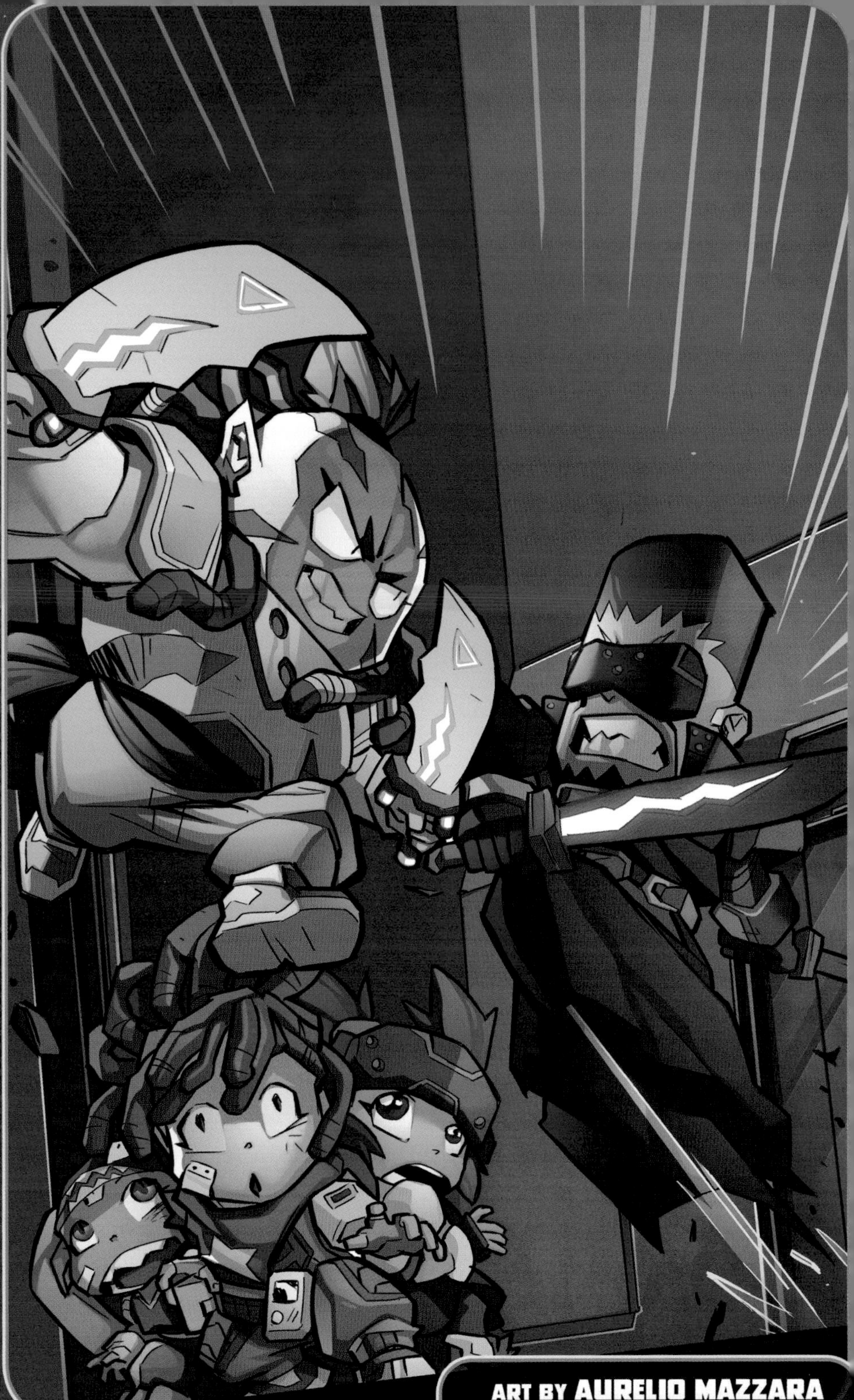
ART BY AURELIO MAZZARA
COLORS BY DAVID GARCIA CRUZ

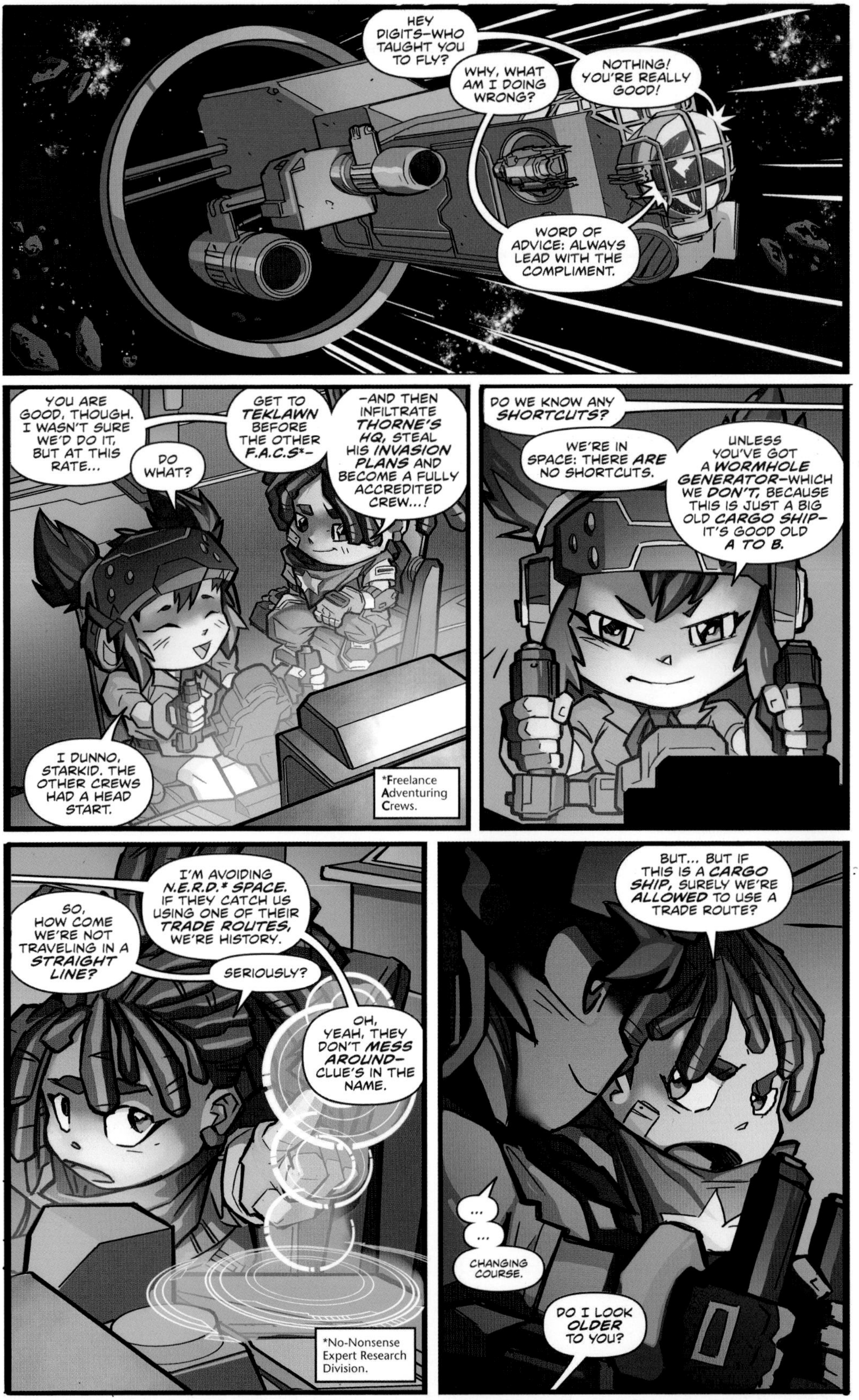
HEY DIGITS—WHO TAUGHT YOU TO FLY?
WHY, WHAT AM I DOING WRONG?
NOTHING! YOU'RE REALLY GOOD!
WORD OF ADVICE: ALWAYS LEAD WITH THE COMPLIMENT.
YOU ARE GOOD, THOUGH. I WASN'T SURE WE'D DO IT, BUT AT THIS RATE...
DO WHAT?
GET TO TEKLAWN BEFORE THE OTHER F.A.C.S*—
—AND THEN INFILTRATE THORNE'S HQ, STEAL HIS INVASION PLANS AND BECOME A FULLY ACCREDITED CREW...!
I DUNNO, STARKID. THE OTHER CREWS HAD A HEAD START.
*Freelance Adventuring Crews.
DO WE KNOW ANY SHORTCUTS?
WE'RE IN SPACE: THERE ARE NO SHORTCUTS.
UNLESS YOU'VE GOT A WORMHOLE GENERATOR—WHICH WE DON'T, BECAUSE THIS IS JUST A BIG OLD CARGO SHIP—IT'S GOOD OLD A TO B.
SO, HOW COME WE'RE NOT TRAVELING IN A STRAIGHT LINE?
I'M AVOIDING N.E.R.D.* SPACE. IF THEY CATCH US USING ONE OF THEIR TRADE ROUTES, WE'RE HISTORY.
SERIOUSLY?
OH, YEAH, THEY DON'T MESS AROUND—CLUE'S IN THE NAME.
*No-Nonsense Expert Research Division.
BUT... BUT IF THIS IS A CARGO SHIP, SURELY WE'RE ALLOWED TO USE A TRADE ROUTE?
...
...
CHANGING COURSE.
DO I LOOK OLDER TO YOU?

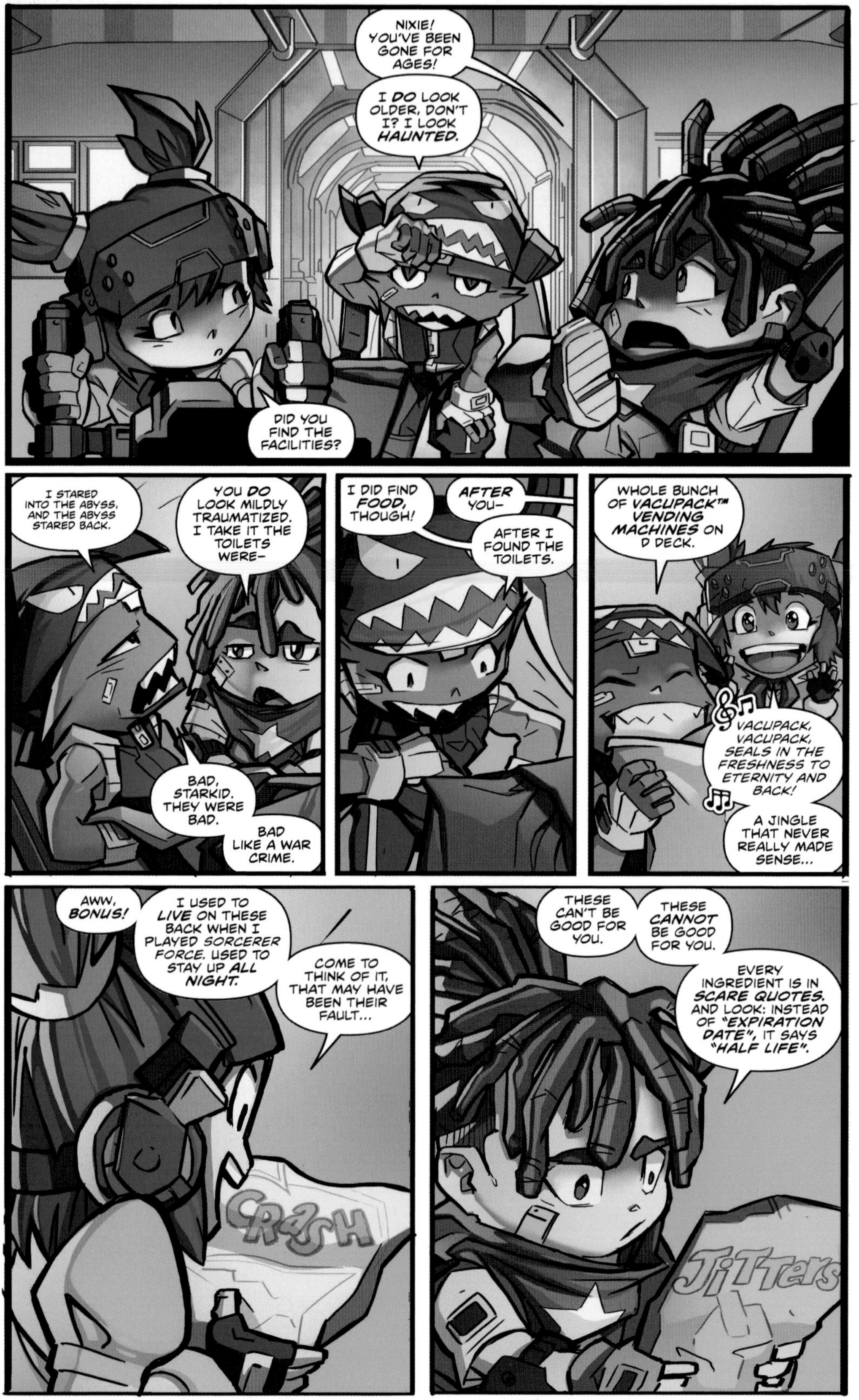

NIXIE! YOU'VE BEEN GONE FOR AGES!
I DO LOOK OLDER, DON'T I? I LOOK HAUNTED.
DID YOU FIND THE FACILITIES?
I STARED INTO THE ABYSS, AND THE ABYSS STARED BACK.
YOU DO LOOK MILDLY TRAUMATIZED. I TAKE IT THE TOILETS WERE–
BAD, STARKID. THEY WERE BAD.
BAD LIKE A WAR CRIME.
I DID FIND FOOD, THOUGH!
AFTER YOU–
AFTER I FOUND THE TOILETS.
WHOLE BUNCH OF VACUPACK™ VENDING MACHINES ON D DECK.
VACUPACK, VACUPACK, SEALS IN THE FRESHNESS TO ETERNITY AND BACK!
A JINGLE THAT NEVER REALLY MADE SENSE...
AWW, BONUS!
I USED TO LIVE ON THESE BACK WHEN I PLAYED SORCERER FORCE. USED TO STAY UP ALL NIGHT.
COME TO THINK OF IT, THAT MAY HAVE BEEN THEIR FAULT...
CRASH
THESE CAN'T BE GOOD FOR YOU.
THESE CANNOT BE GOOD FOR YOU.
EVERY INGREDIENT IS IN SCARE QUOTES. AND LOOK: INSTEAD OF "EXPIRATION DATE", IT SAYS "HALF LIFE".
JiTTers

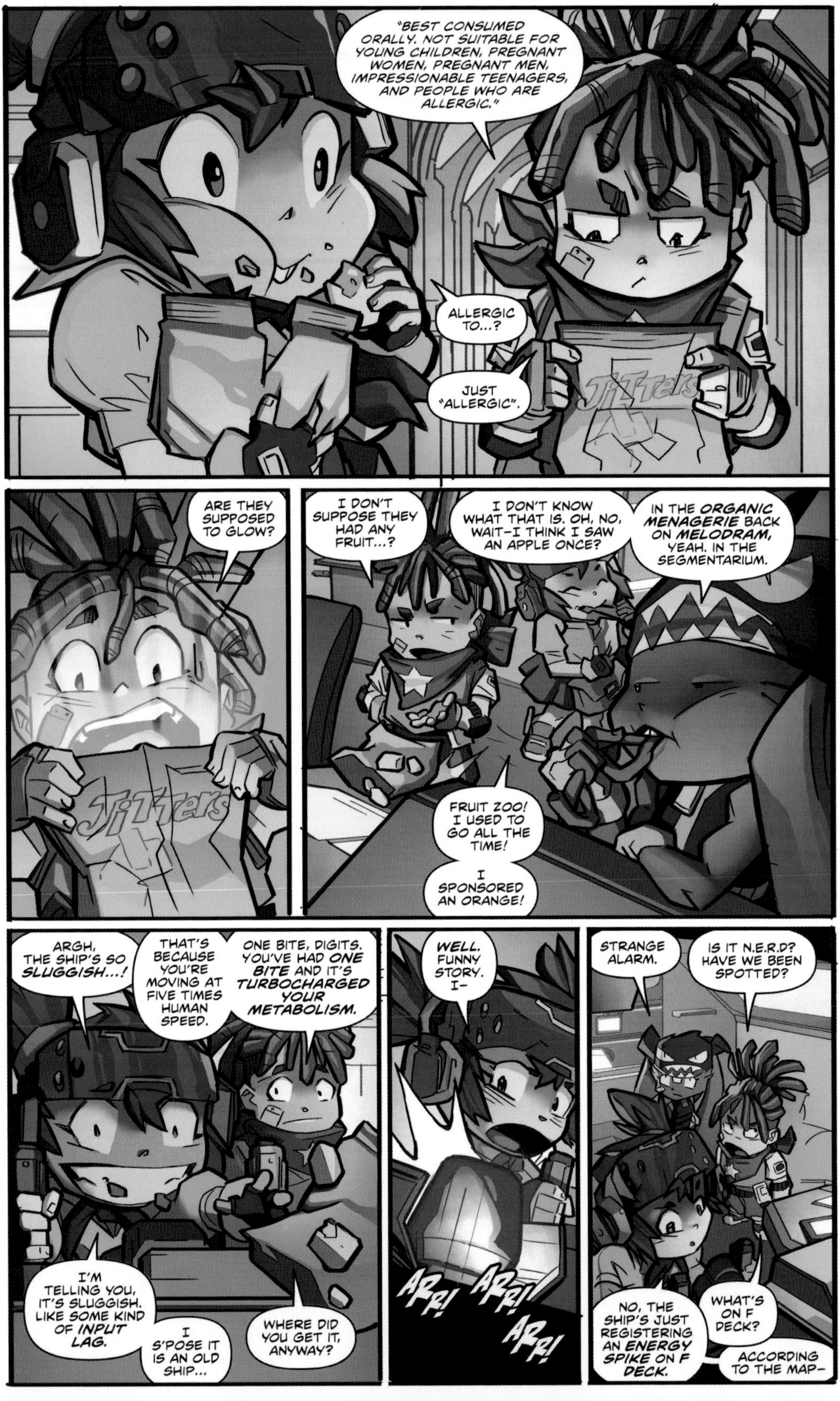
"BEST CONSUMED ORALLY. NOT SUITABLE FOR YOUNG CHILDREN, PREGNANT WOMEN, PREGNANT MEN, IMPRESSIONABLE TEENAGERS, AND PEOPLE WHO ARE ALLERGIC."
ALLERGIC TO...?
JUST "ALLERGIC".
JiTTers
ARE THEY SUPPOSED TO GLOW?
JiTTers
I DON'T SUPPOSE THEY HAD ANY FRUIT...?
I DON'T KNOW WHAT THAT IS. OH, NO, WAIT–I THINK I SAW AN APPLE ONCE?
IN THE ORGANIC MENAGERIE BACK ON MELODRAM, YEAH. IN THE SEGMENTARIUM.
FRUIT ZOO! I USED TO GO ALL THE TIME!
I SPONSORED AN ORANGE!
ARGH, THE SHIP'S SO SLUGGISH...!
THAT'S BECAUSE YOU'RE MOVING AT FIVE TIMES HUMAN SPEED.
ONE BITE, DIGITS. YOU'VE HAD ONE BITE AND IT'S TURBOCHARGED YOUR METABOLISM.
I'M TELLING YOU, IT'S SLUGGISH. LIKE SOME KIND OF INPUT LAG.
I S'POSE IT IS AN OLD SHIP...
WHERE DID YOU GET IT, ANYWAY?
WELL. FUNNY STORY. I–
ARR! ARR! ARR!
STRANGE ALARM.
IS IT N.E.R.D? HAVE WE BEEN SPOTTED?
NO, THE SHIP'S JUST REGISTERING AN ENERGY SPIKE ON F DECK.
WHAT'S ON F DECK?
ACCORDING TO THE MAP–

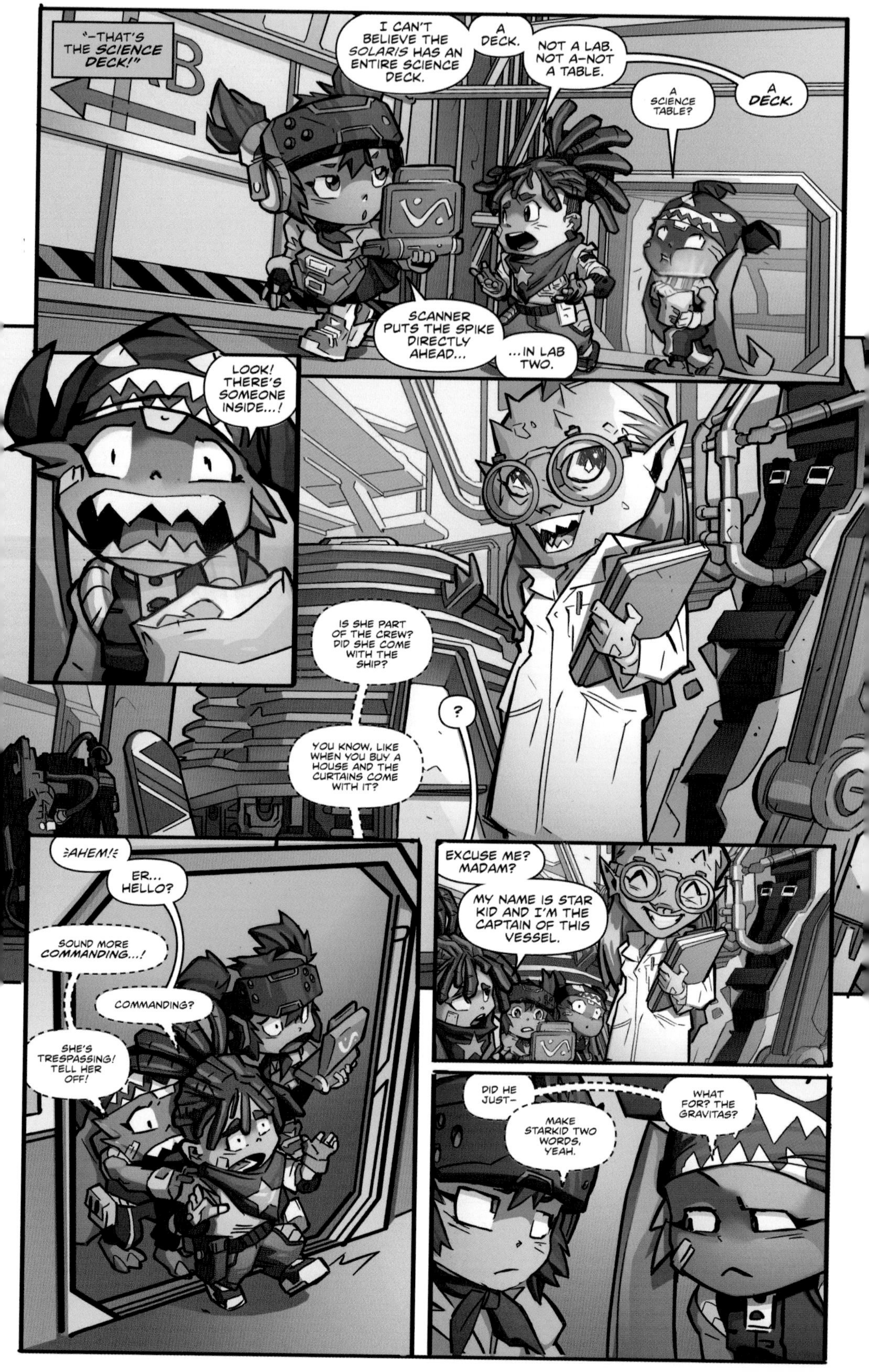
"–THAT'S THE SCIENCE DECK!"
I CAN'T BELIEVE THE SOLARIS HAS AN ENTIRE SCIENCE DECK.
A DECK.
NOT A LAB. NOT A–NOT A TABLE.
A SCIENCE TABLE?
A DECK.
SCANNER PUTS THE SPIKE DIRECTLY AHEAD...
...IN LAB TWO.
LOOK! THERE'S SOMEONE INSIDE...!
IS SHE PART OF THE CREW? DID SHE COME WITH THE SHIP?
?
YOU KNOW, LIKE WHEN YOU BUY A HOUSE AND THE CURTAINS COME WITH IT?
AHEM!
ER... HELLO?
SOUND MORE COMMANDING...!
COMMANDING?
SHE'S TRESPASSING! TELL HER OFF!
EXCUSE ME? MADAM?
MY NAME IS STAR KID AND I'M THE CAPTAIN OF THIS VESSEL.
DID HE JUST–
MAKE STARKID TWO WORDS, YEAH.
WHAT FOR? THE GRAVITAS?

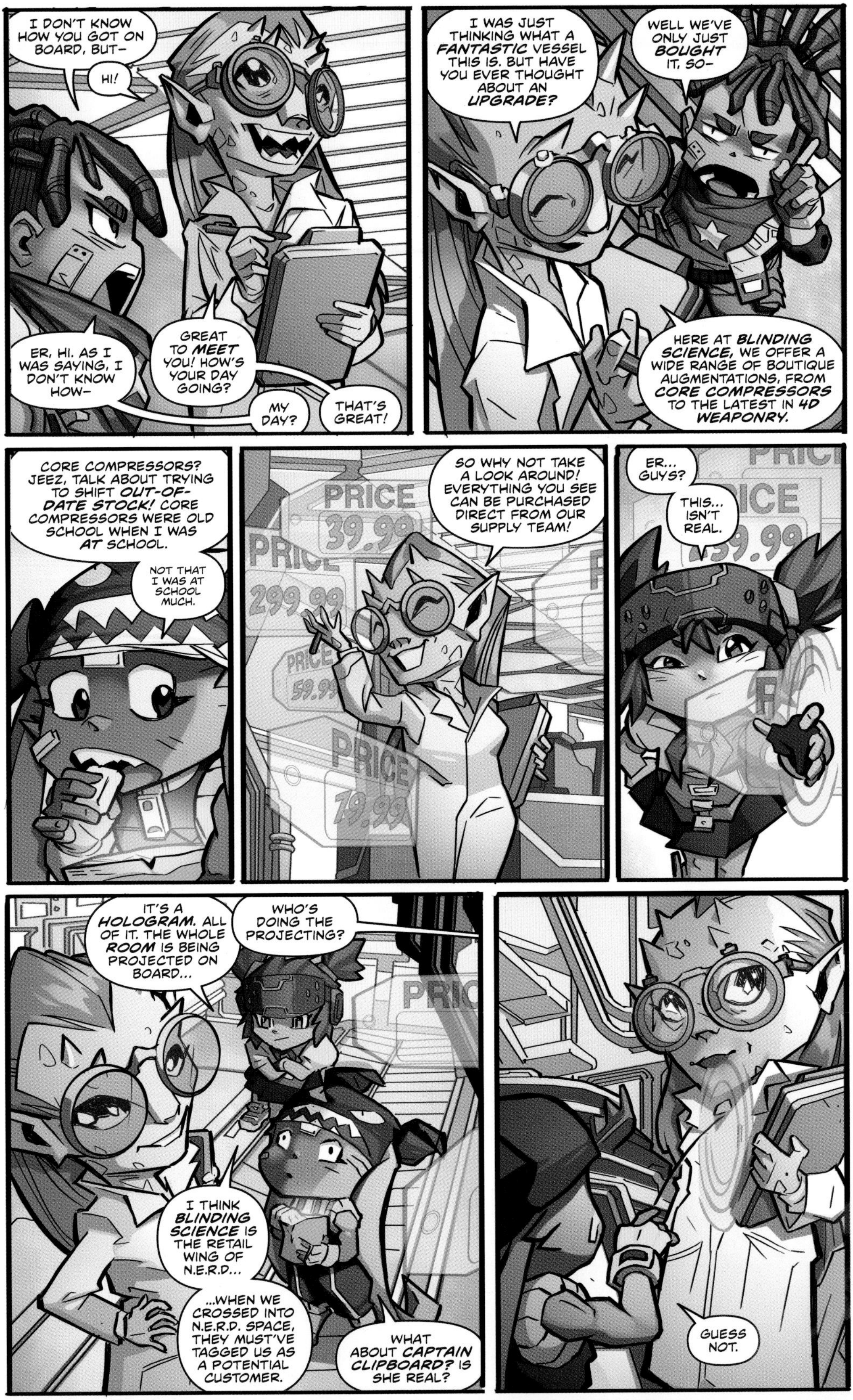
I DON'T KNOW HOW YOU GOT ON BOARD, BUT–
HI!
ER, HI. AS I WAS SAYING, I DON'T KNOW HOW–
GREAT TO MEET YOU! HOW'S YOUR DAY GOING?
MY DAY?
THAT'S GREAT!
I WAS JUST THINKING WHAT A FANTASTIC VESSEL THIS IS. BUT HAVE YOU EVER THOUGHT ABOUT AN UPGRADE?
WELL WE'VE ONLY JUST BOUGHT IT, SO–
HERE AT BLINDING SCIENCE, WE OFFER A WIDE RANGE OF BOUTIQUE AUGMENTATIONS, FROM CORE COMPRESSORS TO THE LATEST IN 4D WEAPONRY.
CORE COMPRESSORS? JEEZ, TALK ABOUT TRYING TO SHIFT OUT-OF-DATE STOCK! CORE COMPRESSORS WERE OLD SCHOOL WHEN I WAS AT SCHOOL.
NOT THAT I WAS AT SCHOOL MUCH.
SO WHY NOT TAKE A LOOK AROUND! EVERYTHING YOU SEE CAN BE PURCHASED DIRECT FROM OUR SUPPLY TEAM!
PRICE 39.99
PRICE 299.99
PRICE 59.99
PRICE 79.99
ER... GUYS?
THIS... ISN'T REAL.
IT'S A HOLOGRAM. ALL OF IT. THE WHOLE ROOM IS BEING PROJECTED ON BOARD...
WHO'S DOING THE PROJECTING?
I THINK BLINDING SCIENCE IS THE RETAIL WING OF N.E.R.D...
...WHEN WE CROSSED INTO N.E.R.D. SPACE, THEY MUST'VE TAGGED US AS A POTENTIAL CUSTOMER.
WHAT ABOUT CAPTAIN CLIPBOARD? IS SHE REAL?
GUESS NOT.

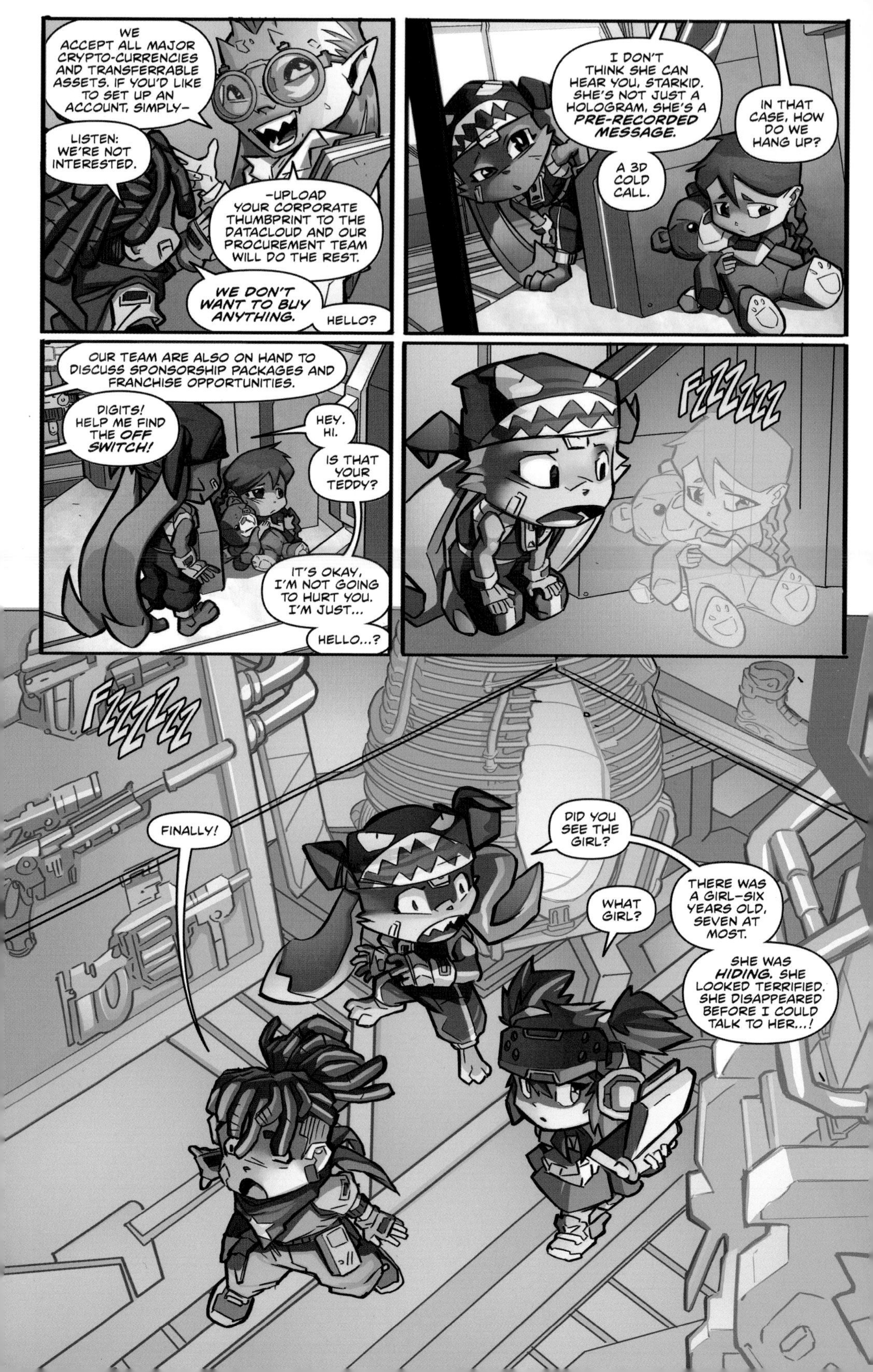
WE ACCEPT ALL MAJOR CRYPTO-CURRENCIES AND TRANSFERRABLE ASSETS. IF YOU'D LIKE TO SET UP AN ACCOUNT, SIMPLY–
LISTEN: WE'RE NOT INTERESTED.
–UPLOAD YOUR CORPORATE THUMBPRINT TO THE DATACLOUD AND OUR PROCUREMENT TEAM WILL DO THE REST.
WE DON'T WANT TO BUY ANYTHING.
HELLO?
I DON'T THINK SHE CAN HEAR YOU, STARKID. SHE'S NOT JUST A HOLOGRAM, SHE'S A PRE-RECORDED MESSAGE.
A 3D COLD CALL.
IN THAT CASE, HOW DO WE HANG UP?
OUR TEAM ARE ALSO ON HAND TO DISCUSS SPONSORSHIP PACKAGES AND FRANCHISE OPPORTUNITIES.
DIGITS! HELP ME FIND THE OFF SWITCH!
HEY. HI.
IS THAT YOUR TEDDY?
IT'S OKAY, I'M NOT GOING TO HURT YOU. I'M JUST...
HELLO...?
FZZZZZZ
FZZZZZZ
FINALLY!
DID YOU SEE THE GIRL?
WHAT GIRL?
THERE WAS A GIRL–SIX YEARS OLD, SEVEN AT MOST.
SHE WAS HIDING. SHE LOOKED TERRIFIED. SHE DISAPPEARED BEFORE I COULD TALK TO HER...!

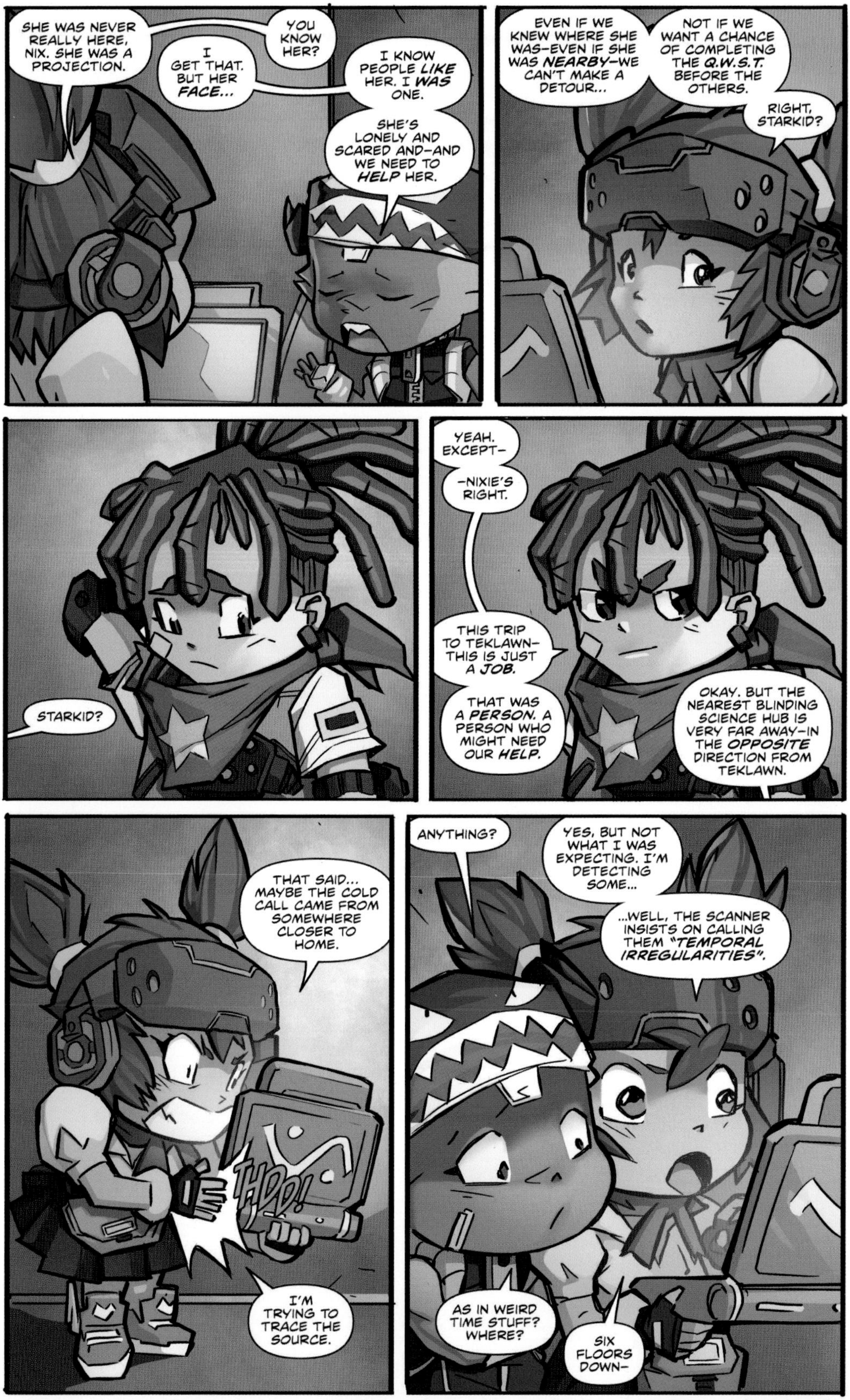

SHE WAS NEVER REALLY HERE, NIX. SHE WAS A PROJECTION.
YOU KNOW HER?
I GET THAT. BUT HER FACE...
I KNOW PEOPLE LIKE HER. I WAS ONE.
SHE'S LONELY AND SCARED AND—AND WE NEED TO HELP HER.
EVEN IF WE KNEW WHERE SHE WAS—EVEN IF SHE WAS NEARBY—WE CAN'T MAKE A DETOUR...
NOT IF WE WANT A CHANCE OF COMPLETING THE Q.W.S.T. BEFORE THE OTHERS.
RIGHT, STARKID?
STARKID?
YEAH. EXCEPT—
—NIXIE'S RIGHT.
THIS TRIP TO TEKLAWN—THIS IS JUST A JOB.
THAT WAS A PERSON. A PERSON WHO MIGHT NEED OUR HELP.
OKAY. BUT THE NEAREST BLINDING SCIENCE HUB IS VERY FAR AWAY—IN THE OPPOSITE DIRECTION FROM TEKLAWN.
THAT SAID... MAYBE THE COLD CALL CAME FROM SOMEWHERE CLOSER TO HOME.
THDD!
I'M TRYING TO TRACE THE SOURCE.
ANYTHING?
YES, BUT NOT WHAT I WAS EXPECTING. I'M DETECTING SOME...
...WELL, THE SCANNER INSISTS ON CALLING THEM "TEMPORAL IRREGULARITIES".
AS IN WEIRD TIME STUFF? WHERE?
SIX FLOORS DOWN—

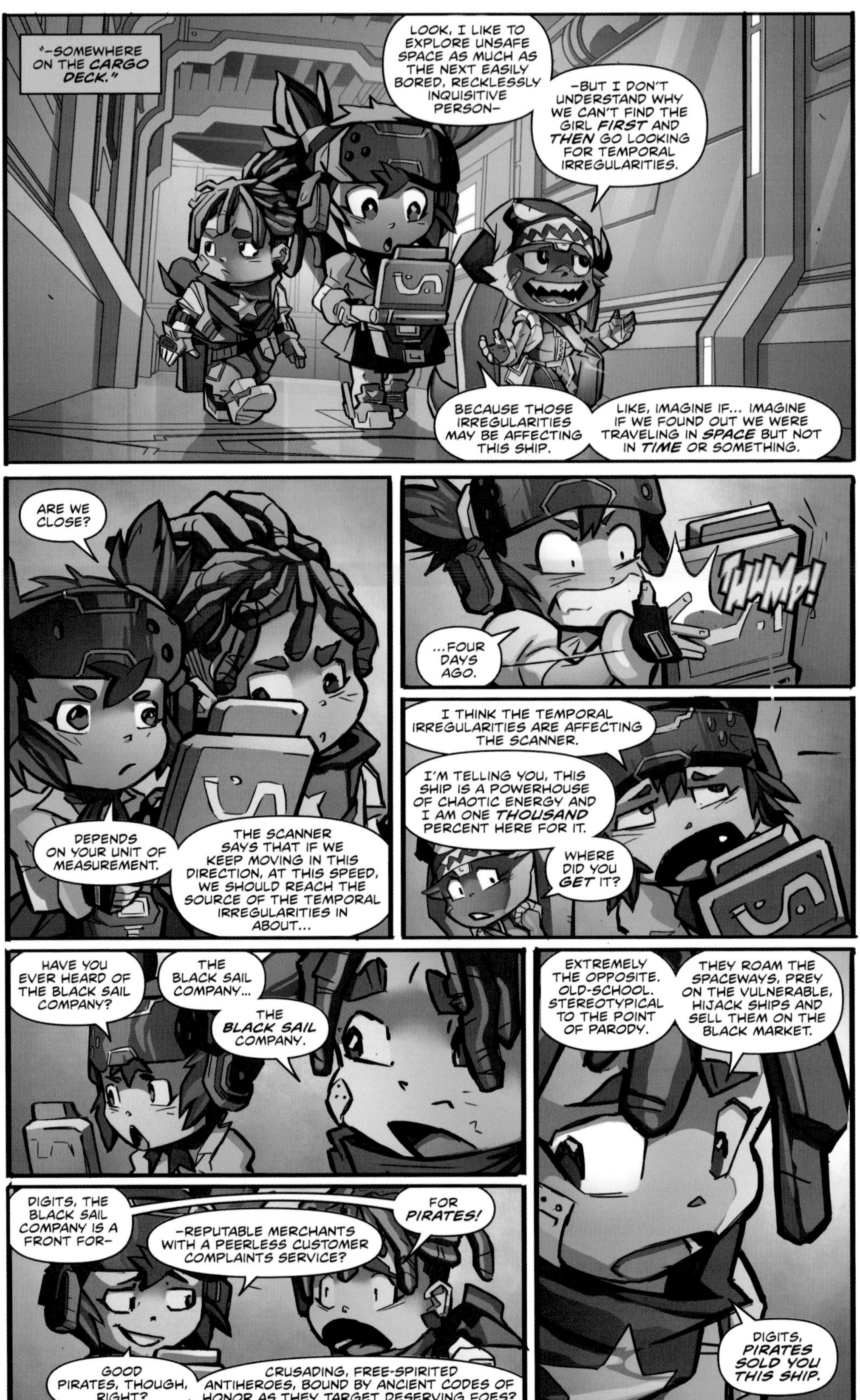
"–SOMEWHERE ON THE CARGO DECK."
LOOK, I LIKE TO EXPLORE UNSAFE SPACE AS MUCH AS THE NEXT EASILY BORED, RECKLESSLY INQUISITIVE PERSON–
–BUT I DON'T UNDERSTAND WHY WE CAN'T FIND THE GIRL FIRST AND THEN GO LOOKING FOR TEMPORAL IRREGULARITIES.
BECAUSE THOSE IRREGULARITIES MAY BE AFFECTING THIS SHIP.
LIKE, IMAGINE IF... IMAGINE IF WE FOUND OUT WE WERE TRAVELING IN SPACE BUT NOT IN TIME OR SOMETHING.
ARE WE CLOSE?
DEPENDS ON YOUR UNIT OF MEASUREMENT.
THE SCANNER SAYS THAT IF WE KEEP MOVING IN THIS DIRECTION, AT THIS SPEED, WE SHOULD REACH THE SOURCE OF THE TEMPORAL IRREGULARITIES IN ABOUT...
THUMP!
...FOUR DAYS AGO.
I THINK THE TEMPORAL IRREGULARITIES ARE AFFECTING THE SCANNER.
I'M TELLING YOU, THIS SHIP IS A POWERHOUSE OF CHAOTIC ENERGY AND I AM ONE THOUSAND PERCENT HERE FOR IT.
WHERE DID YOU GET IT?
HAVE YOU EVER HEARD OF THE BLACK SAIL COMPANY?
THE BLACK SAIL COMPANY...
THE BLACK SAIL COMPANY.
DIGITS, THE BLACK SAIL COMPANY IS A FRONT FOR–
–REPUTABLE MERCHANTS WITH A PEERLESS CUSTOMER COMPLAINTS SERVICE?
FOR PIRATES!
GOOD PIRATES, THOUGH, RIGHT?
CRUSADING, FREE-SPIRITED ANTIHEROES, BOUND BY ANCIENT CODES OF HONOR AS THEY TARGET DESERVING FOES?
EXTREMELY THE OPPOSITE. OLD-SCHOOL. STEREOTYPICAL TO THE POINT OF PARODY.
THEY ROAM THE SPACEWAYS, PREY ON THE VULNERABLE, HIJACK SHIPS AND SELL THEM ON THE BLACK MARKET.
DIGITS, PIRATES SOLD YOU THIS SHIP.

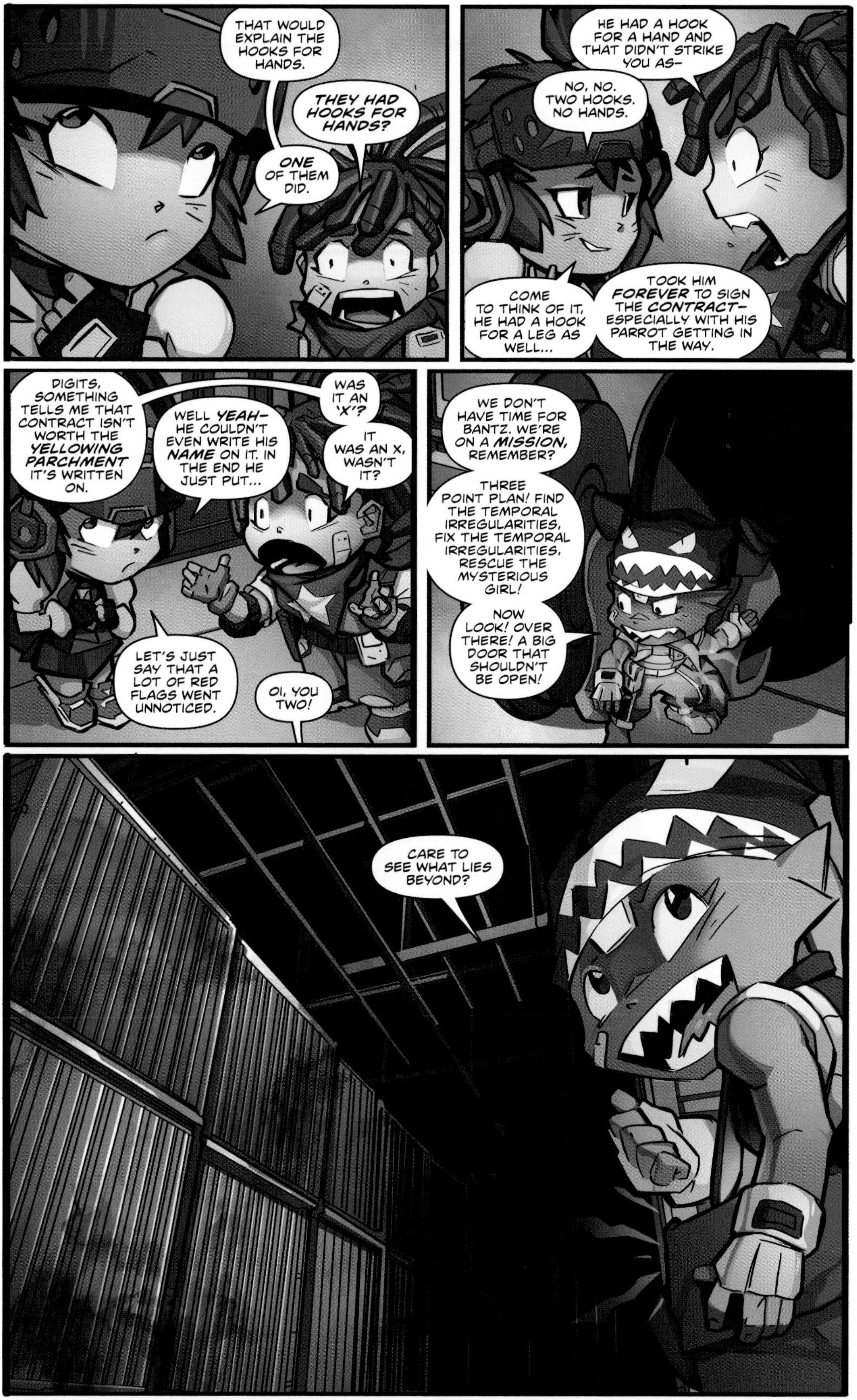
THAT WOULD EXPLAIN THE HOOKS FOR HANDS.
THEY HAD HOOKS FOR HANDS?
ONE OF THEM DID.
HE HAD A HOOK FOR A HAND AND THAT DIDN'T STRIKE YOU AS–
NO, NO. TWO HOOKS. NO HANDS.
COME TO THINK OF IT, HE HAD A HOOK FOR A LEG AS WELL...
TOOK HIM FOREVER TO SIGN THE CONTRACT– ESPECIALLY WITH HIS PARROT GETTING IN THE WAY.
DIGITS, SOMETHING TELLS ME THAT CONTRACT ISN'T WORTH THE YELLOWING PARCHMENT IT'S WRITTEN ON.
WELL YEAH– HE COULDN'T EVEN WRITE HIS NAME ON IT. IN THE END HE JUST PUT...
WAS IT AN 'X'?
IT WAS AN X, WASN'T IT?
LET'S JUST SAY THAT A LOT OF RED FLAGS WENT UNNOTICED.
OI, YOU TWO!
WE DON'T HAVE TIME FOR BANTZ. WE'RE ON A MISSION, REMEMBER?
THREE POINT PLAN! FIND THE TEMPORAL IRREGULARITIES, FIX THE TEMPORAL IRREGULARITIES, RESCUE THE MYSTERIOUS GIRL!
NOW LOOK! OVER THERE! A BIG DOOR THAT SHOULDN'T BE OPEN!
CARE TO SEE WHAT LIES BEYOND?

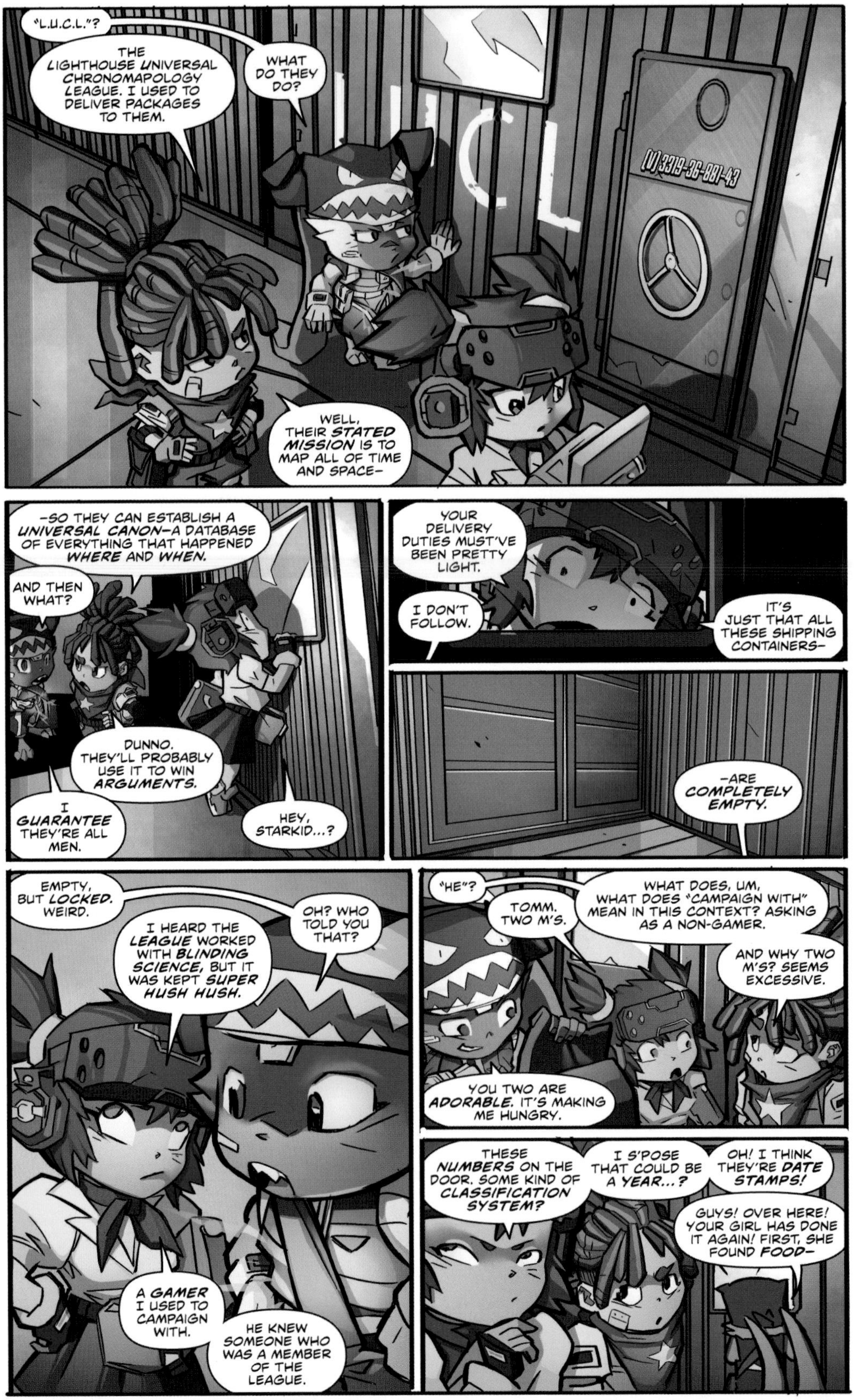
"L.U.C.L."?
THE LIGHTHOUSE UNIVERSAL CHRONOMAPOLOGY LEAGUE. I USED TO DELIVER PACKAGES TO THEM.
WHAT DO THEY DO?
(V) 3319-36-881-43
WELL, THEIR STATED MISSION IS TO MAP ALL OF TIME AND SPACE–
–SO THEY CAN ESTABLISH A UNIVERSAL CANON–A DATABASE OF EVERYTHING THAT HAPPENED WHERE AND WHEN.
AND THEN WHAT?
DUNNO. THEY'LL PROBABLY USE IT TO WIN ARGUMENTS.
I GUARANTEE THEY'RE ALL MEN.
HEY, STARKID...?
YOUR DELIVERY DUTIES MUST'VE BEEN PRETTY LIGHT.
I DON'T FOLLOW.
IT'S JUST THAT ALL THESE SHIPPING CONTAINERS–
–ARE COMPLETELY EMPTY.
EMPTY, BUT LOCKED. WEIRD.
I HEARD THE LEAGUE WORKED WITH BLINDING SCIENCE, BUT IT WAS KEPT SUPER HUSH HUSH.
OH? WHO TOLD YOU THAT?
A GAMER I USED TO CAMPAIGN WITH.
HE KNEW SOMEONE WHO WAS A MEMBER OF THE LEAGUE.
"HE"?
TOMM. TWO M'S.
WHAT DOES, UM, WHAT DOES "CAMPAIGN WITH" MEAN IN THIS CONTEXT? ASKING AS A NON-GAMER.
AND WHY TWO M'S? SEEMS EXCESSIVE.
YOU TWO ARE ADORABLE. IT'S MAKING ME HUNGRY.
THESE NUMBERS ON THE DOOR. SOME KIND OF CLASSIFICATION SYSTEM?
I S'POSE THAT COULD BE A YEAR...?
OH! I THINK THEY'RE DATE STAMPS!
GUYS! OVER HERE! YOUR GIRL HAS DONE IT AGAIN! FIRST, SHE FOUND FOOD–

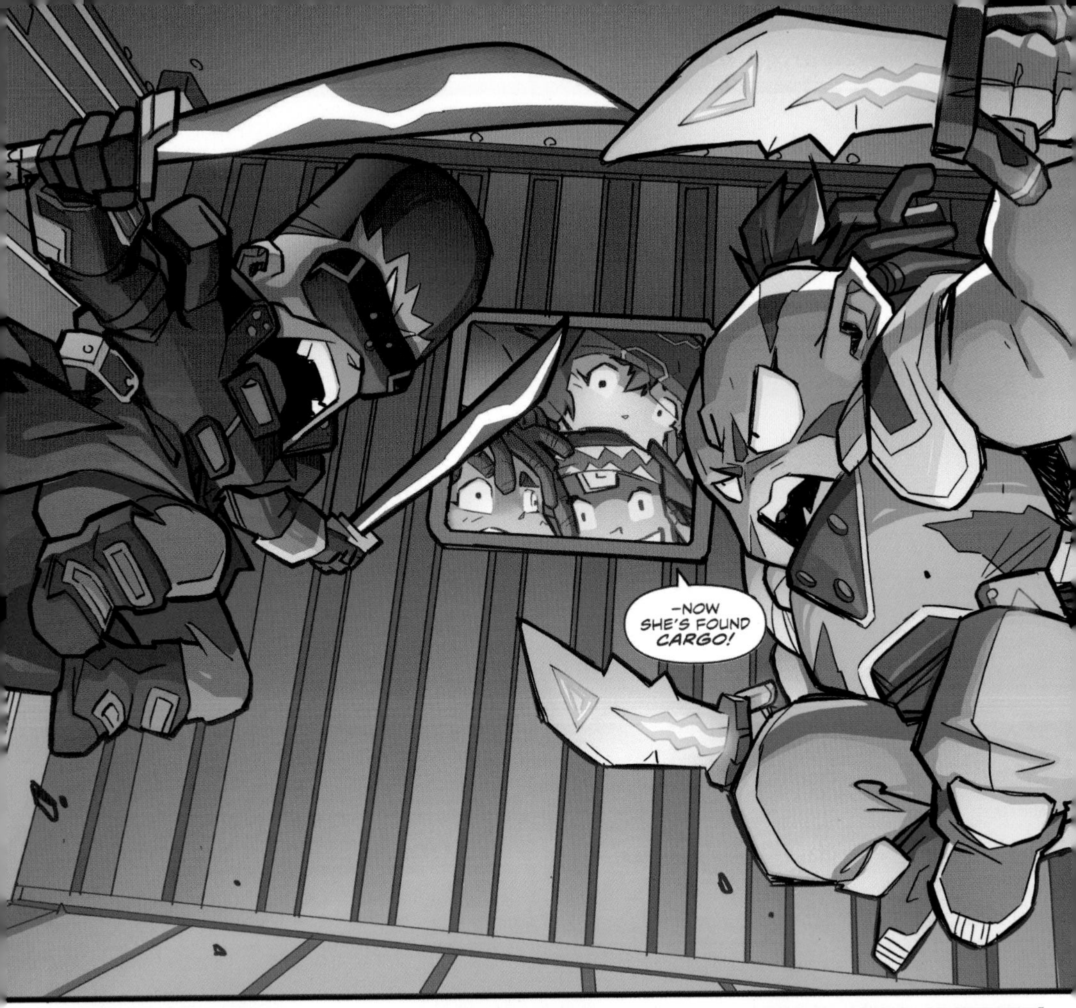
–NOW SHE'S FOUND CARGO!

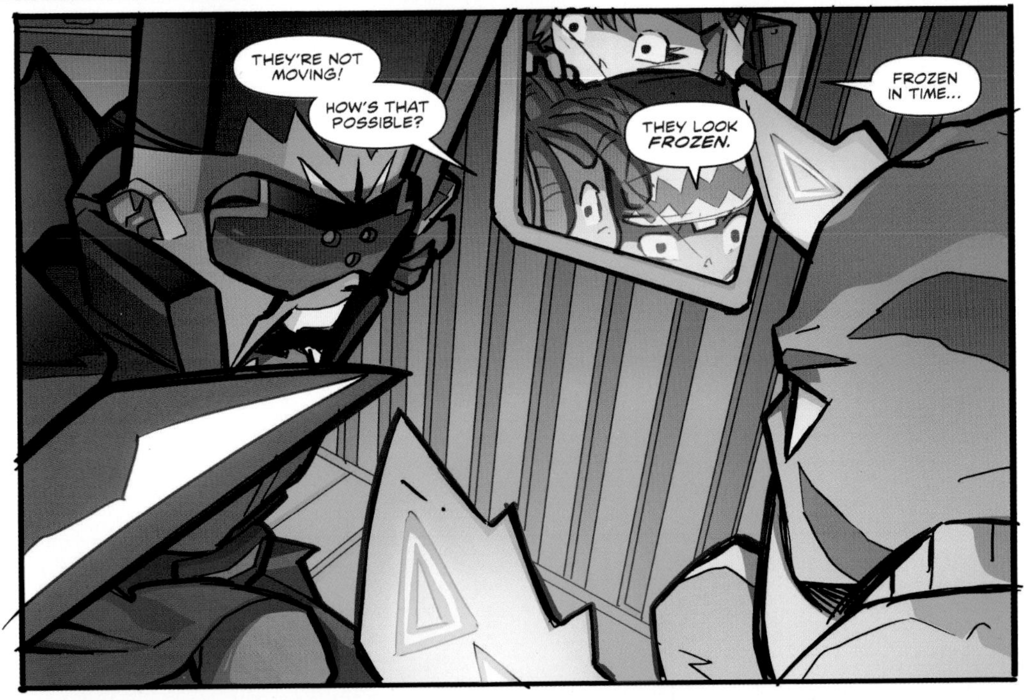
THEY'RE NOT MOVING!
HOW'S THAT POSSIBLE?
THEY LOOK FROZEN.
FROZEN IN TIME...

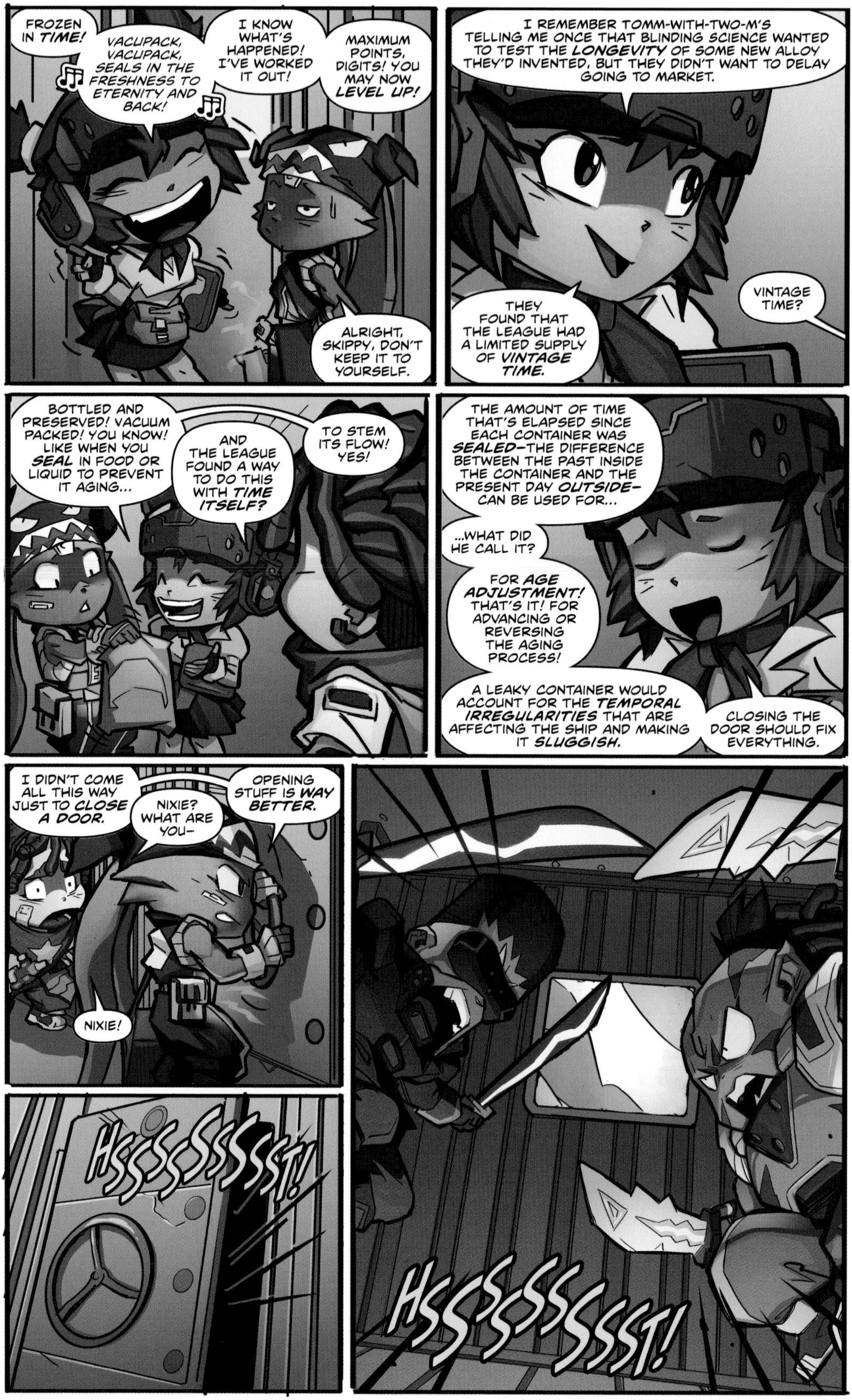

FROZEN IN *TIME!*
VACUPACK, VACUPACK, SEALS IN THE FRESHNESS TO ETERNITY AND BACK!
I KNOW WHAT'S HAPPENED! I'VE WORKED IT OUT!
MAXIMUM POINTS, DIGITS! YOU MAY NOW *LEVEL UP!*
ALRIGHT, SKIPPY, DON'T KEEP IT TO YOURSELF.
I REMEMBER TOMM-WITH-TWO-M'S TELLING ME ONCE THAT BLINDING SCIENCE WANTED TO TEST THE *LONGEVITY* OF SOME NEW ALLOY THEY'D INVENTED, BUT THEY DIDN'T WANT TO DELAY GOING TO MARKET.
THEY FOUND THAT THE LEAGUE HAD A LIMITED SUPPLY OF *VINTAGE TIME.*
VINTAGE TIME?
BOTTLED AND PRESERVED! VACUUM PACKED! YOU KNOW! LIKE WHEN YOU *SEAL* IN FOOD OR LIQUID TO PREVENT IT AGING...
AND THE LEAGUE FOUND A WAY TO DO THIS WITH *TIME ITSELF?*
TO STEM ITS FLOW! YES!
THE AMOUNT OF TIME THAT'S ELAPSED SINCE EACH CONTAINER WAS *SEALED*–THE DIFFERENCE BETWEEN THE PAST INSIDE THE CONTAINER AND THE PRESENT DAY *OUTSIDE*–CAN BE USED FOR...
...WHAT DID HE CALL IT?
FOR *AGE ADJUSTMENT!* THAT'S IT! FOR ADVANCING OR REVERSING THE AGING PROCESS!
A LEAKY CONTAINER WOULD ACCOUNT FOR THE *TEMPORAL IRREGULARITIES* THAT ARE AFFECTING THE SHIP AND MAKING IT *SLUGGISH.*
CLOSING THE DOOR SHOULD FIX EVERYTHING.
I DIDN'T COME ALL THIS WAY JUST TO *CLOSE A DOOR.*
NIXIE? WHAT ARE YOU–
OPENING STUFF IS *WAY BETTER.*
NIXIE!
HSSSSSSSST!
HSSSSSSSST!

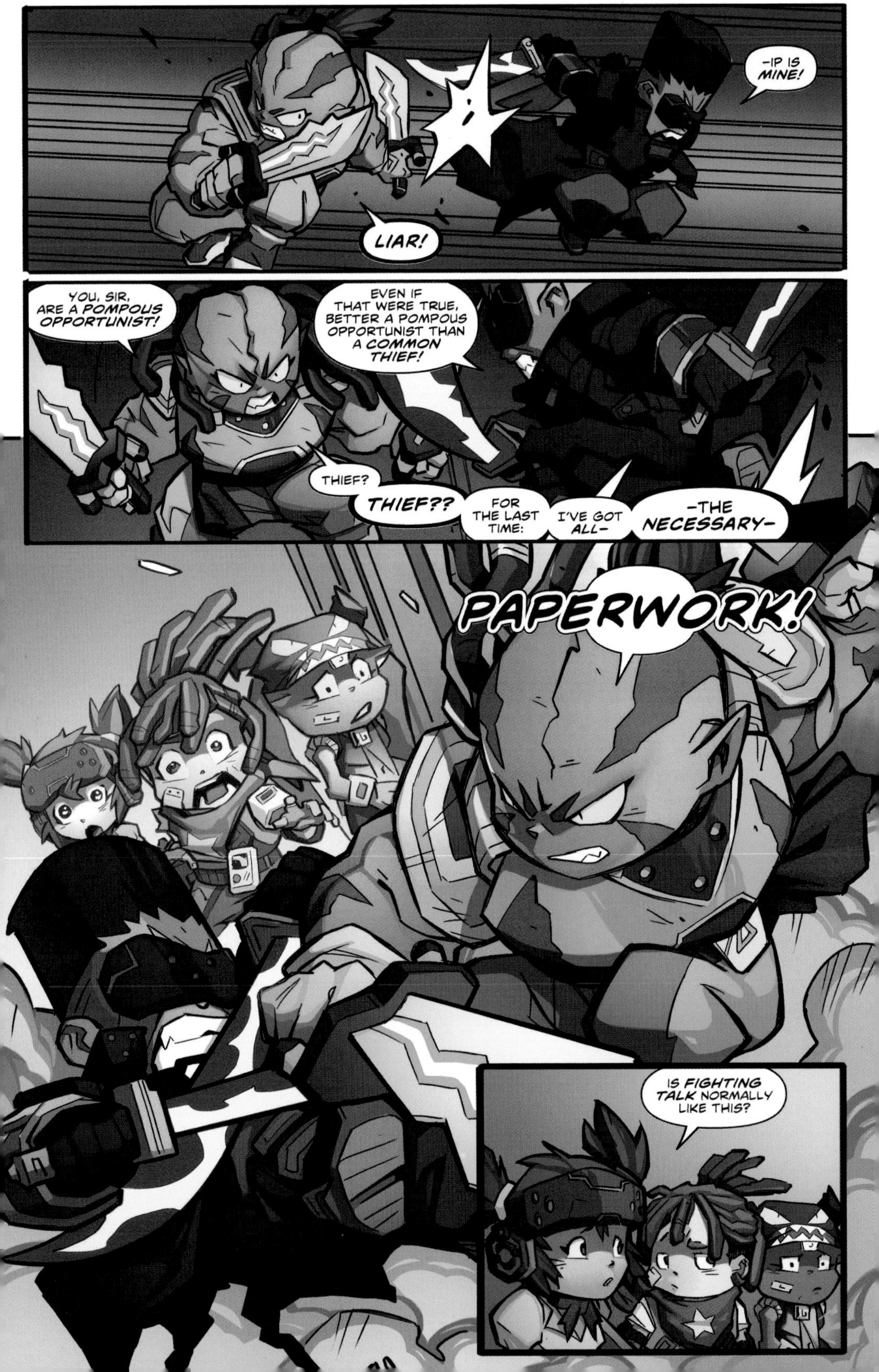
-IP IS MINE!
LIAR!
YOU, SIR, ARE A POMPOUS OPPORTUNIST!
EVEN IF THAT WERE TRUE, BETTER A POMPOUS OPPORTUNIST THAN A COMMON THIEF!
THIEF?
THIEF??
FOR THE LAST TIME:
I'VE GOT ALL-
-THE NECESSARY-
PAPERWORK!
IS FIGHTING TALK NORMALLY LIKE THIS?

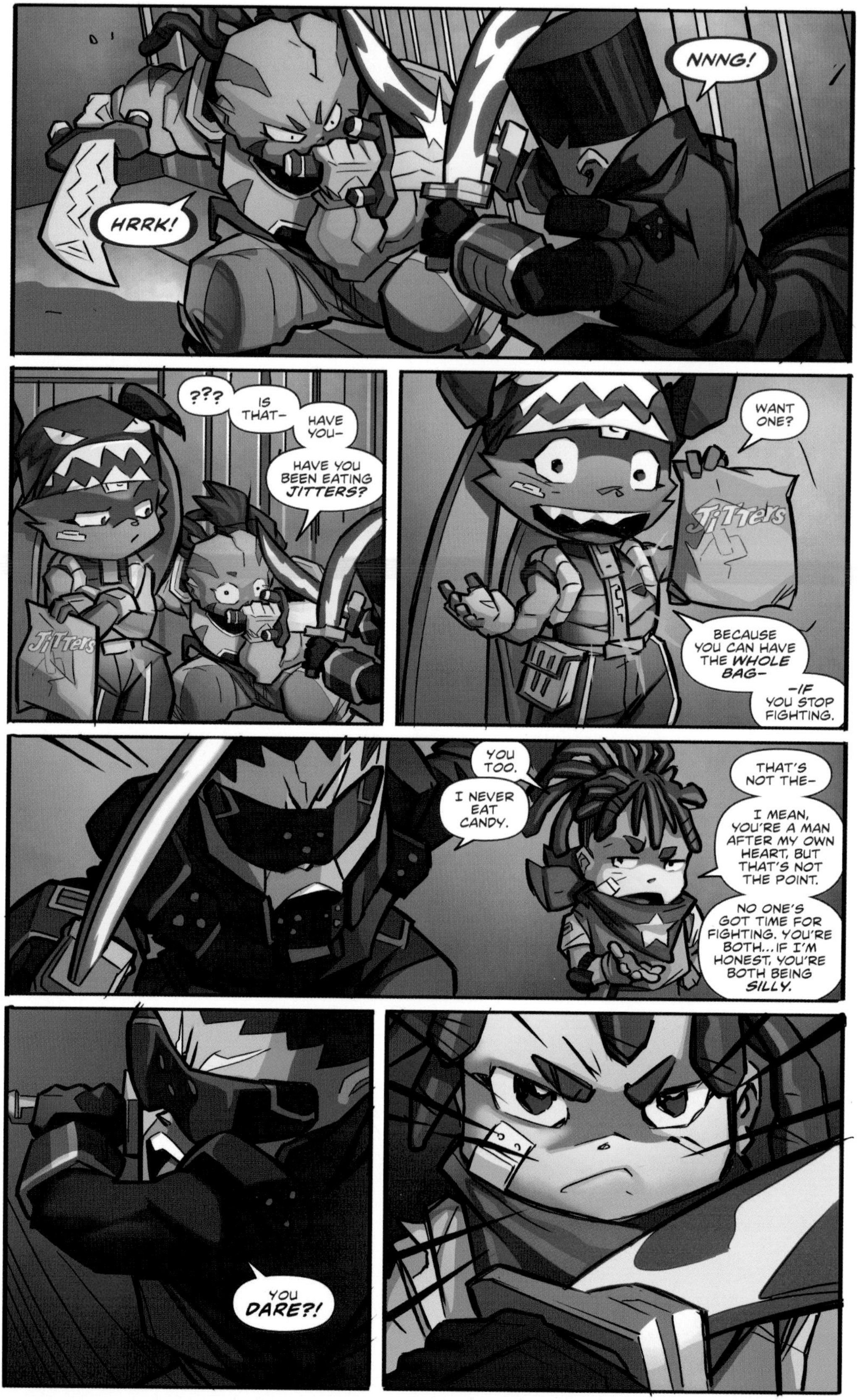
NNNG!
HRRK!
???
IS THAT–
HAVE YOU–
HAVE YOU BEEN EATING JITTERS?
JiTTers
WANT ONE?
JiTTers
BECAUSE YOU CAN HAVE THE WHOLE BAG–
–IF YOU STOP FIGHTING.
YOU TOO.
I NEVER EAT CANDY.
THAT'S NOT THE–
I MEAN, YOU'RE A MAN AFTER MY OWN HEART, BUT THAT'S NOT THE POINT.
NO ONE'S GOT TIME FOR FIGHTING. YOU'RE BOTH... IF I'M HONEST, YOU'RE BOTH BEING SILLY.
YOU DARE?!

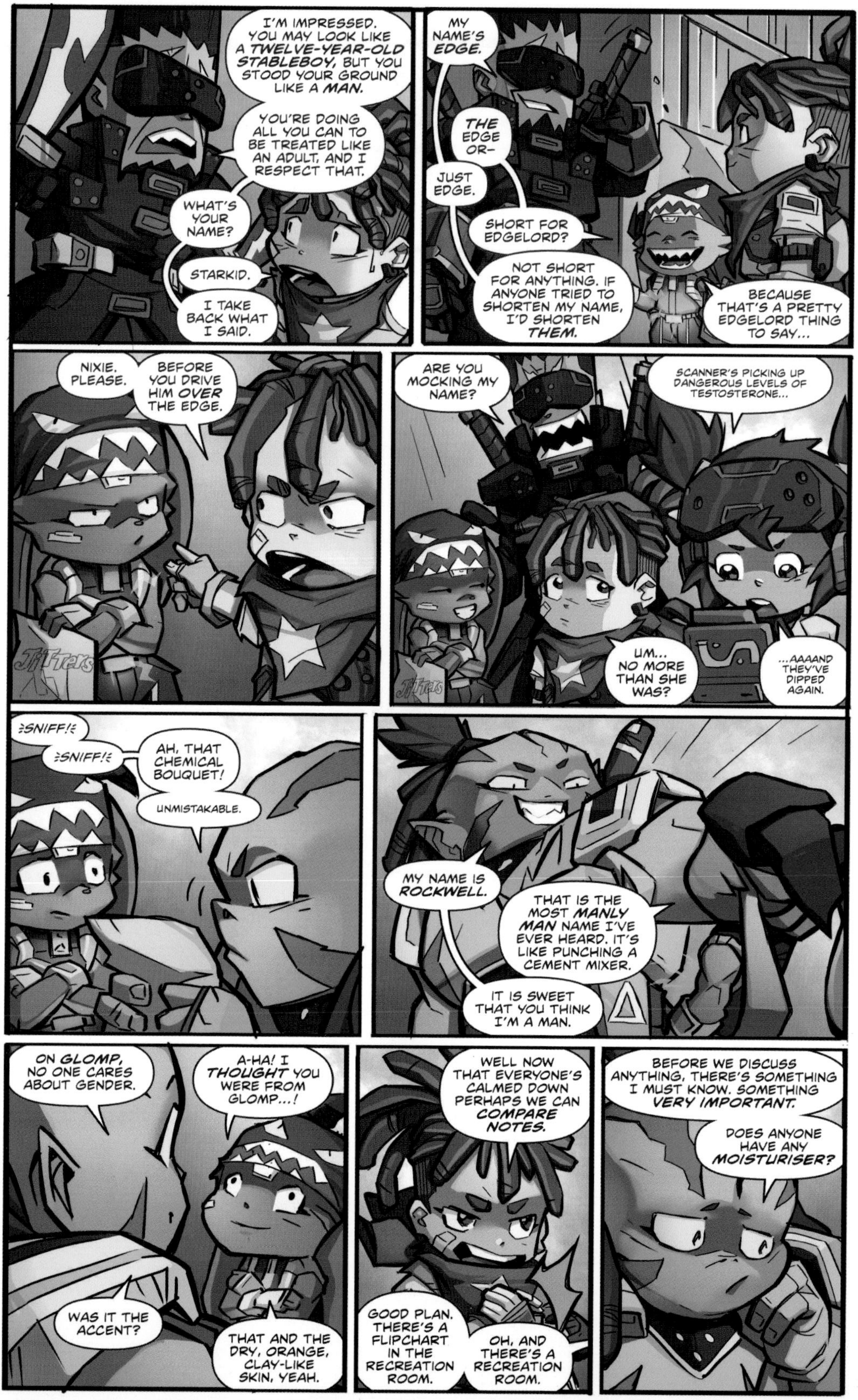

I'M IMPRESSED. YOU MAY LOOK LIKE A TWELVE-YEAR-OLD STABLEBOY, BUT YOU STOOD YOUR GROUND LIKE A MAN.
YOU'RE DOING ALL YOU CAN TO BE TREATED LIKE AN ADULT, AND I RESPECT THAT.
WHAT'S YOUR NAME?
STARKID.
I TAKE BACK WHAT I SAID.
MY NAME'S EDGE.
THE EDGE OR–
JUST EDGE.
SHORT FOR EDGELORD?
NOT SHORT FOR ANYTHING. IF ANYONE TRIED TO SHORTEN MY NAME, I'D SHORTEN THEM.
BECAUSE THAT'S A PRETTY EDGELORD THING TO SAY...
NIXIE. PLEASE.
BEFORE YOU DRIVE HIM OVER THE EDGE.
JITTERS
ARE YOU MOCKING MY NAME?
SCANNER'S PICKING UP DANGEROUS LEVELS OF TESTOSTERONE...
UM... NO MORE THAN SHE WAS?
...AAAAND THEY'VE DIPPED AGAIN.
SNIFF!
SNIFF!
AH, THAT CHEMICAL BOUQUET!
UNMISTAKABLE.
MY NAME IS ROCKWELL.
THAT IS THE MOST MANLY MAN NAME I'VE EVER HEARD. IT'S LIKE PUNCHING A CEMENT MIXER.
IT IS SWEET THAT YOU THINK I'M A MAN.
ON GLOMP, NO ONE CARES ABOUT GENDER.
A-HA! I THOUGHT YOU WERE FROM GLOMP...!
WAS IT THE ACCENT?
THAT AND THE DRY, ORANGE, CLAY-LIKE SKIN, YEAH.
WELL NOW THAT EVERYONE'S CALMED DOWN PERHAPS WE CAN COMPARE NOTES.
GOOD PLAN. THERE'S A FLIPCHART IN THE RECREATION ROOM.
OH, AND THERE'S A RECREATION ROOM.
BEFORE WE DISCUSS ANYTHING, THERE'S SOMETHING I MUST KNOW. SOMETHING VERY IMPORTANT.
DOES ANYONE HAVE ANY MOISTURISER?

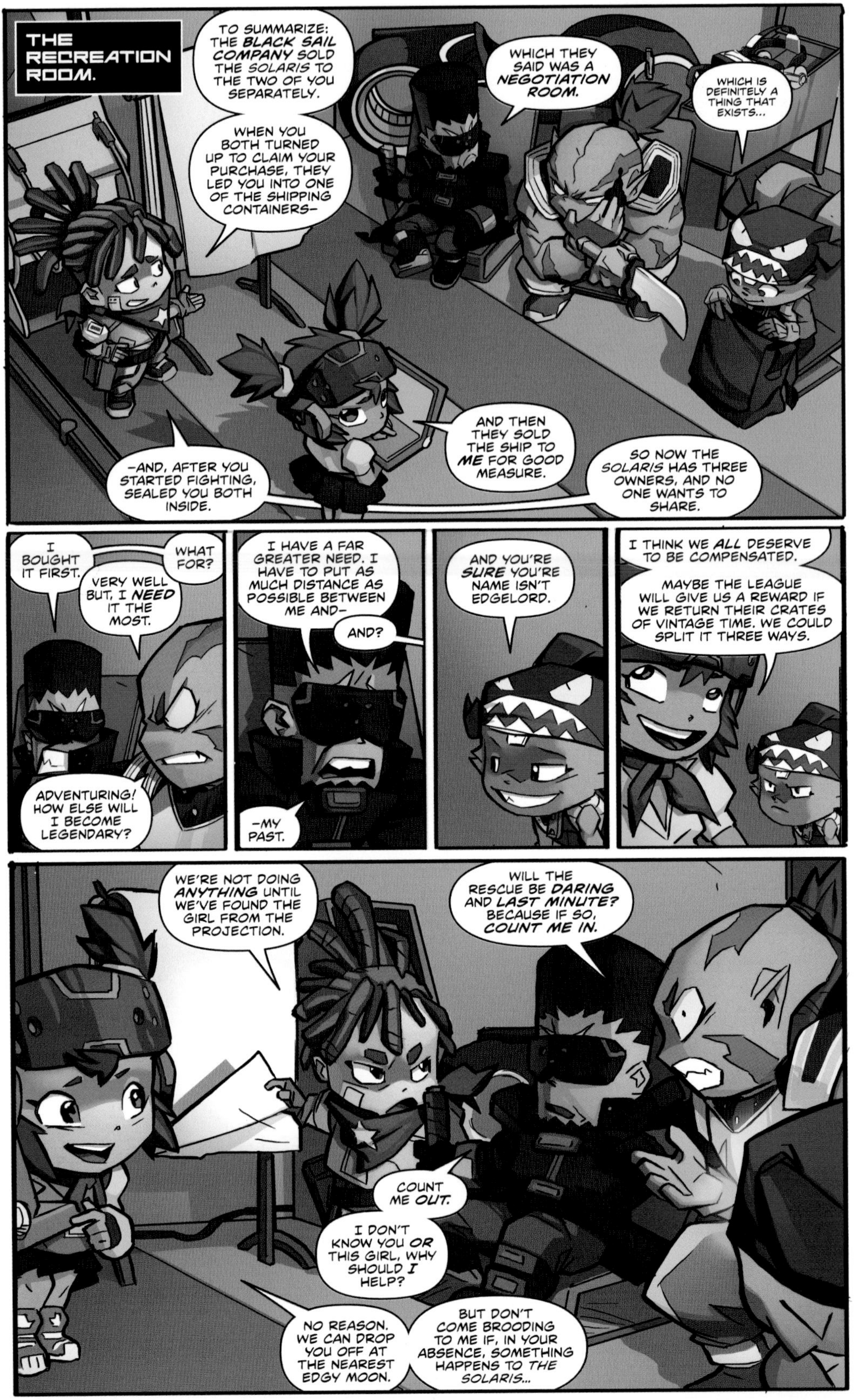
THE RECREATION ROOM.
TO SUMMARIZE: THE BLACK SAIL COMPANY SOLD THE SOLARIS TO THE TWO OF YOU SEPARATELY.
WHEN YOU BOTH TURNED UP TO CLAIM YOUR PURCHASE, THEY LED YOU INTO ONE OF THE SHIPPING CONTAINERS–
WHICH THEY SAID WAS A NEGOTIATION ROOM.
WHICH IS DEFINITELY A THING THAT EXISTS...
–AND, AFTER YOU STARTED FIGHTING, SEALED YOU BOTH INSIDE.
AND THEN THEY SOLD THE SHIP TO ME FOR GOOD MEASURE.
SO NOW THE SOLARIS HAS THREE OWNERS, AND NO ONE WANTS TO SHARE.
I BOUGHT IT FIRST.
VERY WELL BUT, I NEED IT THE MOST.
WHAT FOR?
ADVENTURING! HOW ELSE WILL I BECOME LEGENDARY?
I HAVE A FAR GREATER NEED. I HAVE TO PUT AS MUCH DISTANCE AS POSSIBLE BETWEEN ME AND–
AND?
–MY PAST.
AND YOU'RE SURE YOU'RE NAME ISN'T EDGELORD.
I THINK WE ALL DESERVE TO BE COMPENSATED.
MAYBE THE LEAGUE WILL GIVE US A REWARD IF WE RETURN THEIR CRATES OF VINTAGE TIME. WE COULD SPLIT IT THREE WAYS.
WE'RE NOT DOING ANYTHING UNTIL WE'VE FOUND THE GIRL FROM THE PROJECTION.
WILL THE RESCUE BE DARING AND LAST MINUTE? BECAUSE IF SO, COUNT ME IN.
COUNT ME OUT.
I DON'T KNOW YOU OR THIS GIRL, WHY SHOULD I HELP?
NO REASON. WE CAN DROP YOU OFF AT THE NEAREST EDGY MOON.
BUT DON'T COME BROODING TO ME IF, IN YOUR ABSENCE, SOMETHING HAPPENS TO THE SOLARIS...

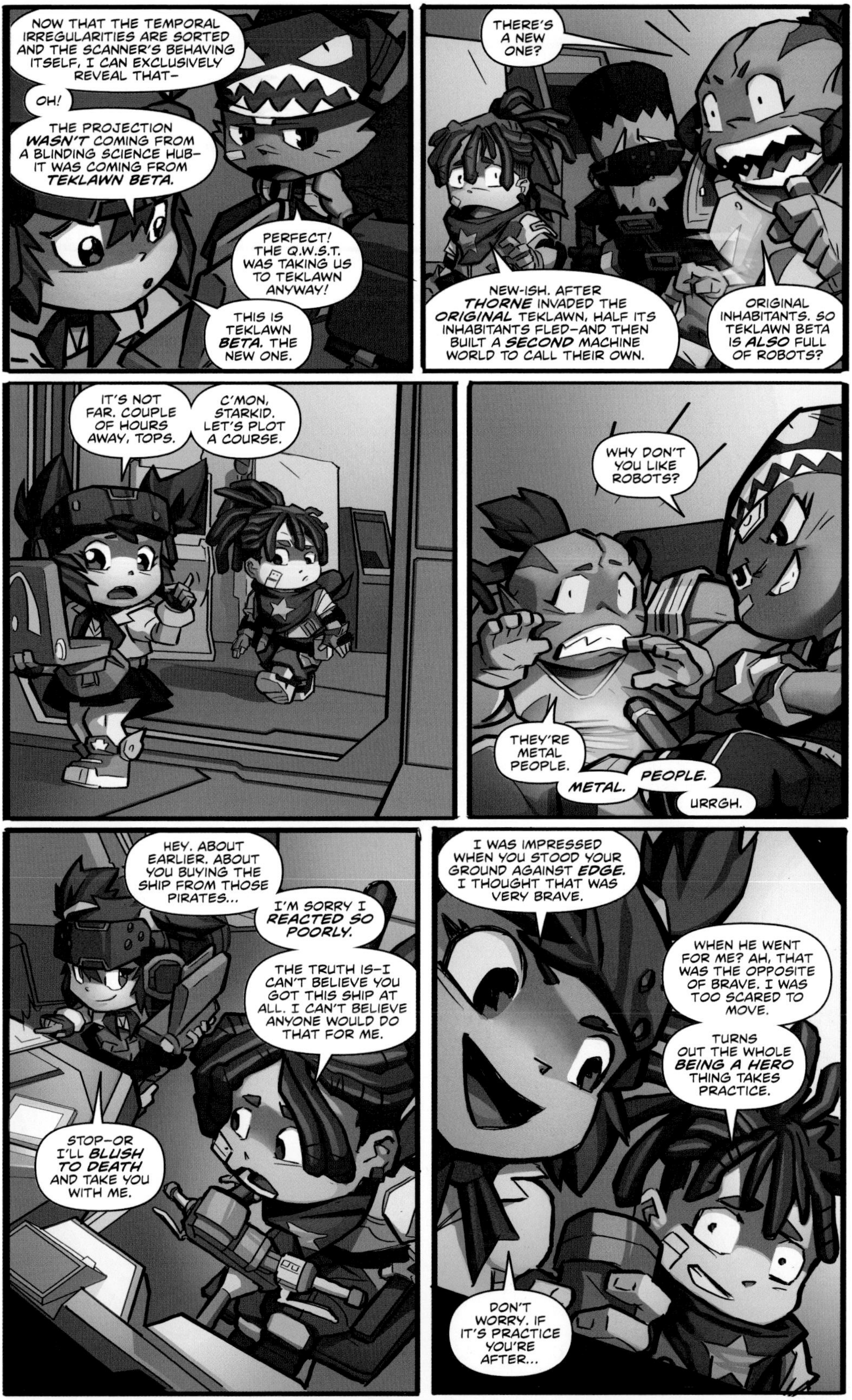

NOW THAT THE TEMPORAL IRREGULARITIES ARE SORTED AND THE SCANNER'S BEHAVING ITSELF, I CAN EXCLUSIVELY REVEAL THAT–
OH!
THE PROJECTION WASN'T COMING FROM A BLINDING SCIENCE HUB– IT WAS COMING FROM TEKLAWN BETA.
PERFECT! THE Q.W.S.T. WAS TAKING US TO TEKLAWN ANYWAY!
THIS IS TEKLAWN BETA. THE NEW ONE.
THERE'S A NEW ONE?
NEW-ISH. AFTER THORNE INVADED THE ORIGINAL TEKLAWN, HALF ITS INHABITANTS FLED–AND THEN BUILT A SECOND MACHINE WORLD TO CALL THEIR OWN.
ORIGINAL INHABITANTS. SO TEKLAWN BETA IS ALSO FULL OF ROBOTS?
IT'S NOT FAR. COUPLE OF HOURS AWAY, TOPS.
C'MON, STARKID. LET'S PLOT A COURSE.
WHY DON'T YOU LIKE ROBOTS?
THEY'RE METAL PEOPLE.
METAL.
PEOPLE.
URRGH.
HEY. ABOUT EARLIER. ABOUT YOU BUYING THE SHIP FROM THOSE PIRATES...
I'M SORRY I REACTED SO POORLY.
THE TRUTH IS–I CAN'T BELIEVE YOU GOT THIS SHIP AT ALL. I CAN'T BELIEVE ANYONE WOULD DO THAT FOR ME.
STOP–OR I'LL BLUSH TO DEATH AND TAKE YOU WITH ME.
I WAS IMPRESSED WHEN YOU STOOD YOUR GROUND AGAINST EDGE. I THOUGHT THAT WAS VERY BRAVE.
WHEN HE WENT FOR ME? AH, THAT WAS THE OPPOSITE OF BRAVE. I WAS TOO SCARED TO MOVE.
TURNS OUT THE WHOLE BEING A HERO THING TAKES PRACTICE.
DON'T WORRY. IF IT'S PRACTICE YOU'RE AFTER...

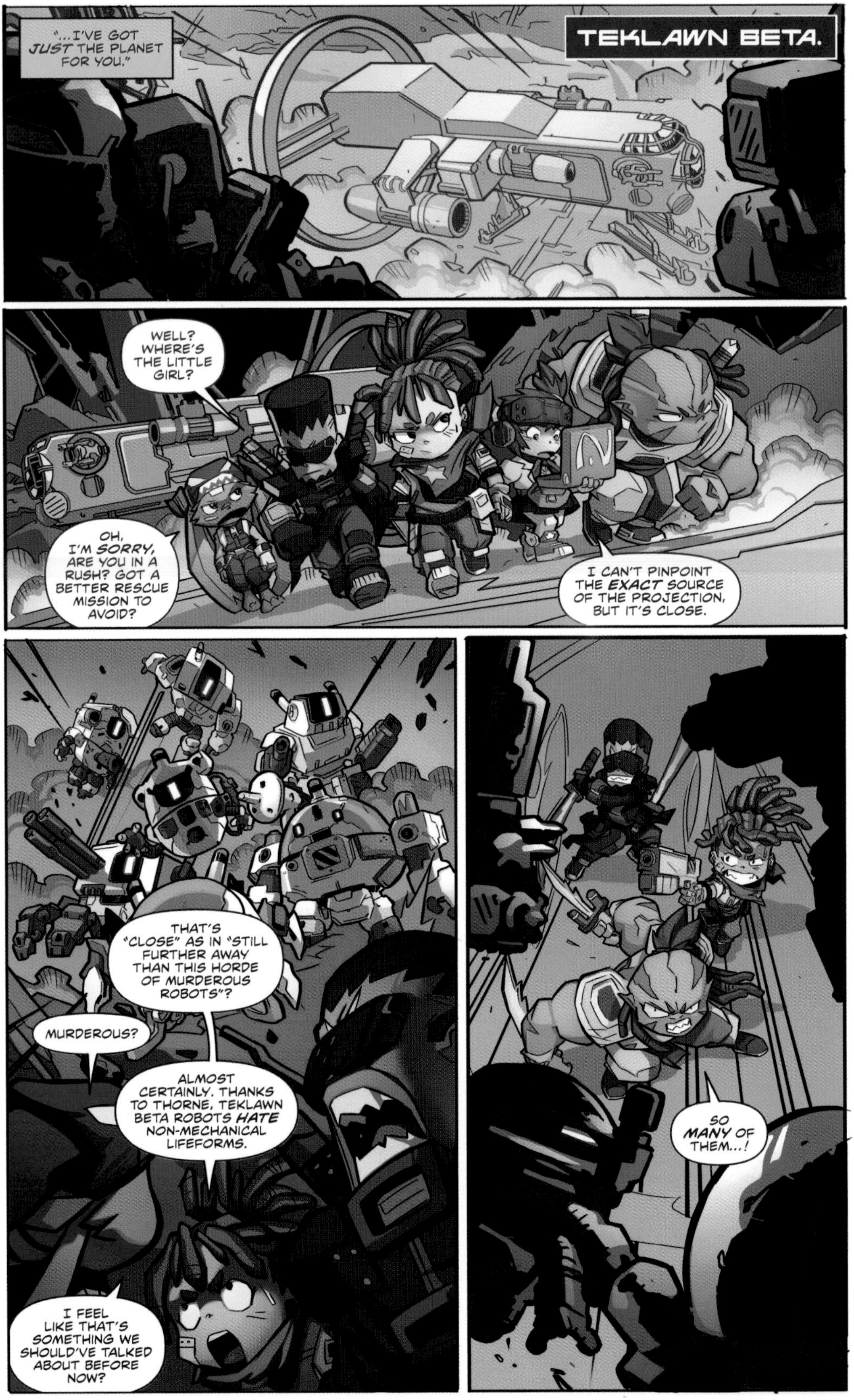

"...I'VE GOT JUST THE PLANET FOR YOU."
TEKLAWN BETA.
WELL? WHERE'S THE LITTLE GIRL?
OH, I'M SORRY, ARE YOU IN A RUSH? GOT A BETTER RESCUE MISSION TO AVOID?
I CAN'T PINPOINT THE EXACT SOURCE OF THE PROJECTION, BUT IT'S CLOSE.
THAT'S "CLOSE" AS IN "STILL FURTHER AWAY THAN THIS HORDE OF MURDEROUS ROBOTS"?
MURDEROUS?
ALMOST CERTAINLY. THANKS TO THORNE, TEKLAWN BETA ROBOTS HATE NON-MECHANICAL LIFEFORMS.
I FEEL LIKE THAT'S SOMETHING WE SHOULD'VE TALKED ABOUT BEFORE NOW?
SO MANY OF THEM...!

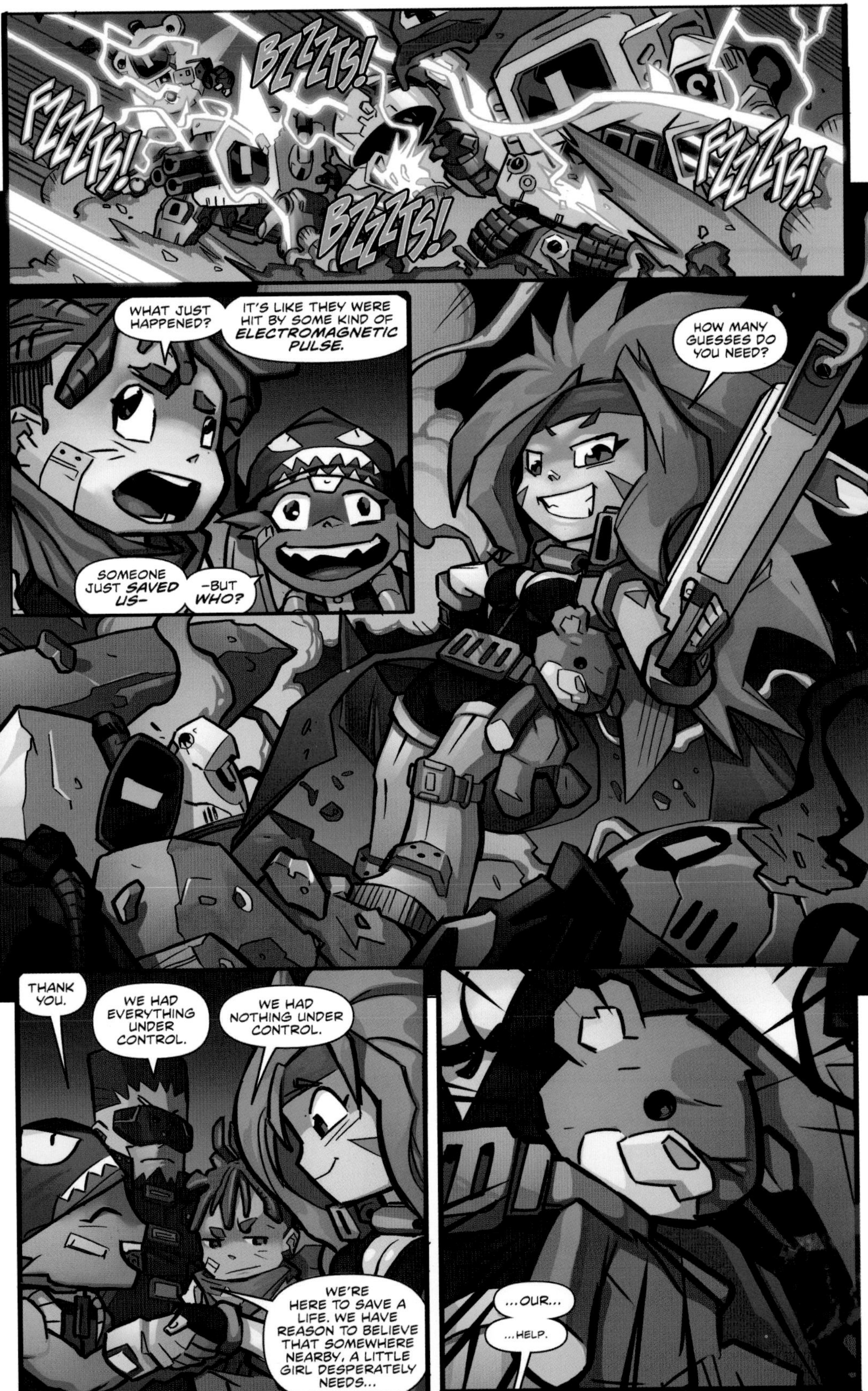
FZZZTS!
BZZZTS!
BZZZTS!
FZZZTS!
WHAT JUST HAPPENED?
IT'S LIKE THEY WERE HIT BY SOME KIND OF ELECTROMAGNETIC PULSE.
SOMEONE JUST SAVED US—
—BUT WHO?
HOW MANY GUESSES DO YOU NEED?
THANK YOU.
WE HAD EVERYTHING UNDER CONTROL.
WE HAD NOTHING UNDER CONTROL.
WE'RE HERE TO SAVE A LIFE. WE HAVE REASON TO BELIEVE THAT SOMEWHERE NEARBY, A LITTLE GIRL DESPERATELY NEEDS...
...OUR...
...HELP.

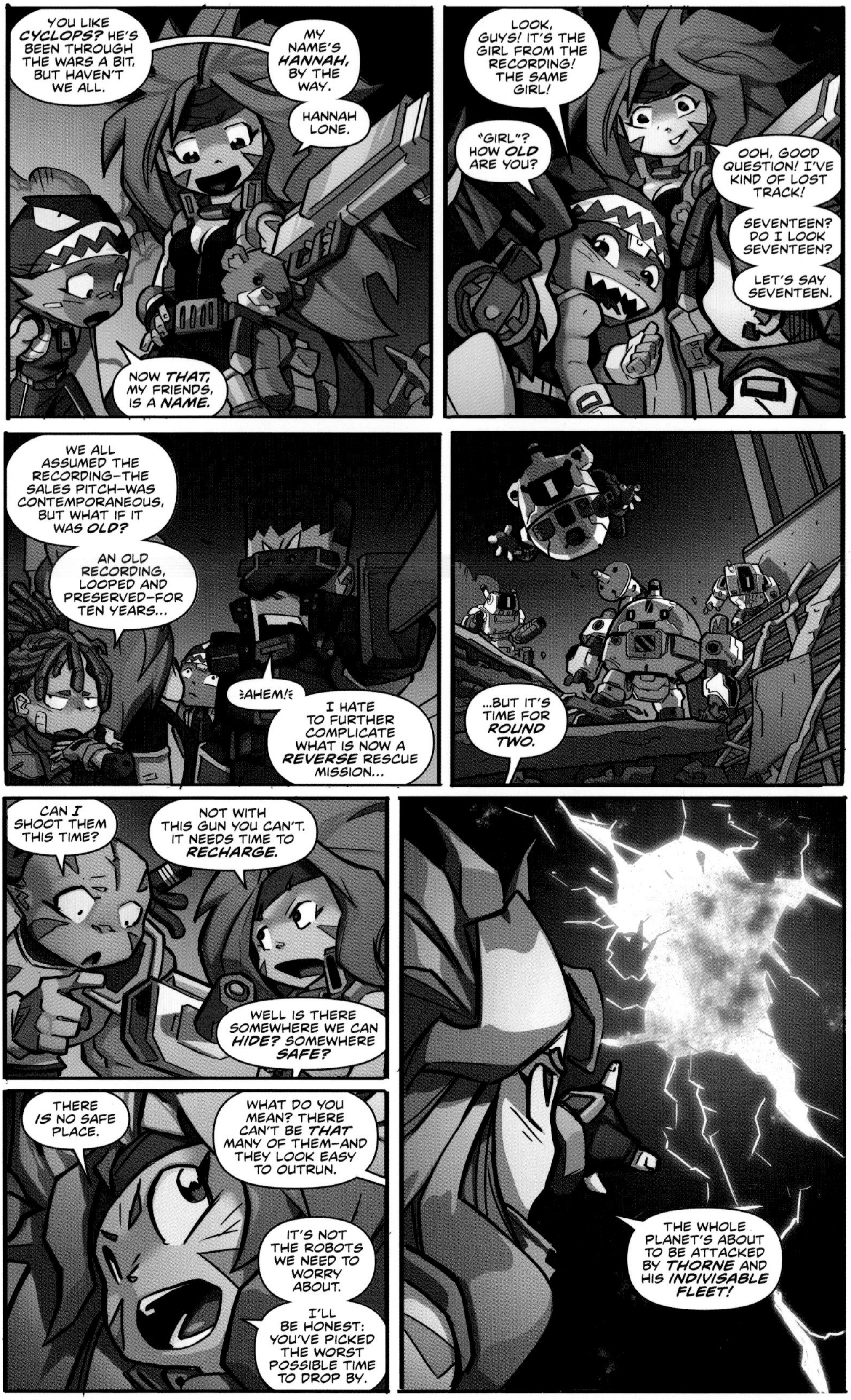
YOU LIKE CYCLOPS? HE'S BEEN THROUGH THE WARS A BIT, BUT HAVEN'T WE ALL.
MY NAME'S HANNAH, BY THE WAY.
HANNAH LONE.
NOW THAT, MY FRIENDS, IS A NAME.
LOOK, GUYS! IT'S THE GIRL FROM THE RECORDING! THE SAME GIRL!
"GIRL"? HOW OLD ARE YOU?
OOH, GOOD QUESTION! I'VE KIND OF LOST TRACK!
SEVENTEEN? DO I LOOK SEVENTEEN?
LET'S SAY SEVENTEEN.
WE ALL ASSUMED THE RECORDING—THE SALES PITCH—WAS CONTEMPORANEOUS, BUT WHAT IF IT WAS OLD?
AN OLD RECORDING, LOOPED AND PRESERVED—FOR TEN YEARS...
AHEM!
I HATE TO FURTHER COMPLICATE WHAT IS NOW A REVERSE RESCUE MISSION...
...BUT IT'S TIME FOR ROUND TWO.
CAN I SHOOT THEM THIS TIME?
NOT WITH THIS GUN YOU CAN'T. IT NEEDS TIME TO RECHARGE.
WELL IS THERE SOMEWHERE WE CAN HIDE? SOMEWHERE SAFE?
THERE IS NO SAFE PLACE.
WHAT DO YOU MEAN? THERE CAN'T BE THAT MANY OF THEM—AND THEY LOOK EASY TO OUTRUN.
IT'S NOT THE ROBOTS WE NEED TO WORRY ABOUT.
I'LL BE HONEST: YOU'VE PICKED THE WORST POSSIBLE TIME TO DROP BY.
THE WHOLE PLANET'S ABOUT TO BE ATTACKED BY THORNE AND HIS INDIVISABLE FLEET!

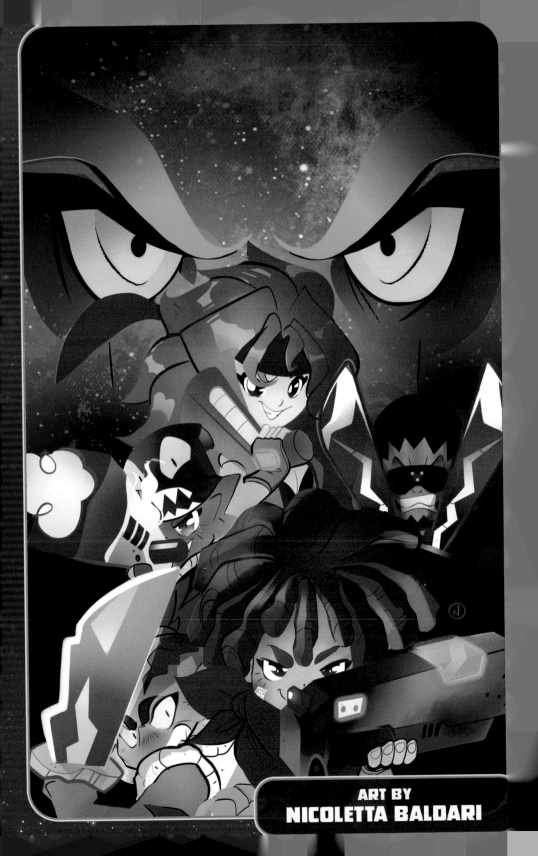

ART BY
NICOLETTA BALDARI

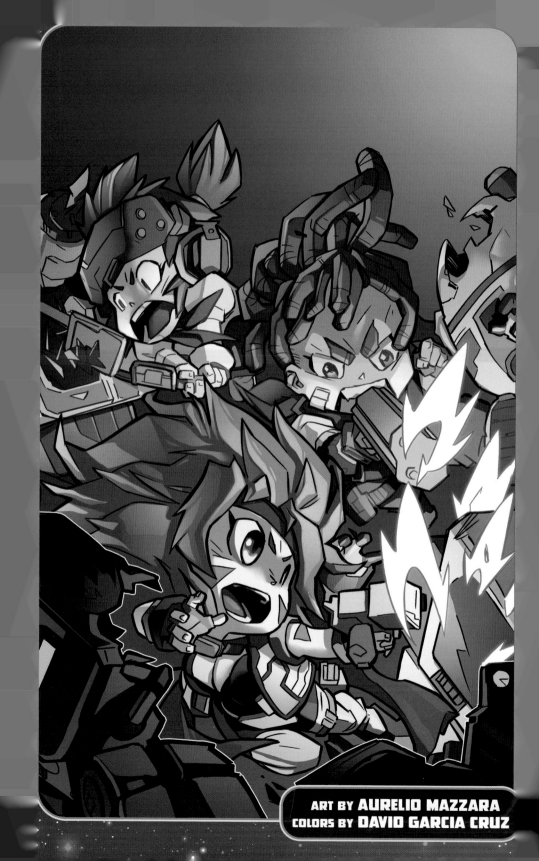

ART BY **AURELIO MAZZARA**
COLORS BY **DAVID GARCIA CRUZ**

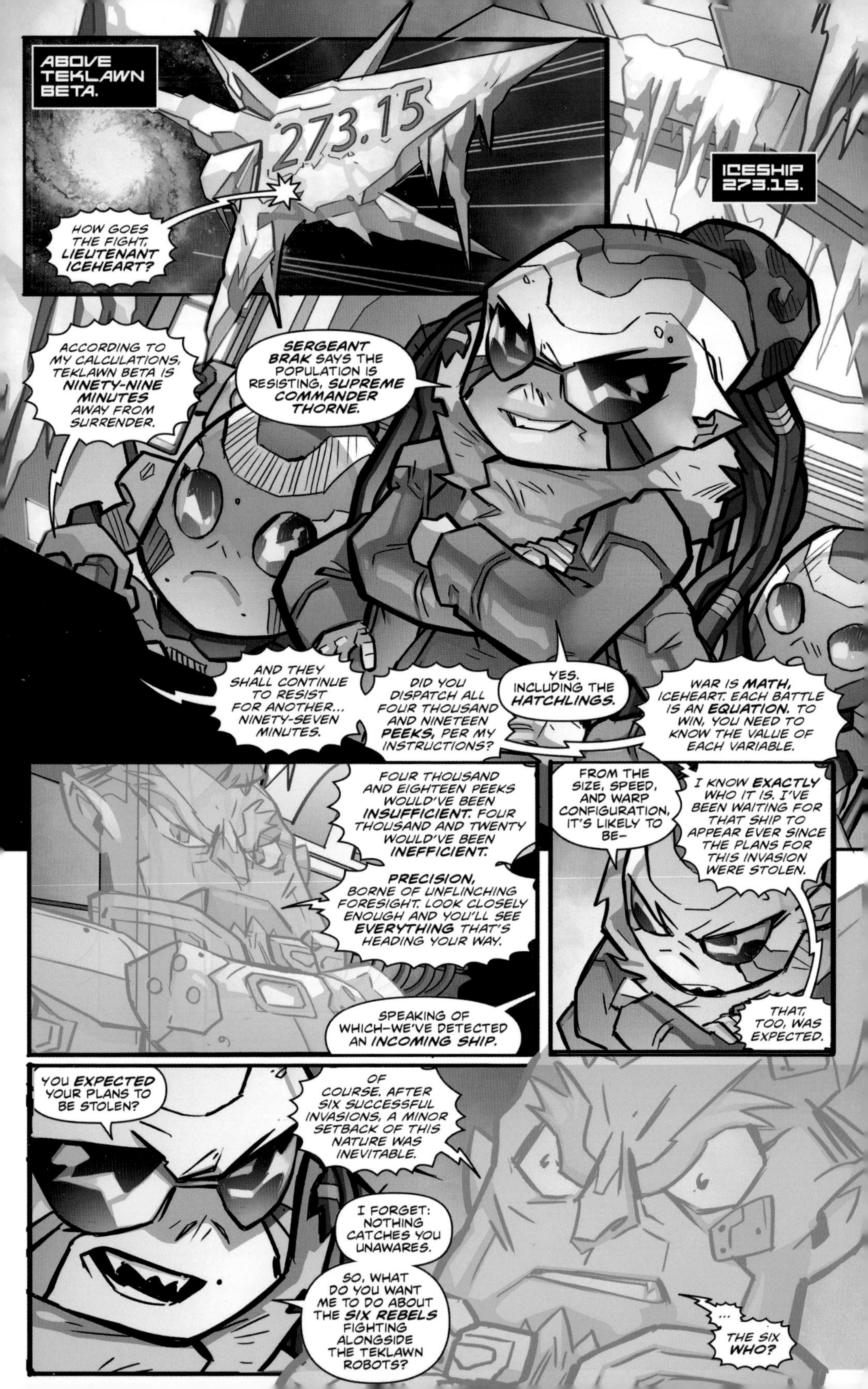

ABOVE TEKLAWN BETA.
273.15
HOW GOES THE FIGHT, LIEUTENANT ICEHEART?
ICESHIP 273.15.
ACCORDING TO MY CALCULATIONS, TEKLAWN BETA IS NINETY-NINE MINUTES AWAY FROM SURRENDER.
SERGEANT BRAK SAYS THE POPULATION IS RESISTING, SUPREME COMMANDER THORNE.
AND THEY SHALL CONTINUE TO RESIST FOR ANOTHER... NINETY-SEVEN MINUTES.
DID YOU DISPATCH ALL FOUR THOUSAND AND NINETEEN PEEKS, PER MY INSTRUCTIONS?
YES. INCLUDING THE HATCHLINGS.
WAR IS MATH, ICEHEART. EACH BATTLE IS AN EQUATION. TO WIN, YOU NEED TO KNOW THE VALUE OF EACH VARIABLE.
FOUR THOUSAND AND EIGHTEEN PEEKS WOULD'VE BEEN INSUFFICIENT. FOUR THOUSAND AND TWENTY WOULD'VE BEEN INEFFICIENT.
PRECISION, BORNE OF UNFLINCHING FORESIGHT. LOOK CLOSELY ENOUGH AND YOU'LL SEE EVERYTHING THAT'S HEADING YOUR WAY.
SPEAKING OF WHICH–WE'VE DETECTED AN INCOMING SHIP.
FROM THE SIZE, SPEED, AND WARP CONFIGURATION, IT'S LIKELY TO BE–
I KNOW EXACTLY WHO IT IS. I'VE BEEN WAITING FOR THAT SHIP TO APPEAR EVER SINCE THE PLANS FOR THIS INVASION WERE STOLEN.
THAT, TOO, WAS EXPECTED.
YOU EXPECTED YOUR PLANS TO BE STOLEN?
OF COURSE. AFTER SIX SUCCESSFUL INVASIONS, A MINOR SETBACK OF THIS NATURE WAS INEVITABLE.
I FORGET: NOTHING CATCHES YOU UNAWARES.
SO, WHAT DO YOU WANT ME TO DO ABOUT THE SIX REBELS FIGHTING ALONGSIDE THE TEKLAWN ROBOTS?
... THE SIX WHO?

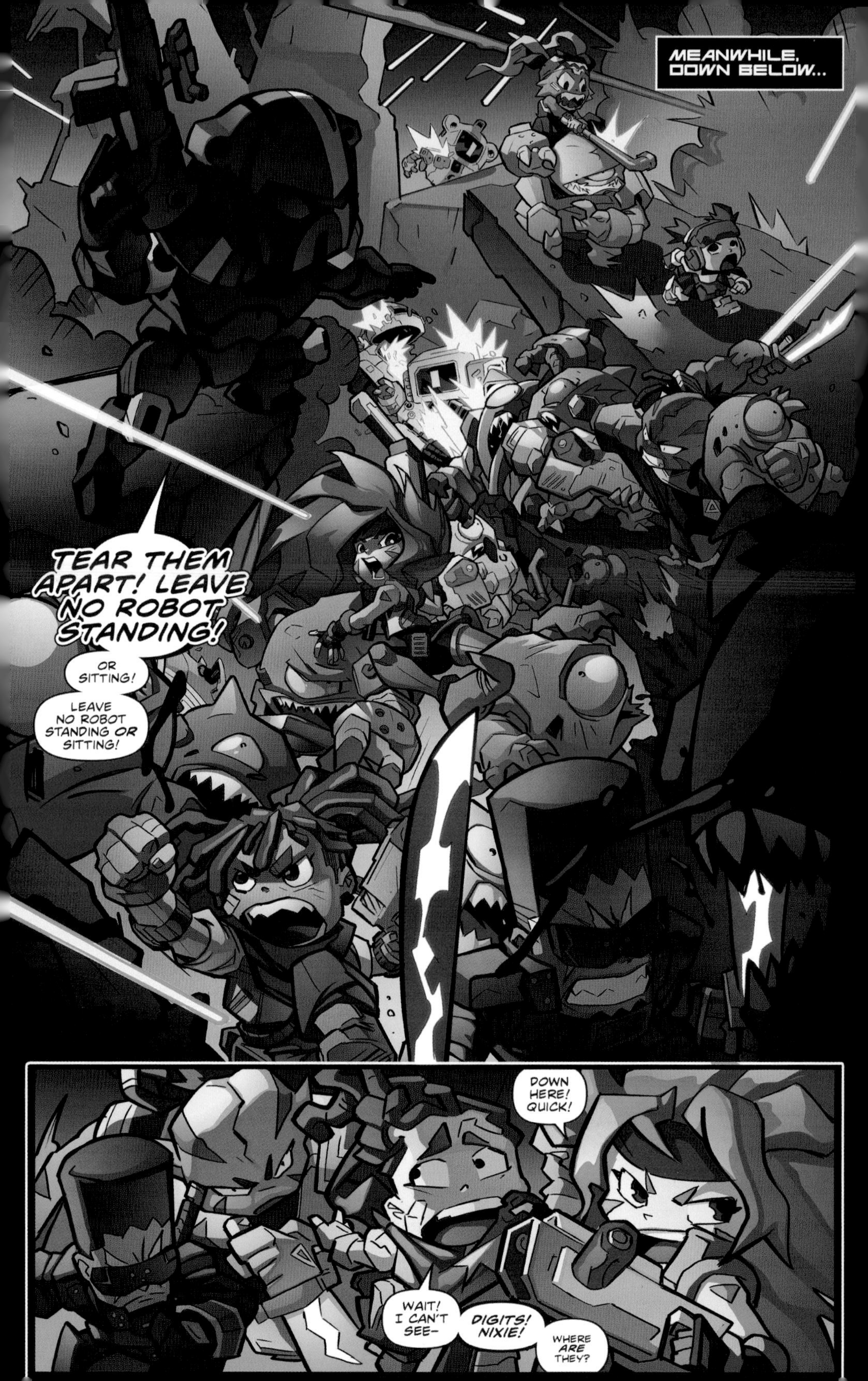
MEANWHILE, DOWN BELOW...
TEAR THEM APART! LEAVE NO ROBOT STANDING!
OR SITTING!
LEAVE NO ROBOT STANDING OR SITTING!
DOWN HERE! QUICK!
WAIT! I CAN'T SEE-
DIGITS! NIXIE!
WHERE ARE THEY?

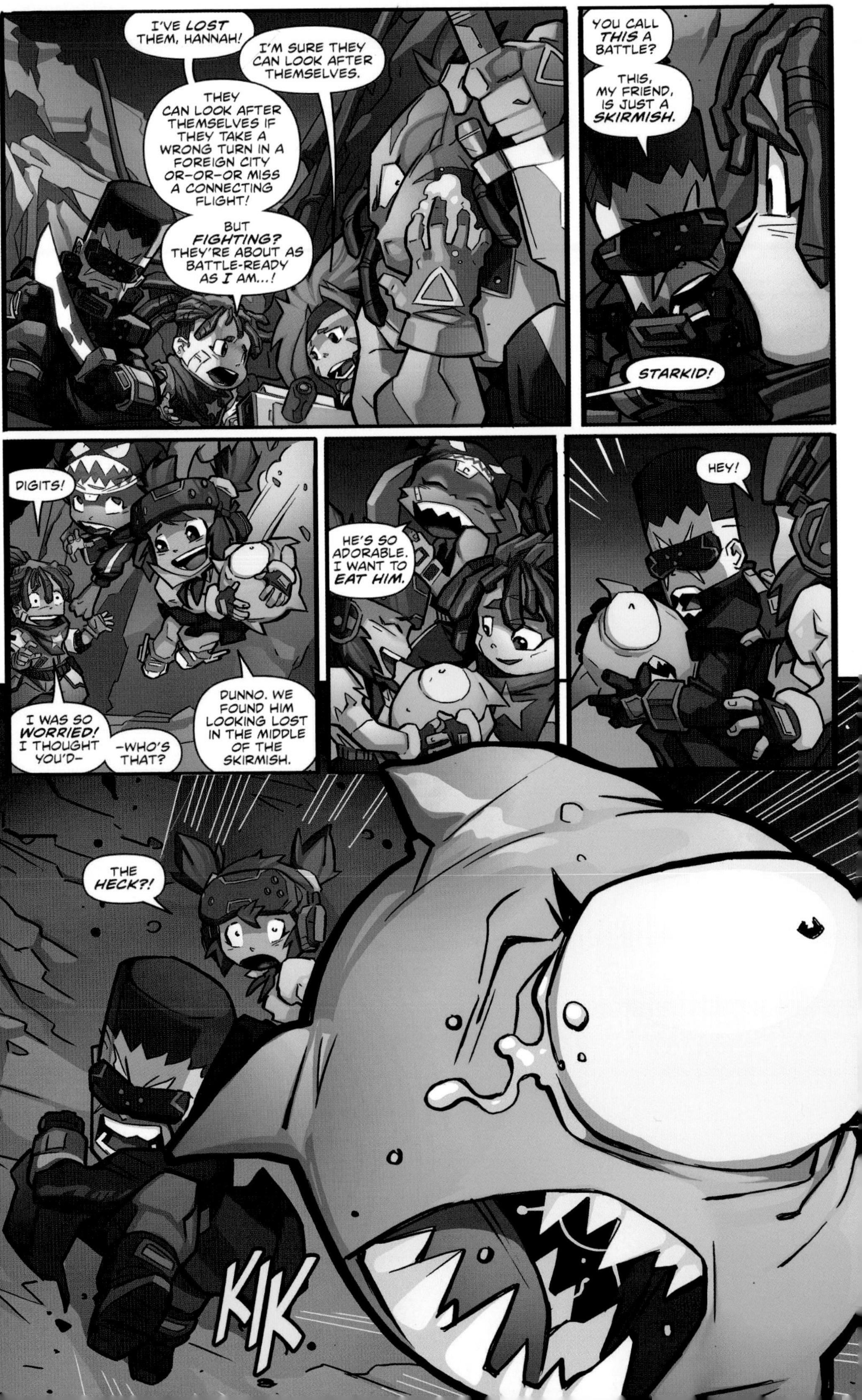

I'VE LOST THEM, HANNAH!
I'M SURE THEY CAN LOOK AFTER THEMSELVES.
THEY CAN LOOK AFTER THEMSELVES IF THEY TAKE A WRONG TURN IN A FOREIGN CITY OR-OR-OR MISS A CONNECTING FLIGHT!
BUT FIGHTING? THEY'RE ABOUT AS BATTLE-READY AS I AM...!
YOU CALL THIS A BATTLE?
THIS, MY FRIEND, IS JUST A SKIRMISH.
STARKID!
DIGITS!
I WAS SO WORRIED! I THOUGHT YOU'D-
-WHO'S THAT?
DUNNO. WE FOUND HIM LOOKING LOST IN THE MIDDLE OF THE SKIRMISH.
HE'S SO ADORABLE. I WANT TO EAT HIM.
HEY!
THE HECK?!
KIK

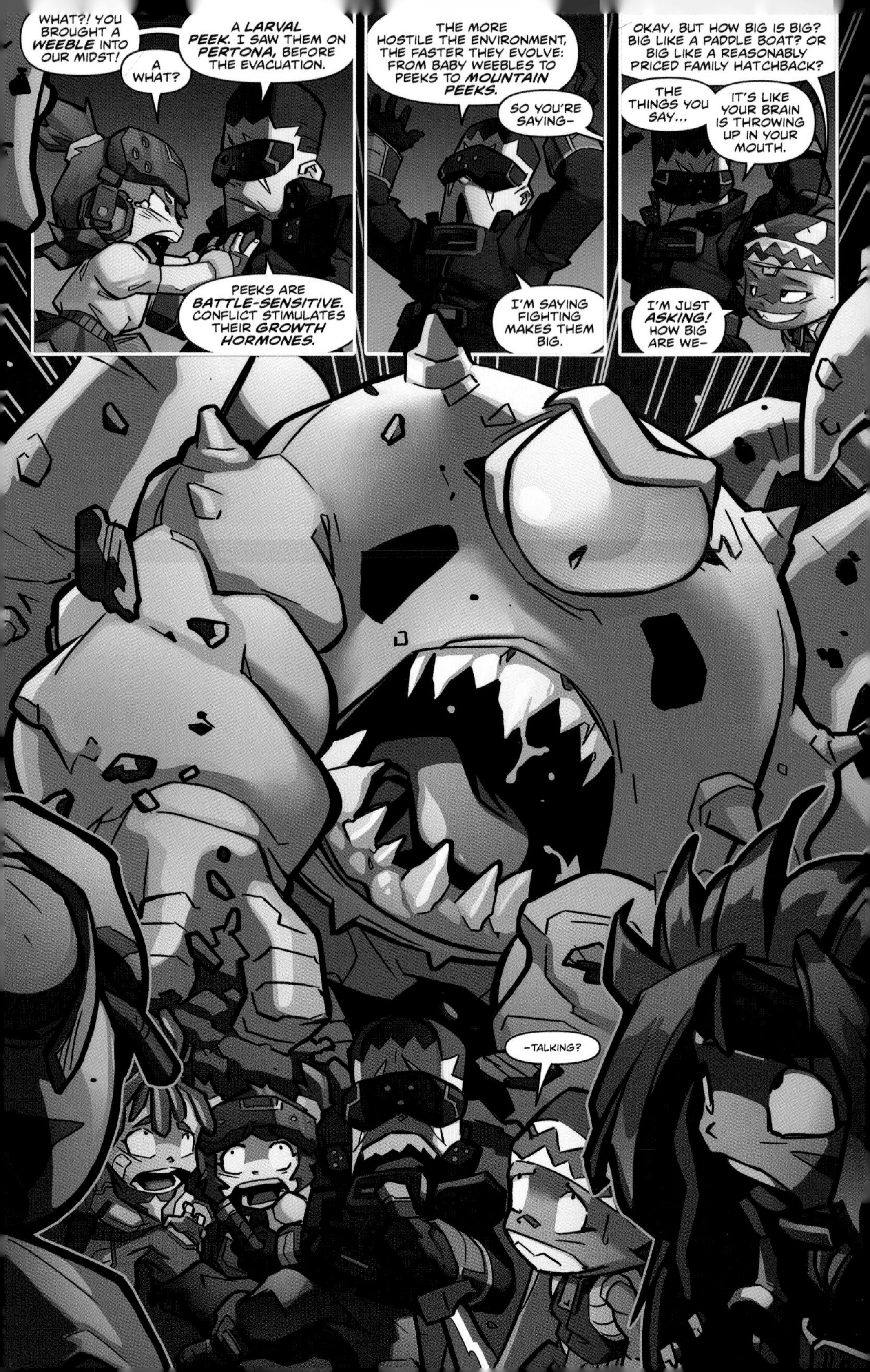

WHAT?! YOU BROUGHT A WEEBLE INTO OUR MIDST!
A WHAT?
A LARVAL PEEK. I SAW THEM ON PERTONA, BEFORE THE EVACUATION.
PEEKS ARE BATTLE-SENSITIVE. CONFLICT STIMULATES THEIR GROWTH HORMONES.
THE MORE HOSTILE THE ENVIRONMENT, THE FASTER THEY EVOLVE: FROM BABY WEEBLES TO PEEKS TO MOUNTAIN PEEKS.
SO YOU'RE SAYING–
I'M SAYING FIGHTING MAKES THEM BIG.
OKAY, BUT HOW BIG IS BIG? BIG LIKE A PADDLE BOAT? OR BIG LIKE A REASONABLY PRICED FAMILY HATCHBACK?
THE THINGS YOU SAY...
IT'S LIKE YOUR BRAIN IS THROWING UP IN YOUR MOUTH.
I'M JUST ASKING! HOW BIG ARE WE–
–TALKING?

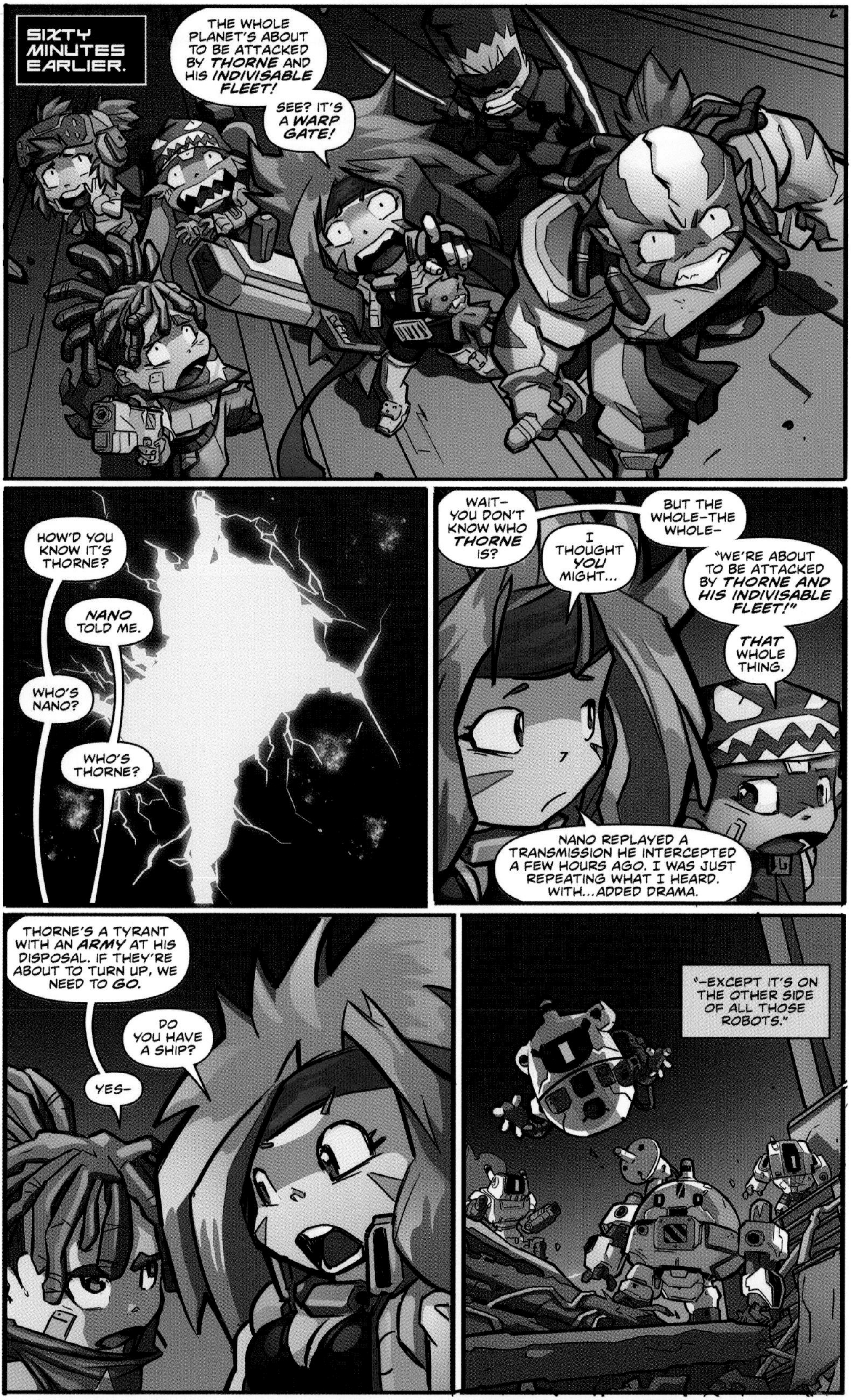
SIXTY MINUTES EARLIER.
THE WHOLE PLANET'S ABOUT TO BE ATTACKED BY THORNE AND HIS INDIVISABLE FLEET!
SEE? IT'S A WARP GATE!
HOW'D YOU KNOW IT'S THORNE?
NANO TOLD ME.
WHO'S NANO?
WHO'S THORNE?
WAIT- YOU DON'T KNOW WHO THORNE IS?
I THOUGHT YOU MIGHT...
BUT THE WHOLE—THE WHOLE-
"WE'RE ABOUT TO BE ATTACKED BY THORNE AND HIS INDIVISABLE FLEET!"
THAT WHOLE THING.
NANO REPLAYED A TRANSMISSION HE INTERCEPTED A FEW HOURS AGO. I WAS JUST REPEATING WHAT I HEARD. WITH...ADDED DRAMA.
THORNE'S A TYRANT WITH AN ARMY AT HIS DISPOSAL. IF THEY'RE ABOUT TO TURN UP, WE NEED TO GO.
DO YOU HAVE A SHIP?
YES-
"-EXCEPT IT'S ON THE OTHER SIDE OF ALL THOSE ROBOTS."

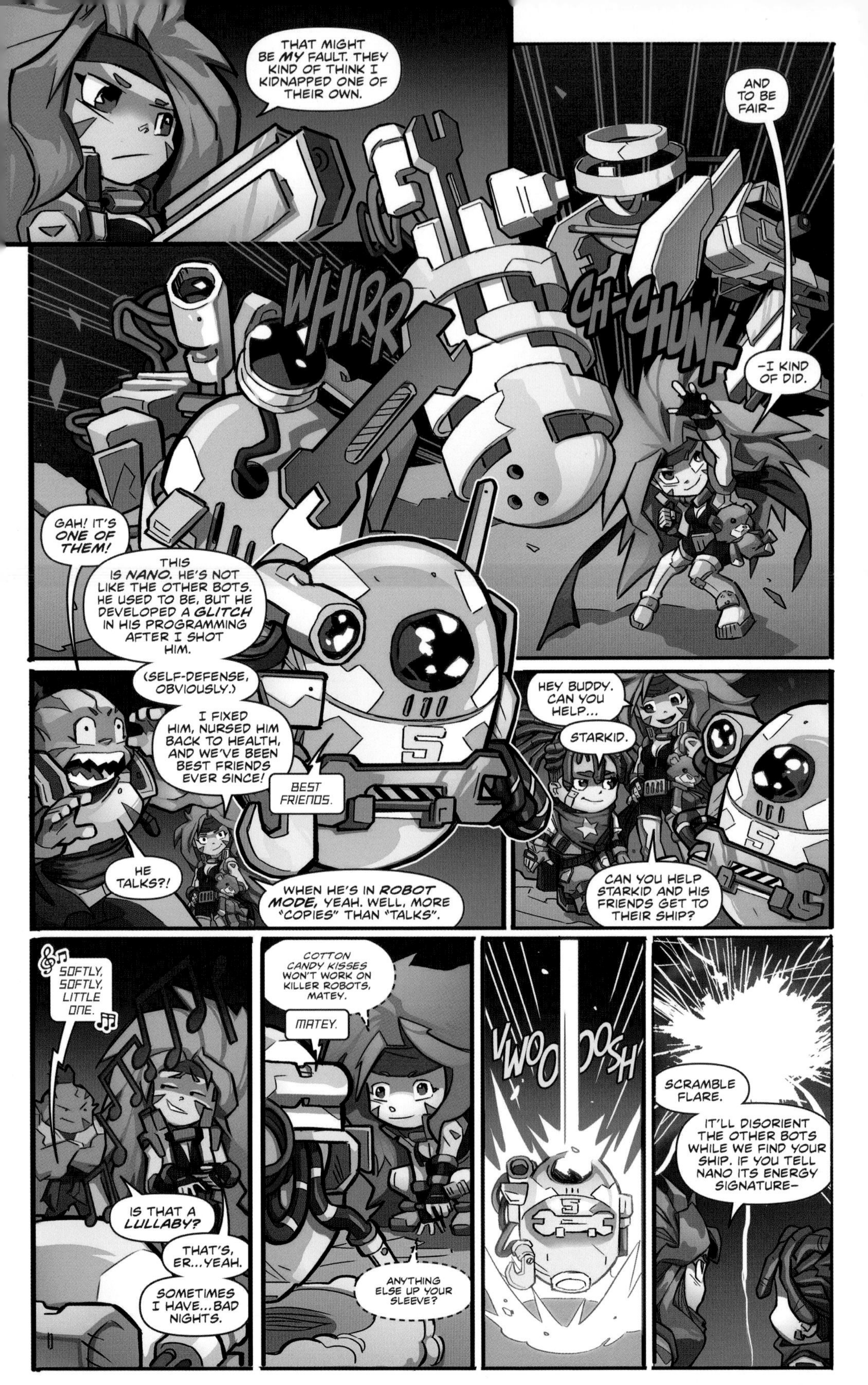
THAT MIGHT BE MY FAULT. THEY KIND OF THINK I KIDNAPPED ONE OF THEIR OWN.
AND TO BE FAIR–
WHIRR
CH-CHUNK
–I KIND OF DID.
GAH! IT'S ONE OF THEM!
THIS IS NANO. HE'S NOT LIKE THE OTHER BOTS. HE USED TO BE, BUT HE DEVELOPED A GLITCH IN HIS PROGRAMMING AFTER I SHOT HIM.
(SELF-DEFENSE, OBVIOUSLY.)
I FIXED HIM, NURSED HIM BACK TO HEALTH, AND WE'VE BEEN BEST FRIENDS EVER SINCE!
BEST FRIENDS.
HE TALKS?!
WHEN HE'S IN ROBOT MODE, YEAH. WELL, MORE "COPIES" THAN "TALKS".
HEY BUDDY. CAN YOU HELP...
STARKID.
CAN YOU HELP STARKID AND HIS FRIENDS GET TO THEIR SHIP?
SOFTLY, SOFTLY, LITTLE ONE.
IS THAT A LULLABY?
THAT'S, ER...YEAH.
SOMETIMES I HAVE...BAD NIGHTS.
COTTON CANDY KISSES WON'T WORK ON KILLER ROBOTS, MATEY.
MATEY.
ANYTHING ELSE UP YOUR SLEEVE?
VWOOOOSH
SCRAMBLE FLARE.
IT'LL DISORIENT THE OTHER BOTS WHILE WE FIND YOUR SHIP. IF YOU TELL NANO ITS ENERGY SIGNATURE–

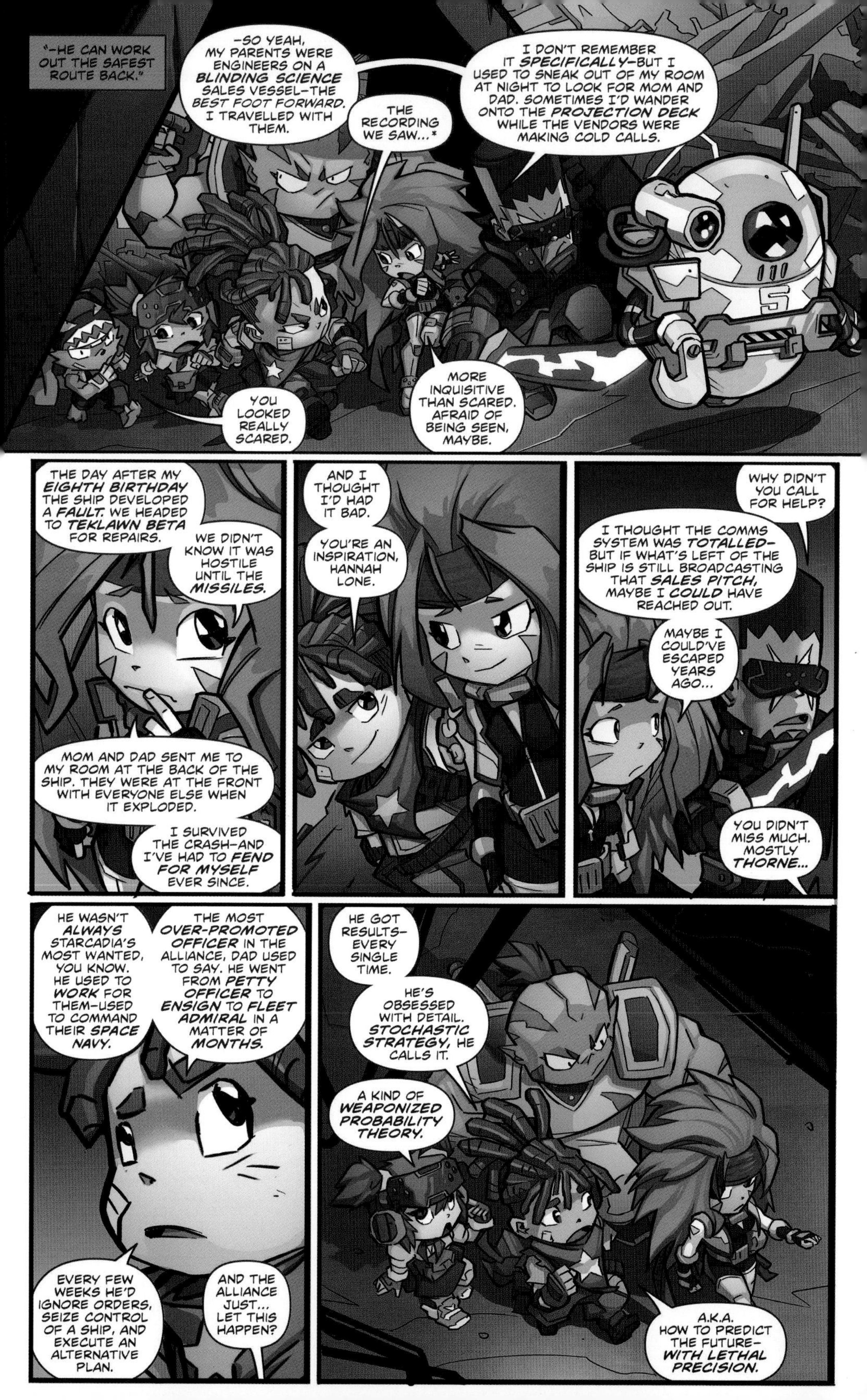
"–HE CAN WORK OUT THE SAFEST ROUTE BACK."
–SO YEAH, MY PARENTS WERE ENGINEERS ON A BLINDING SCIENCE SALES VESSEL–THE BEST FOOT FORWARD. I TRAVELLED WITH THEM.
THE RECORDING WE SAW...*
I DON'T REMEMBER IT SPECIFICALLY–BUT I USED TO SNEAK OUT OF MY ROOM AT NIGHT TO LOOK FOR MOM AND DAD. SOMETIMES I'D WANDER ONTO THE PROJECTION DECK WHILE THE VENDORS WERE MAKING COLD CALLS.
YOU LOOKED REALLY SCARED.
MORE INQUISITIVE THAN SCARED. AFRAID OF BEING SEEN, MAYBE.
THE DAY AFTER MY EIGHTH BIRTHDAY THE SHIP DEVELOPED A FAULT. WE HEADED TO TEKLAWN BETA FOR REPAIRS.
WE DIDN'T KNOW IT WAS HOSTILE UNTIL THE MISSILES.
MOM AND DAD SENT ME TO MY ROOM AT THE BACK OF THE SHIP. THEY WERE AT THE FRONT WITH EVERYONE ELSE WHEN IT EXPLODED.
I SURVIVED THE CRASH–AND I'VE HAD TO FEND FOR MYSELF EVER SINCE.
AND I THOUGHT I'D HAD IT BAD.
YOU'RE AN INSPIRATION, HANNAH LONE.
WHY DIDN'T YOU CALL FOR HELP?
I THOUGHT THE COMMS SYSTEM WAS TOTALLED–BUT IF WHAT'S LEFT OF THE SHIP IS STILL BROADCASTING THAT SALES PITCH, MAYBE I COULD HAVE REACHED OUT.
MAYBE I COULD'VE ESCAPED YEARS AGO...
YOU DIDN'T MISS MUCH. MOSTLY THORNE...
HE WASN'T ALWAYS STARCADIA'S MOST WANTED, YOU KNOW. HE USED TO WORK FOR THEM–USED TO COMMAND THEIR SPACE NAVY.
THE MOST OVER-PROMOTED OFFICER IN THE ALLIANCE, DAD USED TO SAY. HE WENT FROM PETTY OFFICER TO ENSIGN TO FLEET ADMIRAL IN A MATTER OF MONTHS.
EVERY FEW WEEKS HE'D IGNORE ORDERS, SEIZE CONTROL OF A SHIP, AND EXECUTE AN ALTERNATIVE PLAN.
AND THE ALLIANCE JUST... LET THIS HAPPEN?
HE GOT RESULTS–EVERY SINGLE TIME.
HE'S OBSESSED WITH DETAIL. STOCHASTIC STRATEGY, HE CALLS IT.
A KIND OF WEAPONIZED PROBABILITY THEORY.
A.K.A. HOW TO PREDICT THE FUTURE–WITH LETHAL PRECISION.

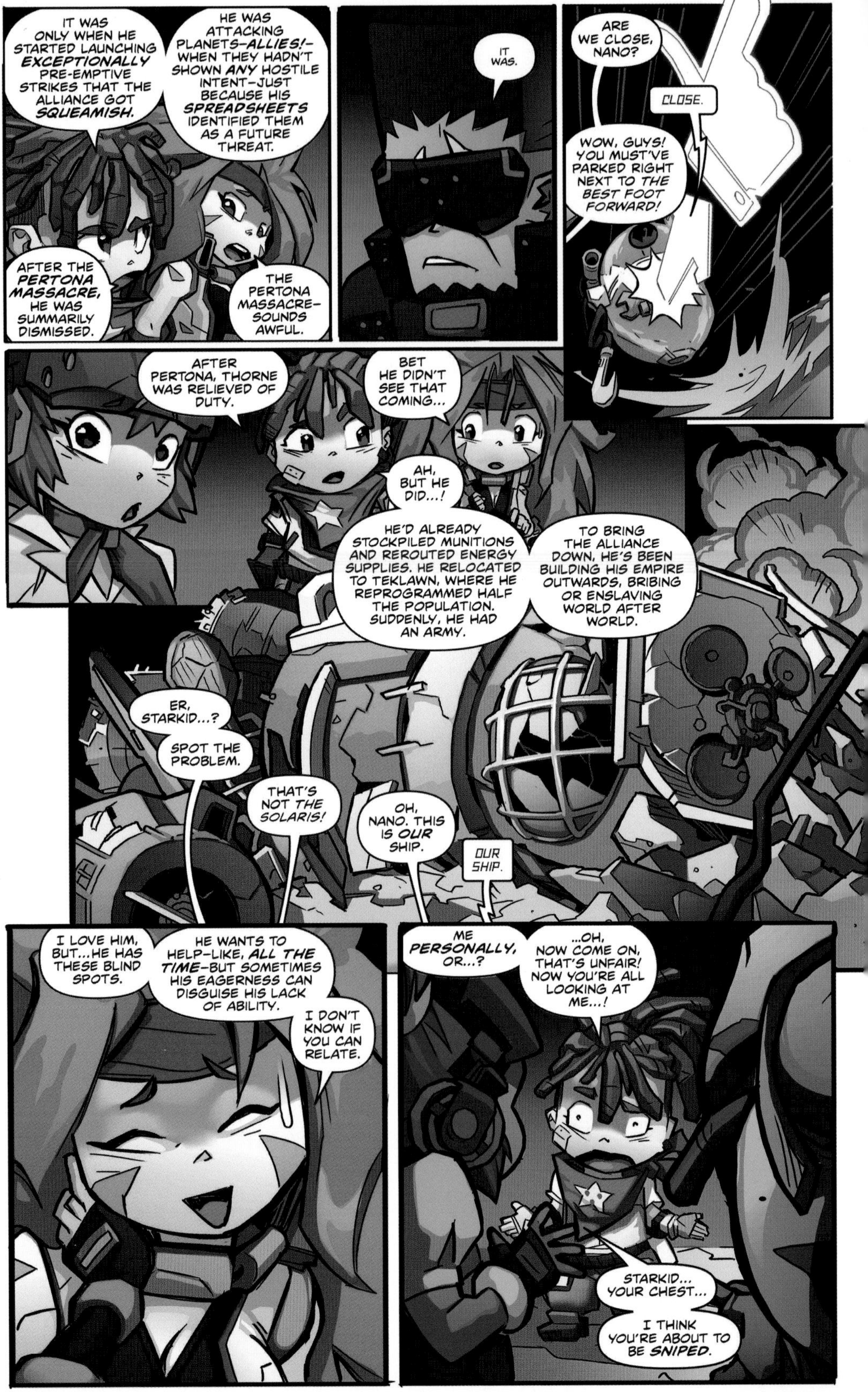
IT WAS ONLY WHEN HE STARTED LAUNCHING *EXCEPTIONALLY* PRE-EMPTIVE STRIKES THAT THE ALLIANCE GOT *SQUEAMISH.*
HE WAS ATTACKING PLANETS–*ALLIES!*–WHEN THEY HADN'T SHOWN *ANY* HOSTILE INTENT–JUST BECAUSE HIS *SPREADSHEETS* IDENTIFIED THEM AS A FUTURE THREAT.
AFTER THE *PERTONA MASSACRE,* HE WAS SUMMARILY DISMISSED.
THE PERTONA MASSACRE-SOUNDS AWFUL.
IT WAS.
ARE WE CLOSE, NANO?
CLOSE.
WOW, GUYS! YOU MUST'VE PARKED RIGHT NEXT TO *THE BEST FOOT FORWARD!*
AFTER PERTONA, THORNE WAS RELIEVED OF DUTY.
BET HE DIDN'T SEE THAT COMING...
AH, BUT HE DID...!
HE'D ALREADY STOCKPILED MUNITIONS AND REROUTED ENERGY SUPPLIES. HE RELOCATED TO TEKLAWN, WHERE HE REPROGRAMMED HALF THE POPULATION. SUDDENLY, HE HAD AN ARMY.
TO BRING THE ALLIANCE DOWN, HE'S BEEN BUILDING HIS EMPIRE OUTWARDS, BRIBING OR ENSLAVING WORLD AFTER WORLD.
ER, STARKID...?
SPOT THE PROBLEM.
THAT'S NOT *THE SOLARIS!*
OH, NANO. THIS IS *OUR* SHIP.
OUR SHIP.
I LOVE HIM, BUT...HE HAS THESE BLIND SPOTS.
HE WANTS TO HELP–LIKE, *ALL THE TIME*–BUT SOMETIMES HIS EAGERNESS CAN DISGUISE HIS LACK OF ABILITY.
I DON'T KNOW IF YOU CAN RELATE.
ME *PERSONALLY,* OR...?
...OH, NOW COME ON, THAT'S UNFAIR! NOW YOU'RE ALL LOOKING AT ME...!
STARKID... YOUR CHEST...
I THINK YOU'RE ABOUT TO BE *SNIPED*.

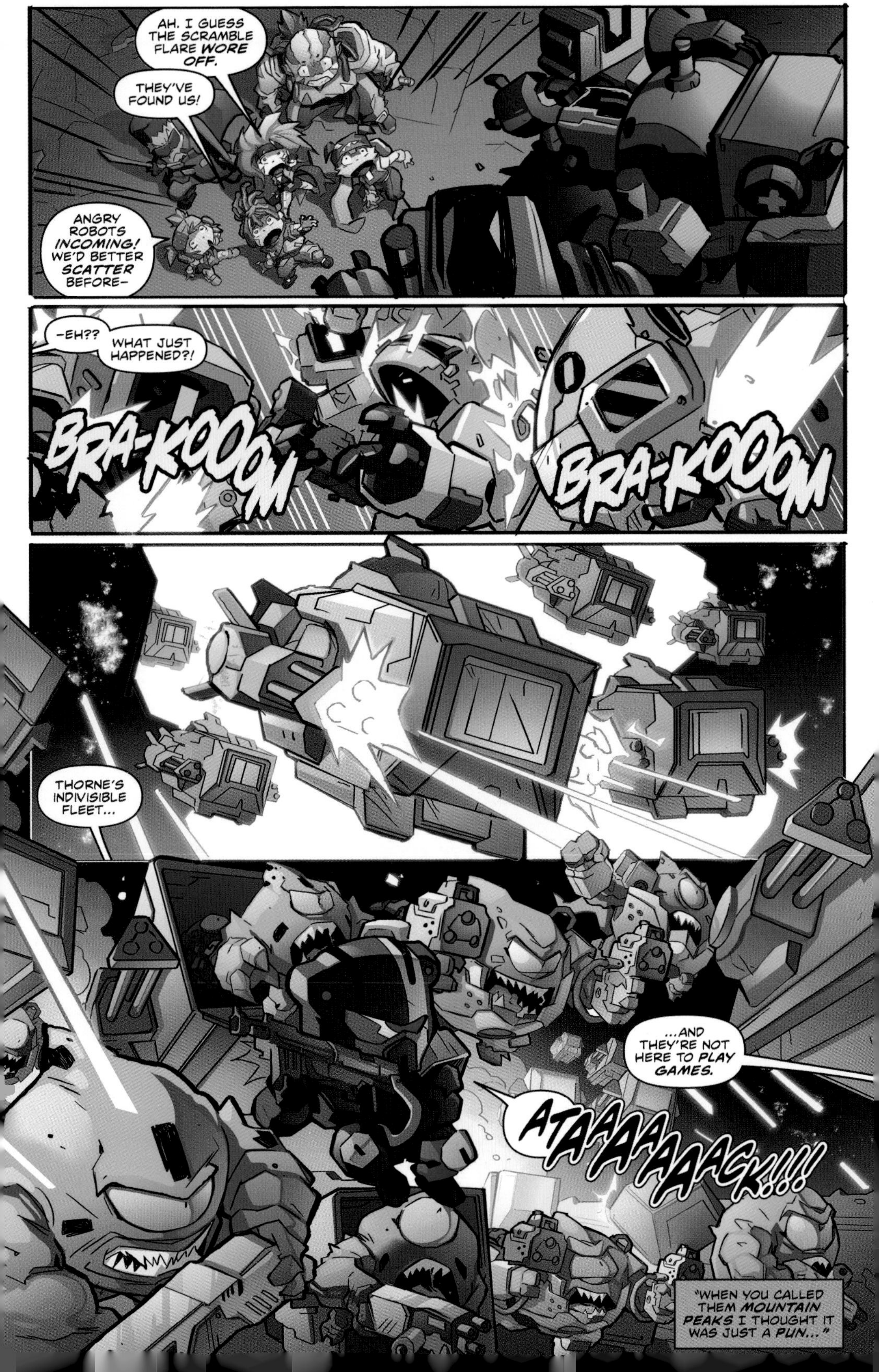
AH. I GUESS THE SCRAMBLE FLARE WORE OFF.
THEY'VE FOUND US!
ANGRY ROBOTS INCOMING! WE'D BETTER SCATTER BEFORE-
-EH??
WHAT JUST HAPPENED?!
BRA-KOOOM
BRA-KOOOM
THORNE'S INDIVISIBLE FLEET...
...AND THEY'RE NOT HERE TO PLAY GAMES.
ATAAAAAAACK!!!
"WHEN YOU CALLED THEM MOUNTAIN PEAKS I THOUGHT IT WAS JUST A PUN..."

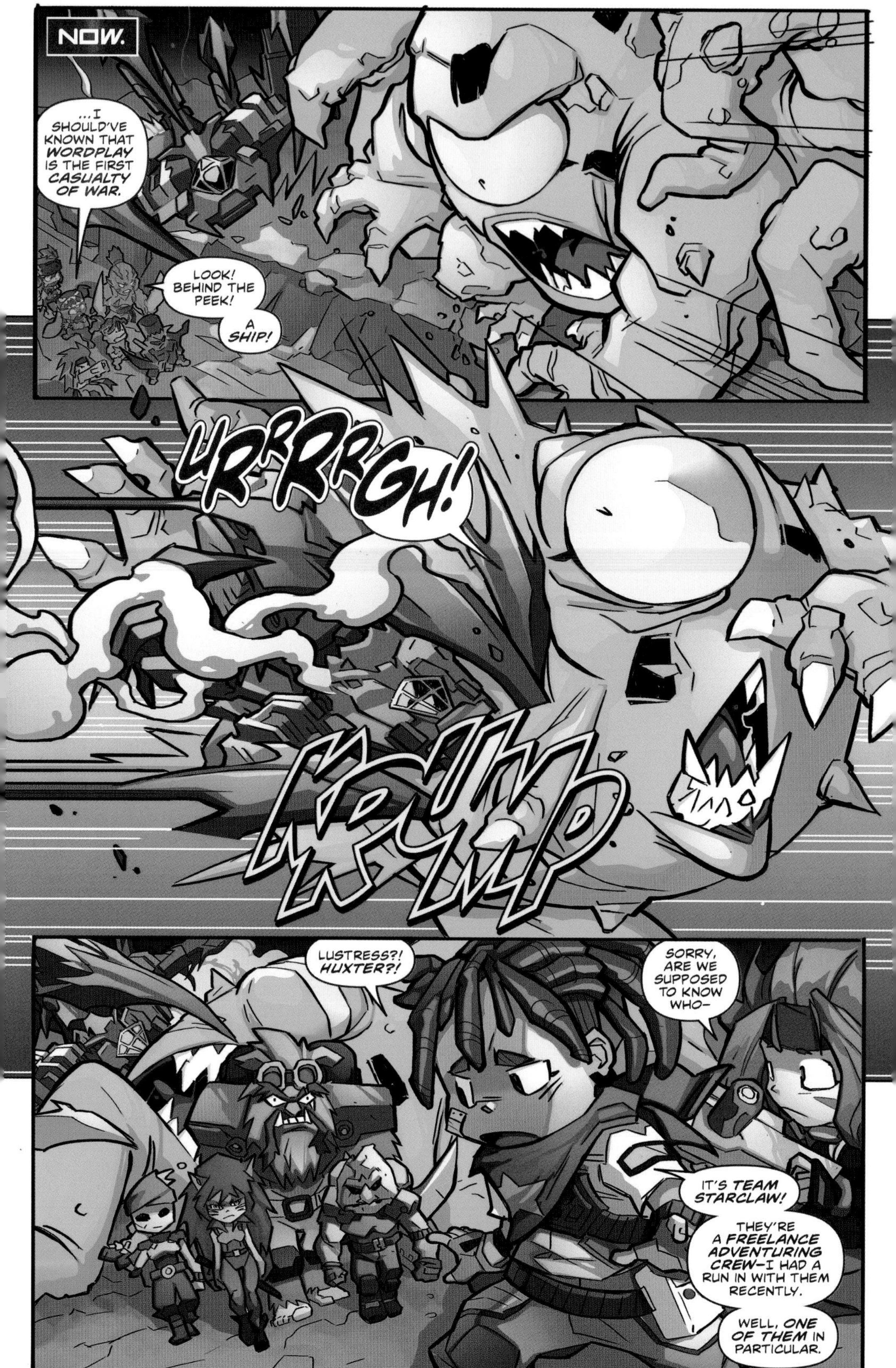
NOW.
...I SHOULD'VE KNOWN THAT WORDPLAY IS THE FIRST CASUALTY OF WAR.
LOOK! BEHIND THE PEEK!
A SHIP!
URRRRRGH!
KRUMP
LUSTRESS?! HUXTER?!
SORRY, ARE WE SUPPOSED TO KNOW WHO–
IT'S TEAM STARCLAW!
THEY'RE A FREELANCE ADVENTURING CREW–I HAD A RUN IN WITH THEM RECENTLY.
WELL, ONE OF THEM IN PARTICULAR.

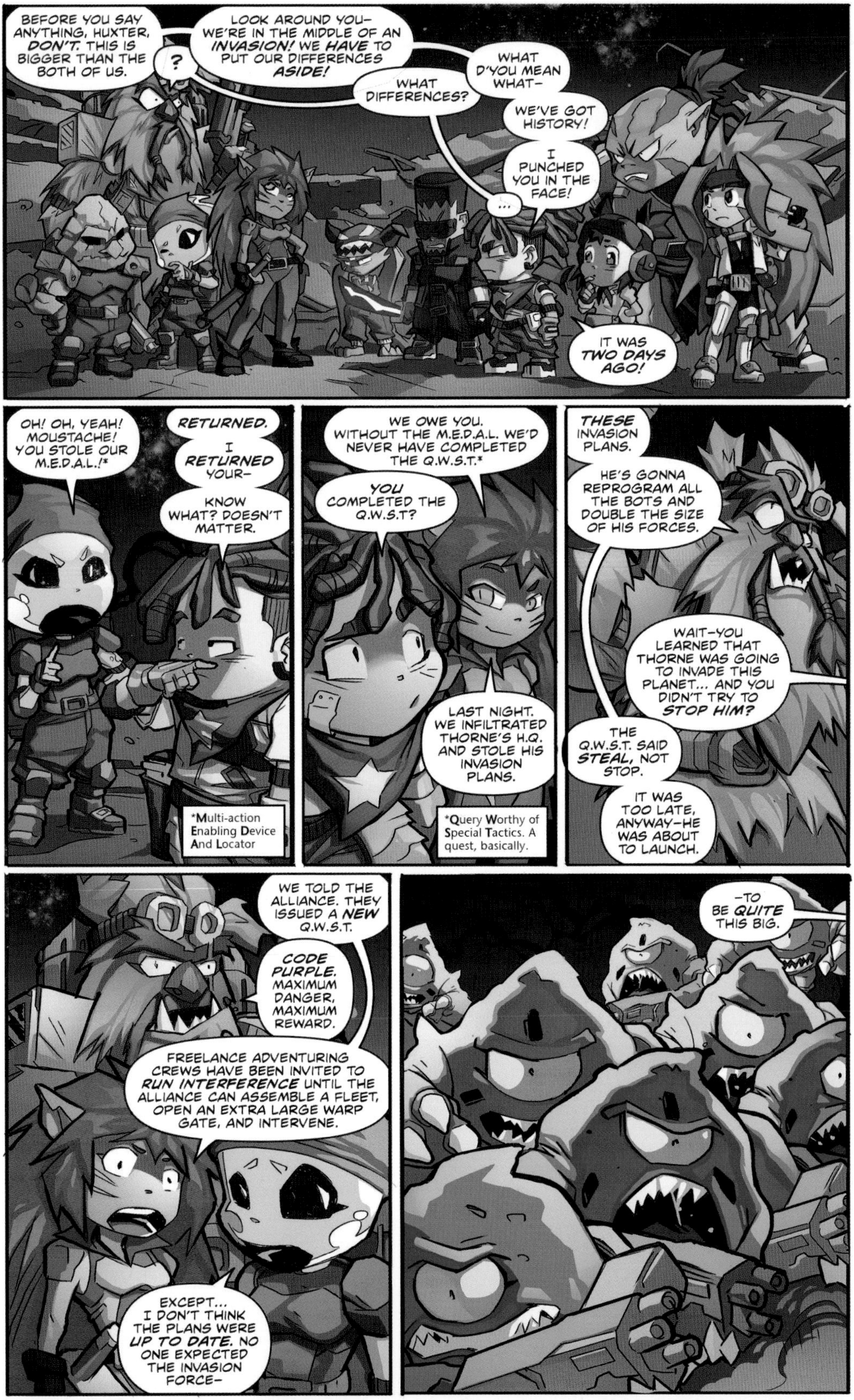

BEFORE YOU SAY ANYTHING, HUXTER, DON'T. THIS IS BIGGER THAN THE BOTH OF US.
?
LOOK AROUND YOU– WE'RE IN THE MIDDLE OF AN INVASION! WE HAVE TO PUT OUR DIFFERENCES ASIDE!
WHAT DIFFERENCES?
WHAT D'YOU MEAN WHAT–
WE'VE GOT HISTORY!
I PUNCHED YOU IN THE FACE!
...
IT WAS TWO DAYS AGO!
OH! OH, YEAH! MOUSTACHE! YOU STOLE OUR M.E.D.A.L.!*
RETURNED.
I RETURNED YOUR–
KNOW WHAT? DOESN'T MATTER.
*Multi-action Enabling Device And Locator
WE OWE YOU. WITHOUT THE M.E.D.A.L. WE'D NEVER HAVE COMPLETED THE Q.W.S.T.*
YOU COMPLETED THE Q.W.S.T?
LAST NIGHT. WE INFILTRATED THORNE'S H.Q. AND STOLE HIS INVASION PLANS.
*Query Worthy of Special Tactics. A quest, basically.
THESE INVASION PLANS.
HE'S GONNA REPROGRAM ALL THE BOTS AND DOUBLE THE SIZE OF HIS FORCES.
WAIT–YOU LEARNED THAT THORNE WAS GOING TO INVADE THIS PLANET... AND YOU DIDN'T TRY TO STOP HIM?
THE Q.W.S.T. SAID STEAL, NOT STOP.
IT WAS TOO LATE, ANYWAY–HE WAS ABOUT TO LAUNCH.
WE TOLD THE ALLIANCE. THEY ISSUED A NEW Q.W.S.T.
CODE PURPLE. MAXIMUM DANGER, MAXIMUM REWARD.
FREELANCE ADVENTURING CREWS HAVE BEEN INVITED TO RUN INTERFERENCE UNTIL THE ALLIANCE CAN ASSEMBLE A FLEET, OPEN AN EXTRA LARGE WARP GATE, AND INTERVENE.
EXCEPT... I DON'T THINK THE PLANS WERE UP TO DATE. NO ONE EXPECTED THE INVASION FORCE–
–TO BE QUITE THIS BIG.

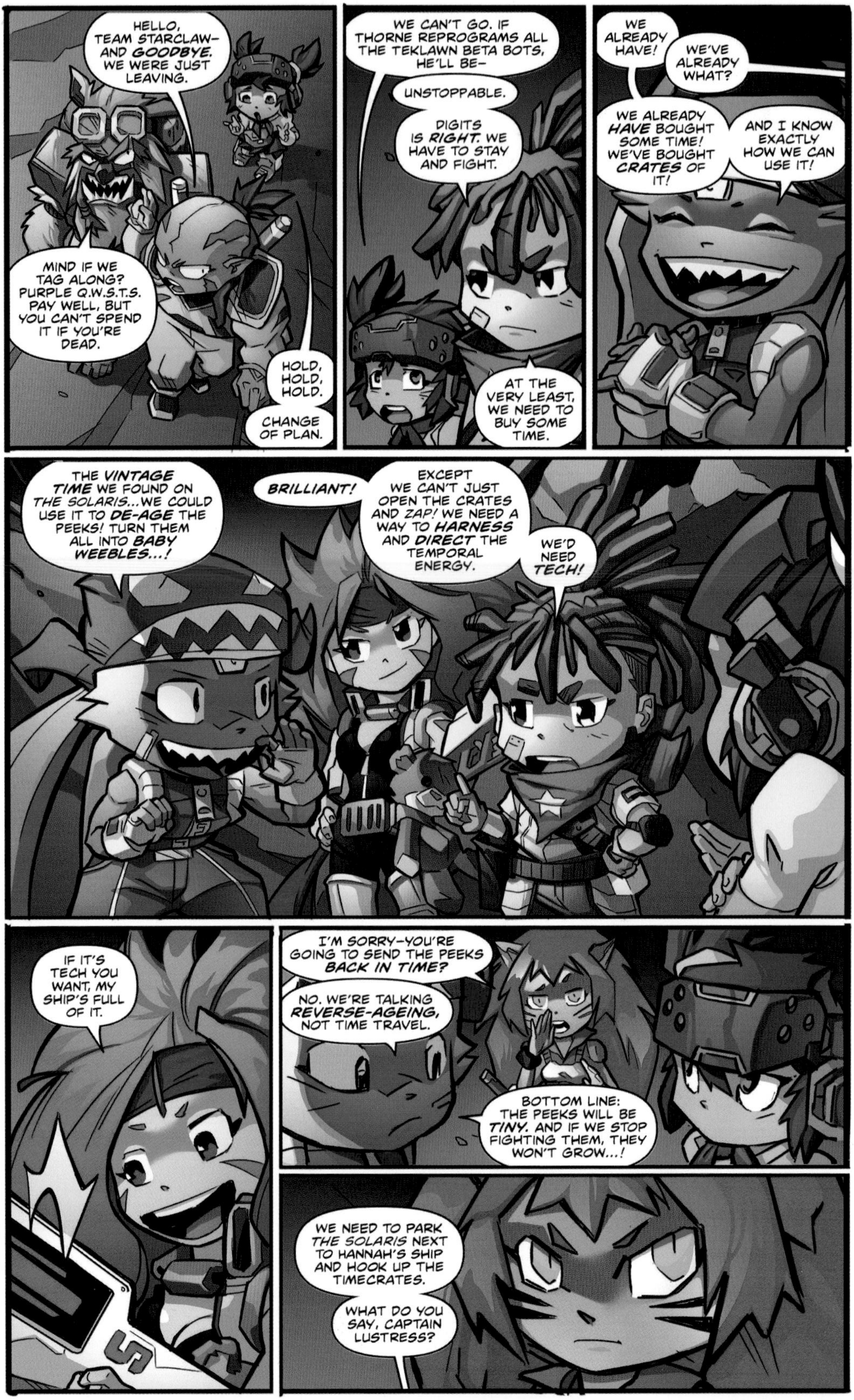
HELLO, TEAM STARCLAW– AND GOODBYE. WE WERE JUST LEAVING.
MIND IF WE TAG ALONG? PURPLE Q.W.S.T.S. PAY WELL, BUT YOU CAN'T SPEND IT IF YOU'RE DEAD.
HOLD, HOLD, HOLD.
CHANGE OF PLAN.
WE CAN'T GO. IF THORNE REPROGRAMS ALL THE TEKLAWN BETA BOTS, HE'LL BE–
UNSTOPPABLE.
DIGITS IS RIGHT. WE HAVE TO STAY AND FIGHT.
AT THE VERY LEAST, WE NEED TO BUY SOME TIME.
WE ALREADY HAVE!
WE'VE ALREADY WHAT?
WE ALREADY HAVE BOUGHT SOME TIME! WE'VE BOUGHT CRATES OF IT!
AND I KNOW EXACTLY HOW WE CAN USE IT!
THE VINTAGE TIME WE FOUND ON THE SOLARIS...WE COULD USE IT TO DE-AGE THE PEEKS! TURN THEM ALL INTO BABY WEEBLES...!
BRILLIANT!
EXCEPT WE CAN'T JUST OPEN THE CRATES AND ZAP! WE NEED A WAY TO HARNESS AND DIRECT THE TEMPORAL ENERGY.
WE'D NEED TECH!
IF IT'S TECH YOU WANT, MY SHIP'S FULL OF IT.
I'M SORRY–YOU'RE GOING TO SEND THE PEEKS BACK IN TIME?
NO. WE'RE TALKING REVERSE-AGEING, NOT TIME TRAVEL.
BOTTOM LINE: THE PEEKS WILL BE TINY. AND IF WE STOP FIGHTING THEM, THEY WON'T GROW...!
WE NEED TO PARK THE SOLARIS NEXT TO HANNAH'S SHIP AND HOOK UP THE TIMECRATES.
WHAT DO YOU SAY, CAPTAIN LUSTRESS?

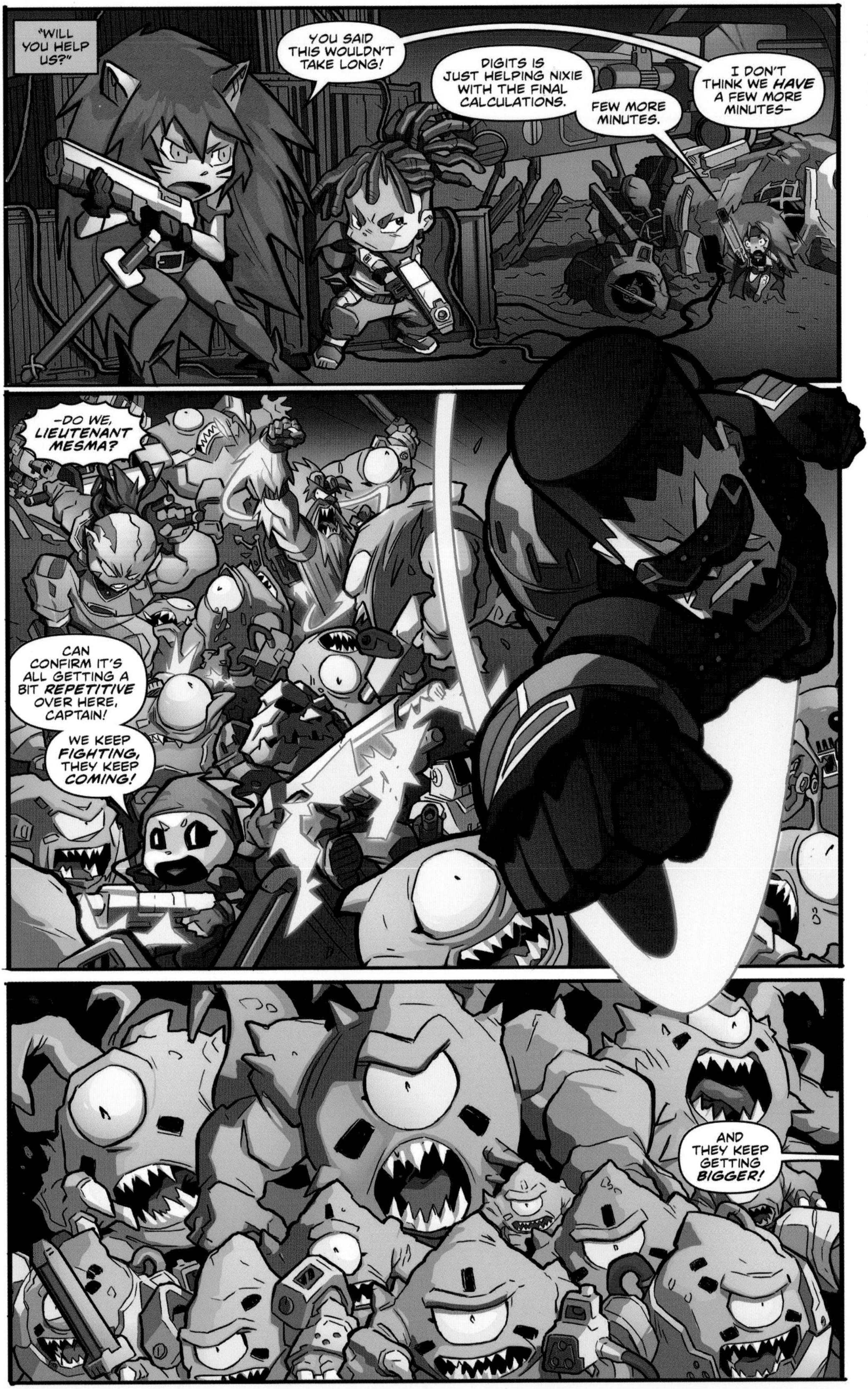
"WILL YOU HELP US?"
YOU SAID THIS WOULDN'T TAKE LONG!
DIGITS IS JUST HELPING NIXIE WITH THE FINAL CALCULATIONS.
FEW MORE MINUTES.
I DON'T THINK WE *HAVE* A FEW MORE MINUTES–
–DO WE, *LIEUTENANT MESMA?*
CAN CONFIRM IT'S ALL GETTING A BIT *REPETITIVE* OVER HERE, CAPTAIN!
WE KEEP *FIGHTING,* THEY KEEP *COMING!*
AND THEY KEEP GETTING *BIGGER!*

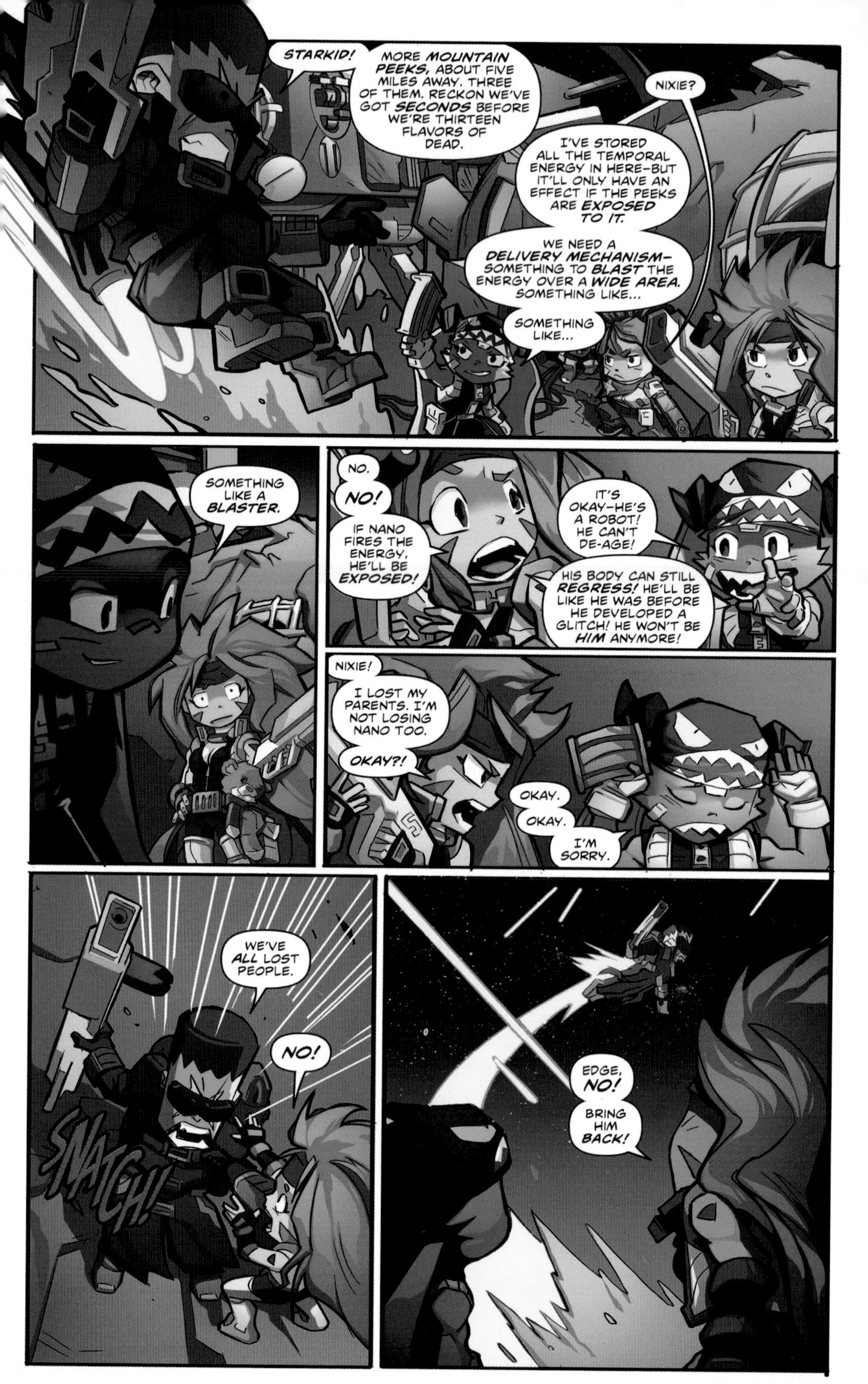
STARKID!
MORE MOUNTAIN PEEKS, ABOUT FIVE MILES AWAY. THREE OF THEM. RECKON WE'VE GOT SECONDS BEFORE WE'RE THIRTEEN FLAVORS OF DEAD.
NIXIE?
I'VE STORED ALL THE TEMPORAL ENERGY IN HERE—BUT IT'LL ONLY HAVE AN EFFECT IF THE PEEKS ARE EXPOSED TO IT.
WE NEED A DELIVERY MECHANISM—SOMETHING TO BLAST THE ENERGY OVER A WIDE AREA. SOMETHING LIKE...
SOMETHING LIKE...
SOMETHING LIKE A BLASTER.
NO.
NO!
IF NANO FIRES THE ENERGY, HE'LL BE EXPOSED!
IT'S OKAY—HE'S A ROBOT! HE CAN'T DE-AGE!
HIS BODY CAN STILL REGRESS! HE'LL BE LIKE HE WAS BEFORE HE DEVELOPED A GLITCH! HE WON'T BE HIM ANYMORE!
NIXIE!
I LOST MY PARENTS. I'M NOT LOSING NANO TOO.
OKAY?!
OKAY.
OKAY.
I'M SORRY.
WE'VE ALL LOST PEOPLE.
NO!
SNATCH!
EDGE, NO!
BRING HIM BACK!

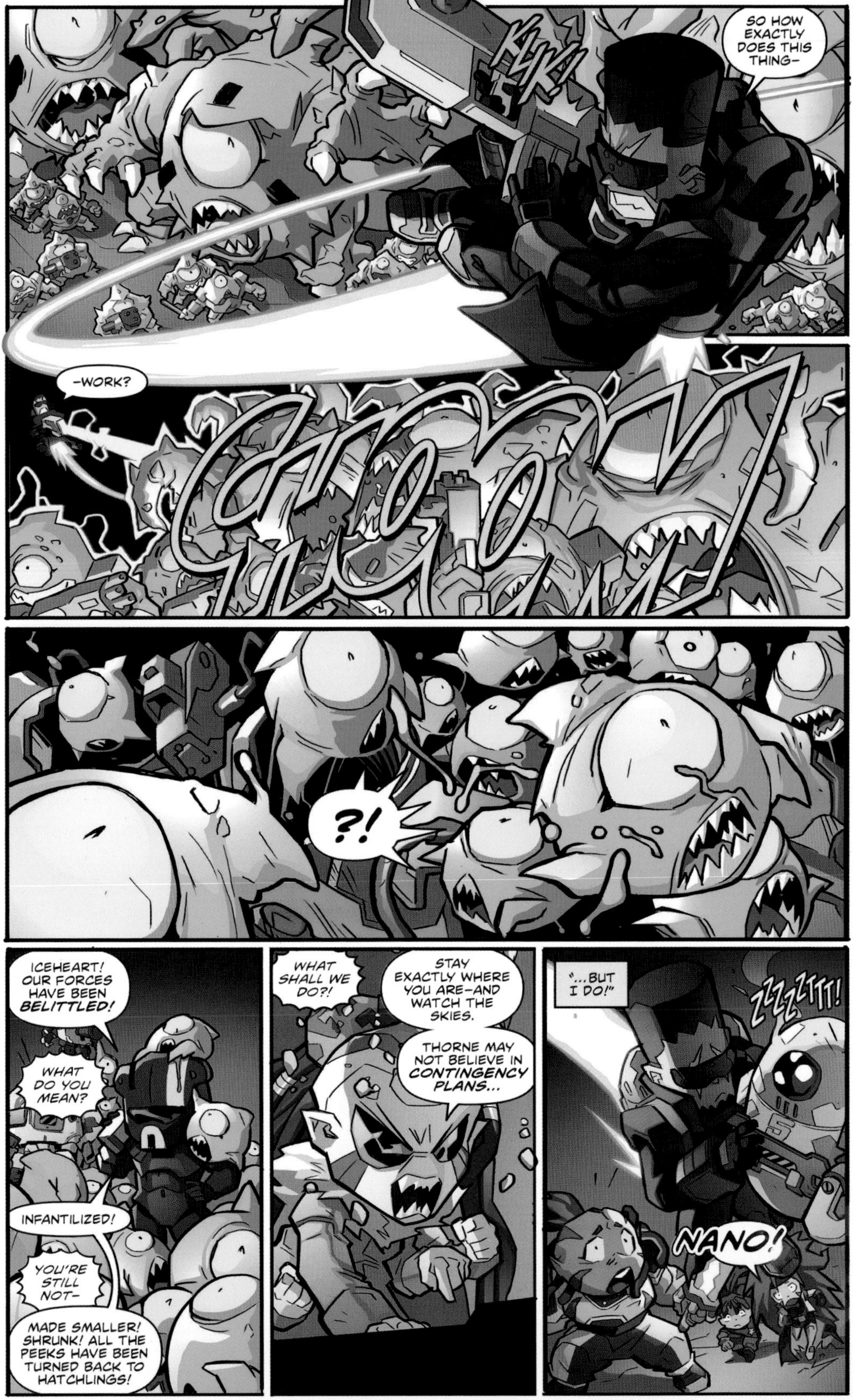
SO HOW EXACTLY DOES THIS THING–
–WORK?
?!
ICEHEART! OUR FORCES HAVE BEEN BELITTLED!
WHAT DO YOU MEAN?
INFANTILIZED!
YOU'RE STILL NOT–
MADE SMALLER! SHRUNK! ALL THE PEEKS HAVE BEEN TURNED BACK TO HATCHLINGS!
WHAT SHALL WE DO?!
STAY EXACTLY WHERE YOU ARE–AND WATCH THE SKIES.
THORNE MAY NOT BELIEVE IN CONTINGENCY PLANS...
"...BUT I DO!"
NANO!

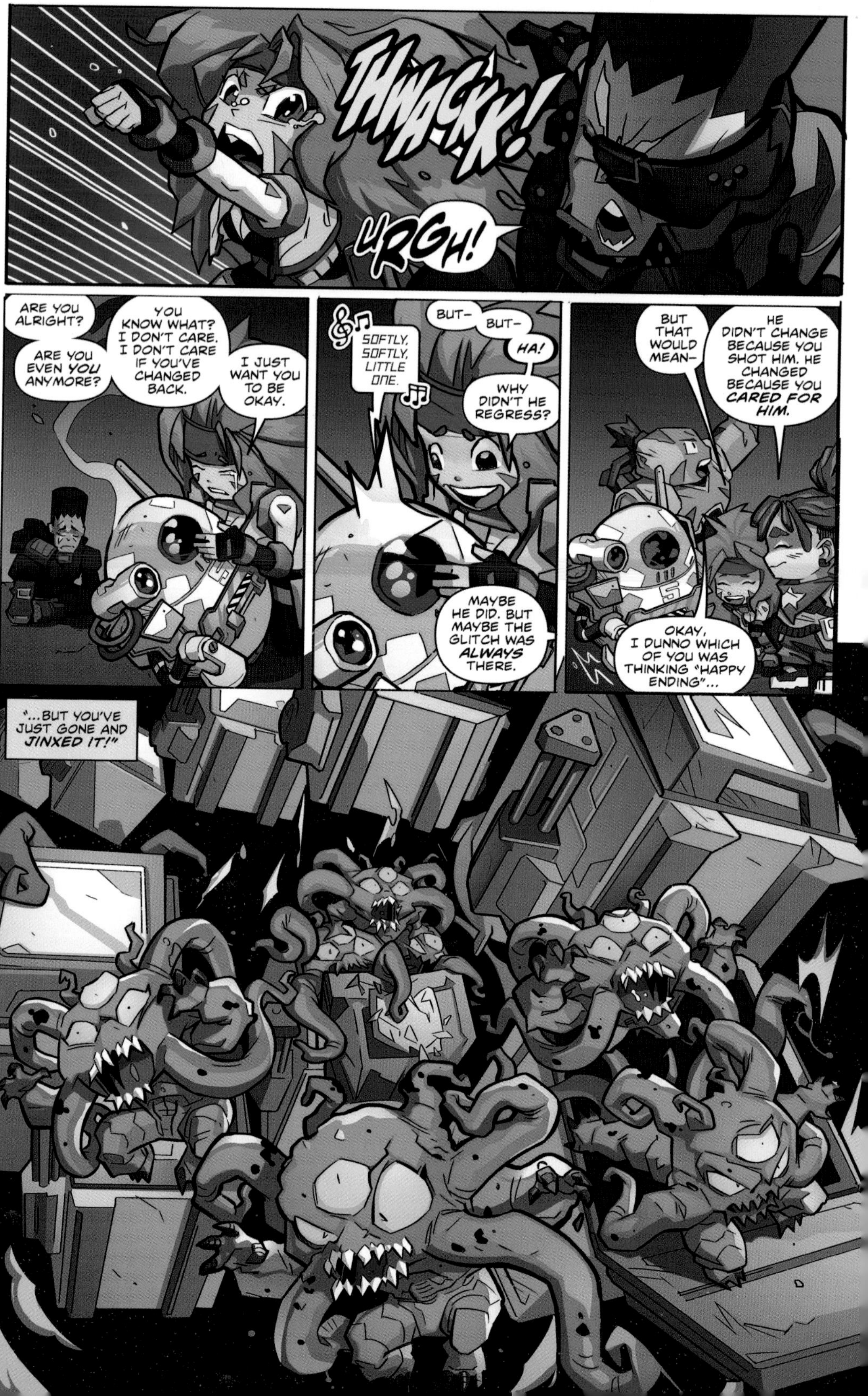
THWACKK!
URGH!
ARE YOU ALRIGHT?
ARE YOU EVEN YOU ANYMORE?
YOU KNOW WHAT? I DON'T CARE. I DON'T CARE IF YOU'VE CHANGED BACK.
I JUST WANT YOU TO BE OKAY.
SOFTLY, SOFTLY, LITTLE ONE.
BUT–
BUT–
HA!
WHY DIDN'T HE REGRESS?
MAYBE HE DID. BUT MAYBE THE GLITCH WAS ALWAYS THERE.
BUT THAT WOULD MEAN–
HE DIDN'T CHANGE BECAUSE YOU SHOT HIM. HE CHANGED BECAUSE YOU CARED FOR HIM.
OKAY, I DUNNO WHICH OF YOU WAS THINKING "HAPPY ENDING"...
"...BUT YOU'VE JUST GONE AND JINXED IT!"

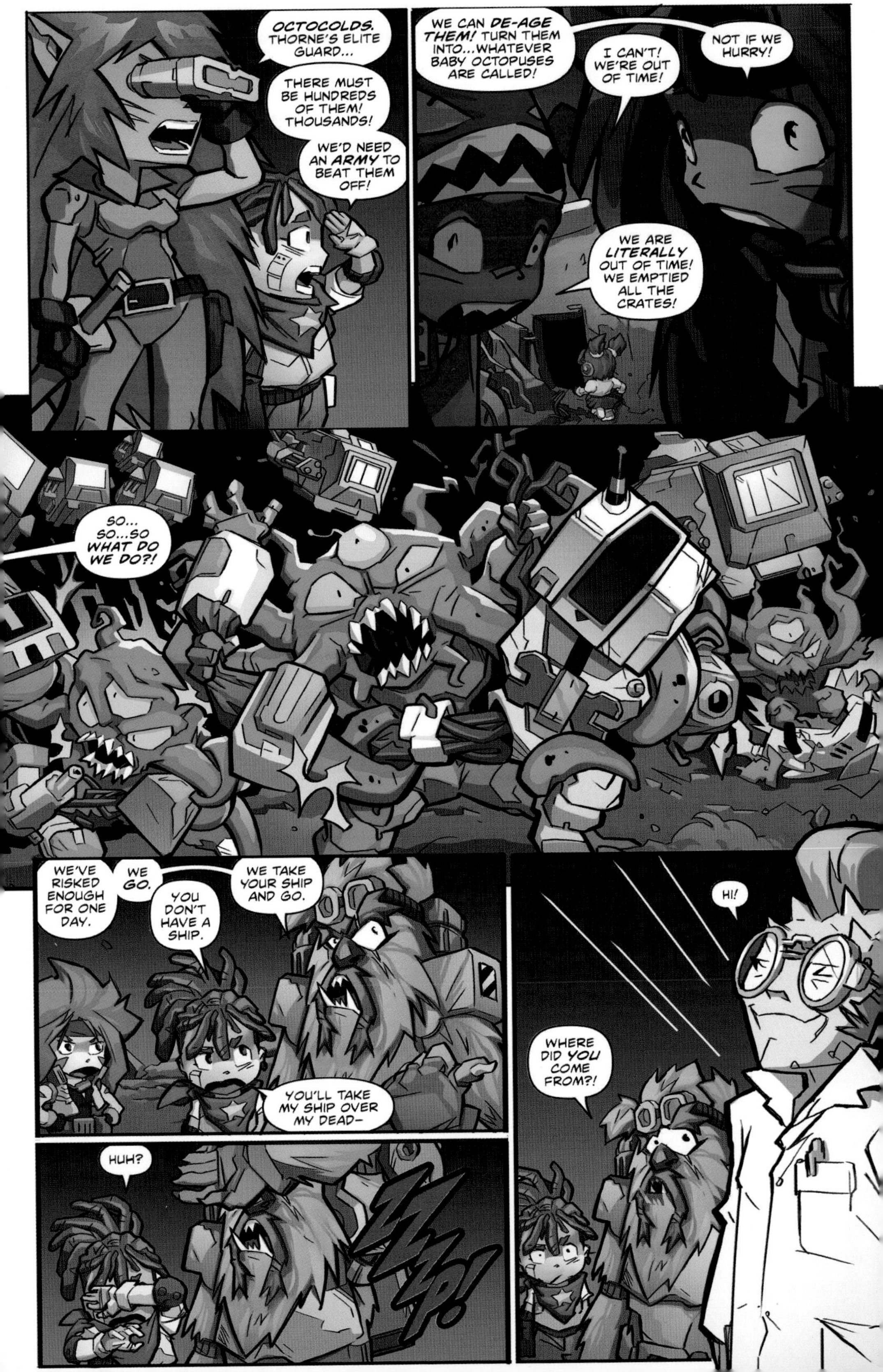
OCTOCOLDS. THORNE'S ELITE GUARD...
THERE MUST BE HUNDREDS OF THEM! THOUSANDS!
WE'D NEED AN ARMY TO BEAT THEM OFF!
WE CAN DE-AGE THEM! TURN THEM INTO...WHATEVER BABY OCTOPUSES ARE CALLED!
I CAN'T! WE'RE OUT OF TIME!
NOT IF WE HURRY!
WE ARE LITERALLY OUT OF TIME! WE EMPTIED ALL THE CRATES!
SO... SO...SO WHAT DO WE DO?!
WE'VE RISKED ENOUGH FOR ONE DAY.
WE GO.
WE TAKE YOUR SHIP AND GO.
YOU DON'T HAVE A SHIP.
YOU'LL TAKE MY SHIP OVER MY DEAD–
HUH?
ZWMP!
HI!
WHERE DID YOU COME FROM?!

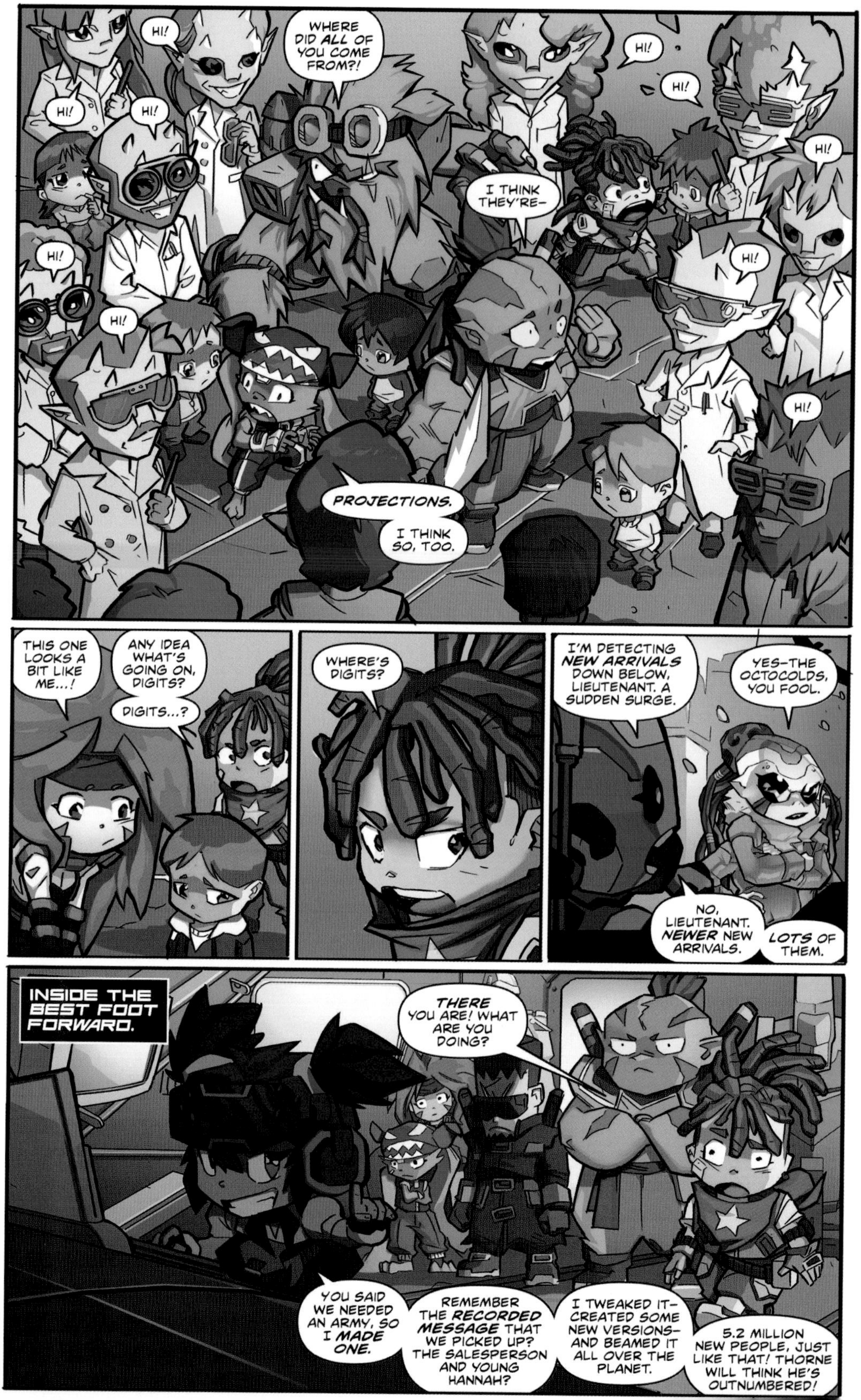
HI!
WHERE DID ALL OF YOU COME FROM?!
HI!
HI!
HI!
HI!
HI!
I THINK THEY'RE-
HI!
HI!
HI!
HI!
HI!
PROJECTIONS.
I THINK SO, TOO.
THIS ONE LOOKS A BIT LIKE ME...!
ANY IDEA WHAT'S GOING ON, DIGITS?
DIGITS...?
WHERE'S DIGITS?
I'M DETECTING NEW ARRIVALS DOWN BELOW, LIEUTENANT. A SUDDEN SURGE.
YES–THE OCTOCOLDS, YOU FOOL.
NO, LIEUTENANT. NEWER NEW ARRIVALS.
LOTS OF THEM.
INSIDE THE BEST FOOT FORWARD.
THERE YOU ARE! WHAT ARE YOU DOING?
YOU SAID WE NEEDED AN ARMY, SO I MADE ONE.
REMEMBER THE RECORDED MESSAGE THAT WE PICKED UP? THE SALESPERSON AND YOUNG HANNAH?
I TWEAKED IT– CREATED SOME NEW VERSIONS– AND BEAMED IT ALL OVER THE PLANET.
5.2 MILLION NEW PEOPLE, JUST LIKE THAT! THORNE WILL THINK HE'S OUTNUMBERED!

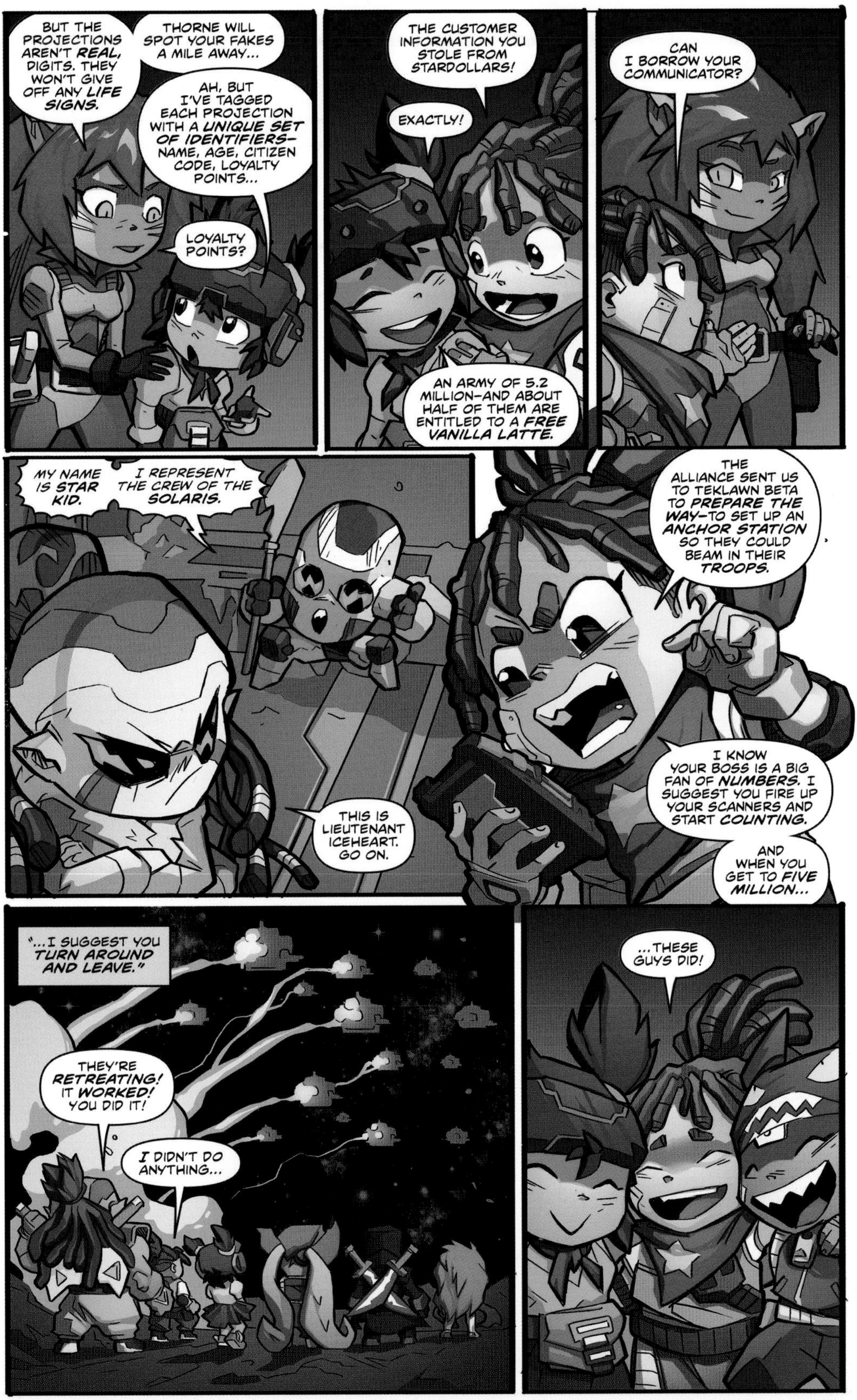

BUT THE PROJECTIONS AREN'T REAL, DIGITS. THEY WON'T GIVE OFF ANY LIFE SIGNS.
THORNE WILL SPOT YOUR FAKES A MILE AWAY...
AH, BUT I'VE TAGGED EACH PROJECTION WITH A UNIQUE SET OF IDENTIFIERS– NAME, AGE, CITIZEN CODE, LOYALTY POINTS...
LOYALTY POINTS?
THE CUSTOMER INFORMATION YOU STOLE FROM STARDOLLARS!
EXACTLY!
AN ARMY OF 5.2 MILLION–AND ABOUT HALF OF THEM ARE ENTITLED TO A FREE VANILLA LATTE.
CAN I BORROW YOUR COMMUNICATOR?
MY NAME IS STAR KID.
I REPRESENT THE CREW OF THE SOLARIS.
THE ALLIANCE SENT US TO TEKLAWN BETA TO PREPARE THE WAY–TO SET UP AN ANCHOR STATION SO THEY COULD BEAM IN THEIR TROOPS.
THIS IS LIEUTENANT ICEHEART. GO ON.
I KNOW YOUR BOSS IS A BIG FAN OF NUMBERS. I SUGGEST YOU FIRE UP YOUR SCANNERS AND START COUNTING.
AND WHEN YOU GET TO FIVE MILLION...
"...I SUGGEST YOU TURN AROUND AND LEAVE."
THEY'RE RETREATING! IT WORKED! YOU DID IT!
I DIDN'T DO ANYTHING...
...THESE GUYS DID!

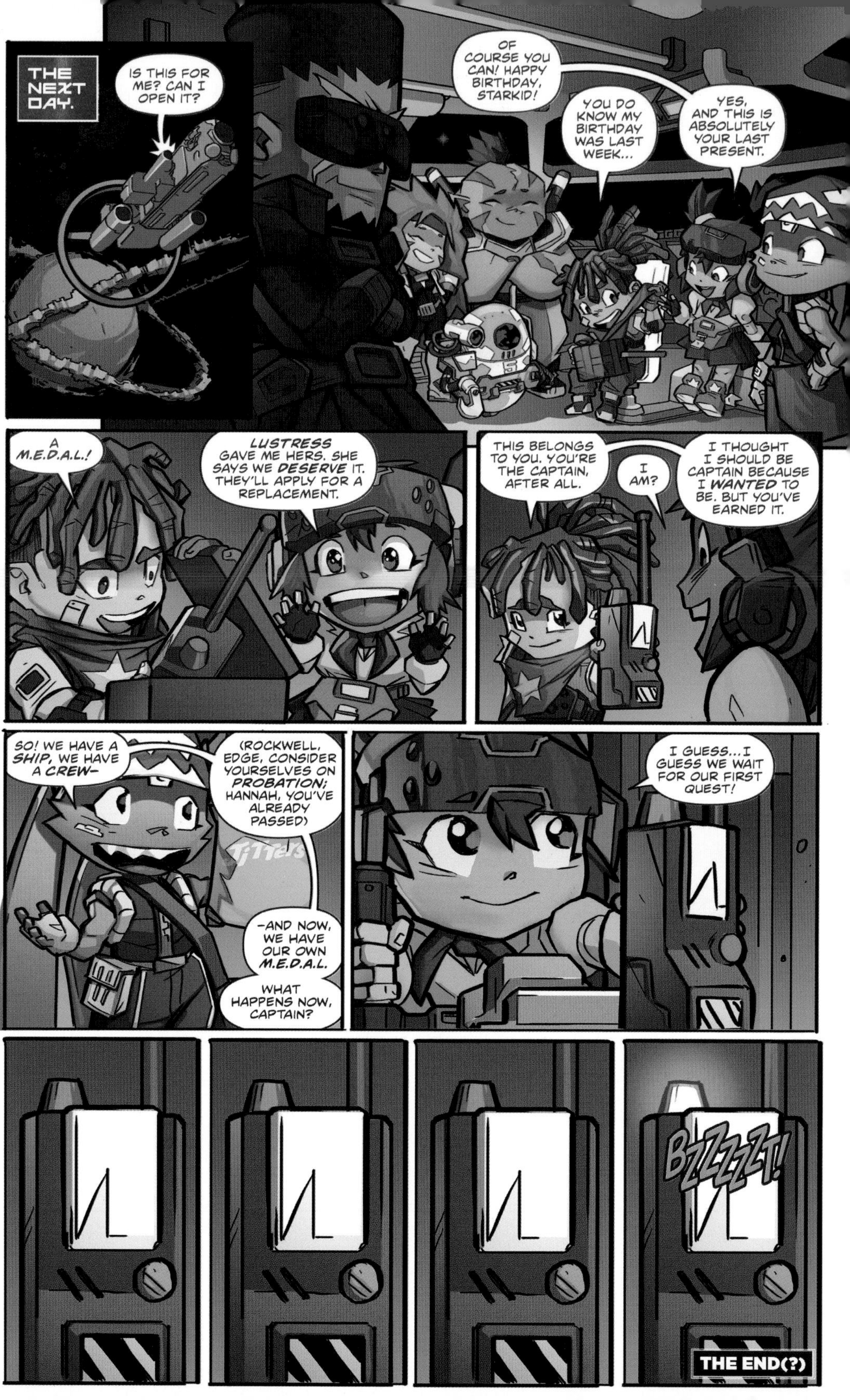
THE NEXT DAY.
IS THIS FOR ME? CAN I OPEN IT?
OF COURSE YOU CAN! HAPPY BIRTHDAY, STARKID!
YOU DO KNOW MY BIRTHDAY WAS LAST WEEK...
YES, AND THIS IS ABSOLUTELY YOUR LAST PRESENT.
A M.E.D.A.L.!
LUSTRESS GAVE ME HERS. SHE SAYS WE DESERVE IT. THEY'LL APPLY FOR A REPLACEMENT.
THIS BELONGS TO YOU. YOU'RE THE CAPTAIN, AFTER ALL.
I AM?
I THOUGHT I SHOULD BE CAPTAIN BECAUSE I WANTED TO BE. BUT YOU'VE EARNED IT.
SO! WE HAVE A SHIP, WE HAVE A CREW–
(ROCKWELL, EDGE, CONSIDER YOURSELVES ON PROBATION; HANNAH, YOU'VE ALREADY PASSED)
–AND NOW, WE HAVE OUR OWN M.E.D.A.L.
WHAT HAPPENS NOW, CAPTAIN?
I GUESS...I GUESS WE WAIT FOR OUR FIRST QUEST!
BZZZZZT!
THE END(?)

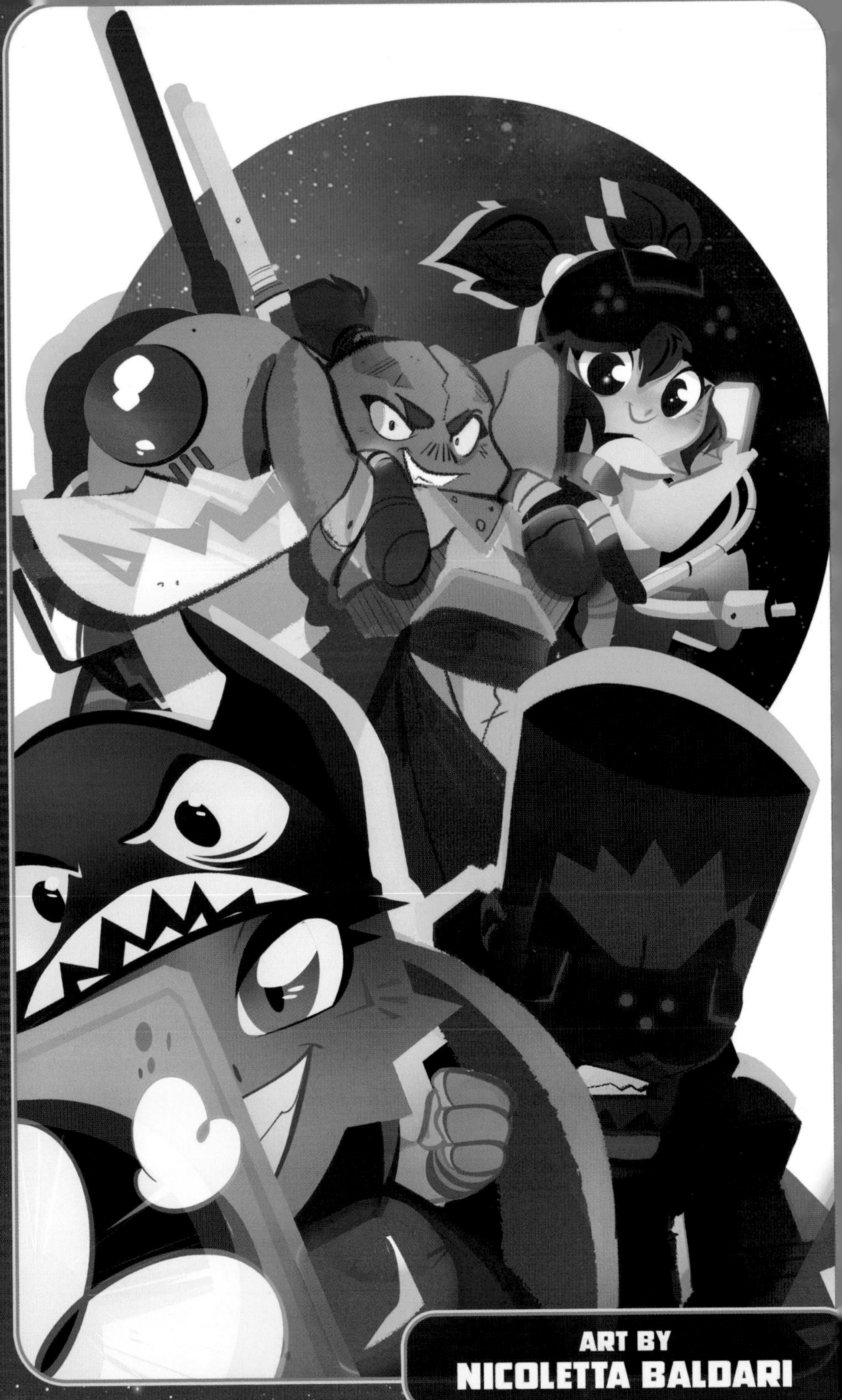

ART BY
NICOLETTA BALDARI

THE FOLLOWING PAGES FEATURE THREE
EXCLUSIVE STARCADIA QUEST GAME
SCENARIOS INSPIRED BY THE COMIC!

HAPPY BIRTHDAY, STARKID

SCENARIO 1 - SETUP

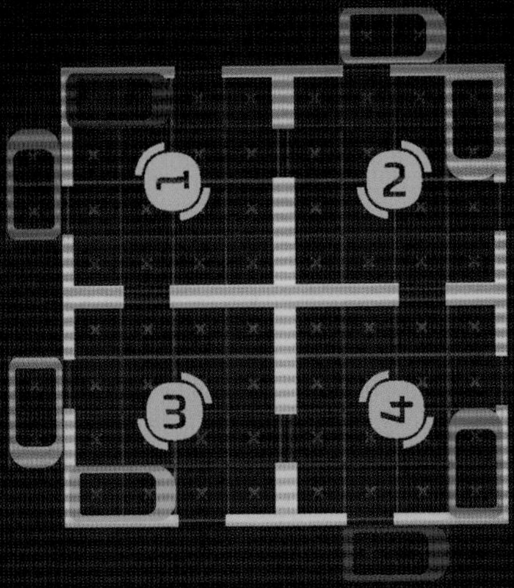

- Place 1 **Blue Quest token** ⬤ on each **Computer Terminal** in Tiles 1, 2, 3 and 4, these tokens are **Data Guardians.**

▷ SPECIAL RULE

Players can choose the starting position of their Shuttle, corresponding to their Crew's colors.

HAPPY BIRTHDAY, STARKID

SCENARIO 1 - SETUP

MONSTER SETUP

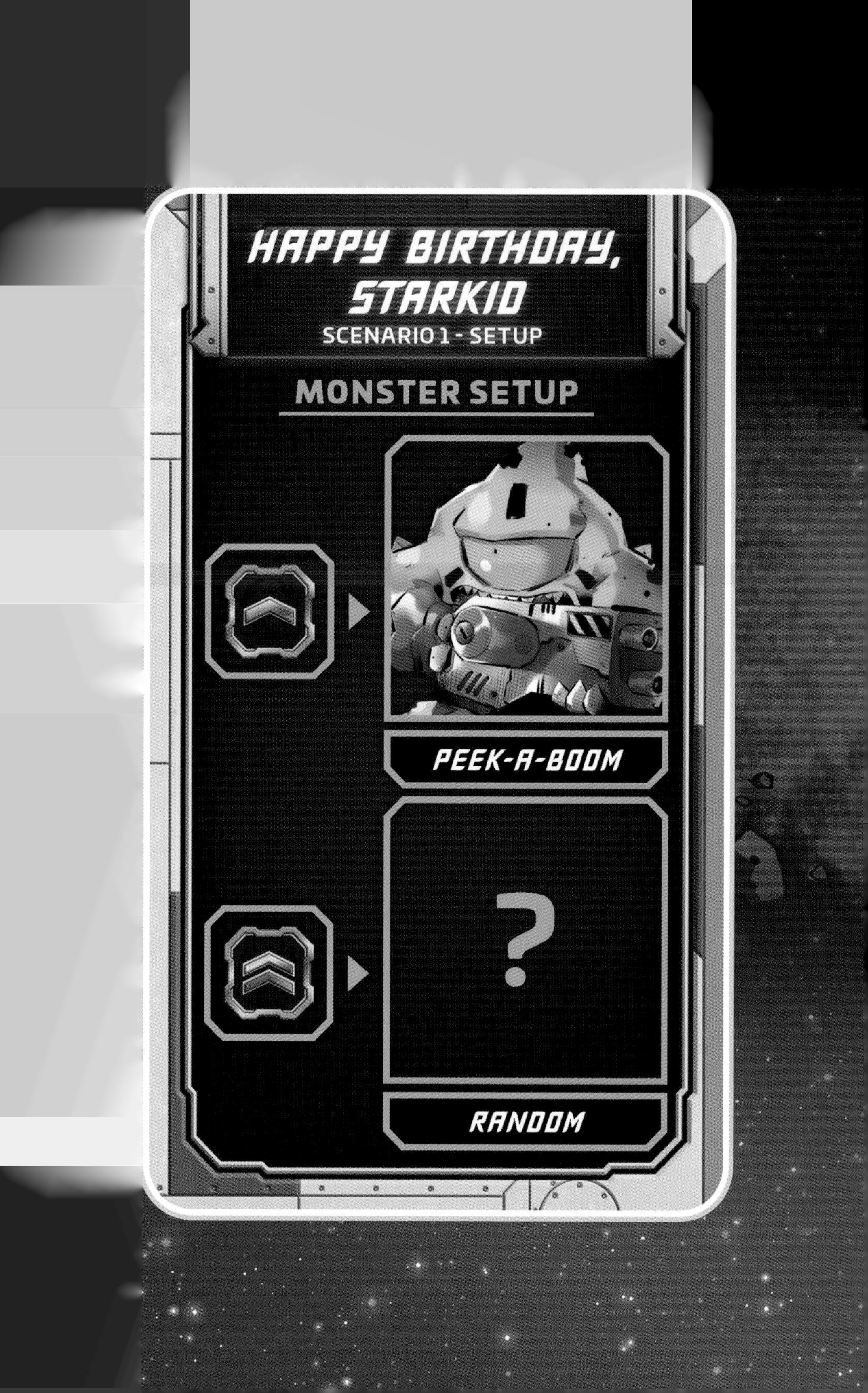

PEEK-A-BOOM

?

RANDOM

HAPPY BIRTHDAY, STARKID

SCENARIO 1

- QUEST 1 -
DELAY DATA GUARDIANS

(PVE QUEST)

- **Blue Quest tokens** 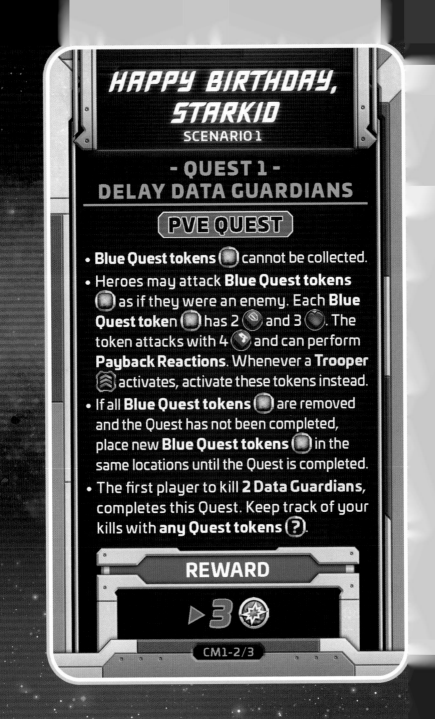 cannot be collected.

- Heroes may attack **Blue Quest tokens** as if they were an enemy. Each **Blue Quest token** has 2 and 3 . The token attacks with 4 and can perform **Payback Reactions**. Whenever a **Trooper** activates, activate these tokens instead.

- If all **Blue Quest tokens** are removed and the Quest has not been completed, place new **Blue Quest tokens** in the same locations until the Quest is completed.

- The first player to kill **2 Data Guardians**, completes this Quest. Keep track of your kills with **any Quest tokens** (?).

REWARD

▶ 3 ✦

CM1-2/3

HAPPY BIRTHDAY, STARKID

SCENARIO 1

- QUEST 2 -
ESCAPE TO SOLARIS

PVE QUEST

• The first player to end activation of both their Heroes on their Crew's Shuttle completes this Quest.

REWARD

▷ 4 ✦

CM1-3/3

TO TEKLAWN
SCENARIO 2 - SETUP

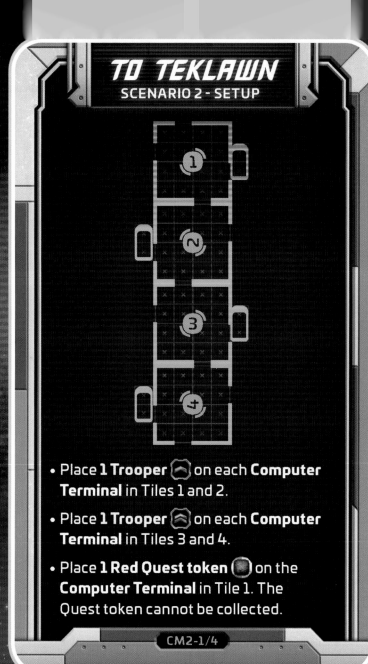

- Place **1 Trooper** 🛡 on each **Computer Terminal** in Tiles 1 and 2.

- Place **1 Trooper** 🛡 on each **Computer Terminal** in Tiles 3 and 4.

- Place **1 Red Quest token** 🔴 on the **Computer Terminal** in Tile 1. The Quest token cannot be collected.

TO TEKLAWN
SCENARIO 2

MONSTER SETUP

?

RANDOM

?

RANDOM

?

RANDOM

TO TEKLAWN
SCENARIO 2

- QUEST 1 -
CLEAR OUT THE SHIP

PVE QUEST

- The first player to kill **2 Troopers**, completes this Quest. Keep track of your kills with any **Quest tokens** (?).

REWARD

▶ 4 ✦

CM2-2/4

TO TEKLAWN
SCENARIO 2

- QUEST 2 -
ASSUME COMMAND

PVE QUEST

- The first player to kill **1 Hero of each Crew** completes this Quest. Heroes killed before this Quest was active do not count towards the objective.

REWARD

▶ 5 ✦

CM2-3/4

TO TEKLAWN
SCENARIO 2

- QUEST 3 -
SET A COURSE

PVE QUEST

- The first player to end the activation of both their Heroes on the Space containing the **Red Quest token** 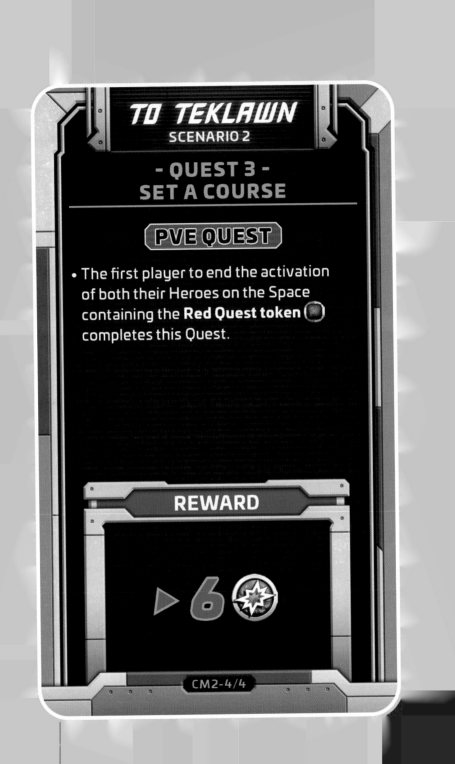 completes this Quest.

REWARD

▶ 6 ✦

CM2-4/4

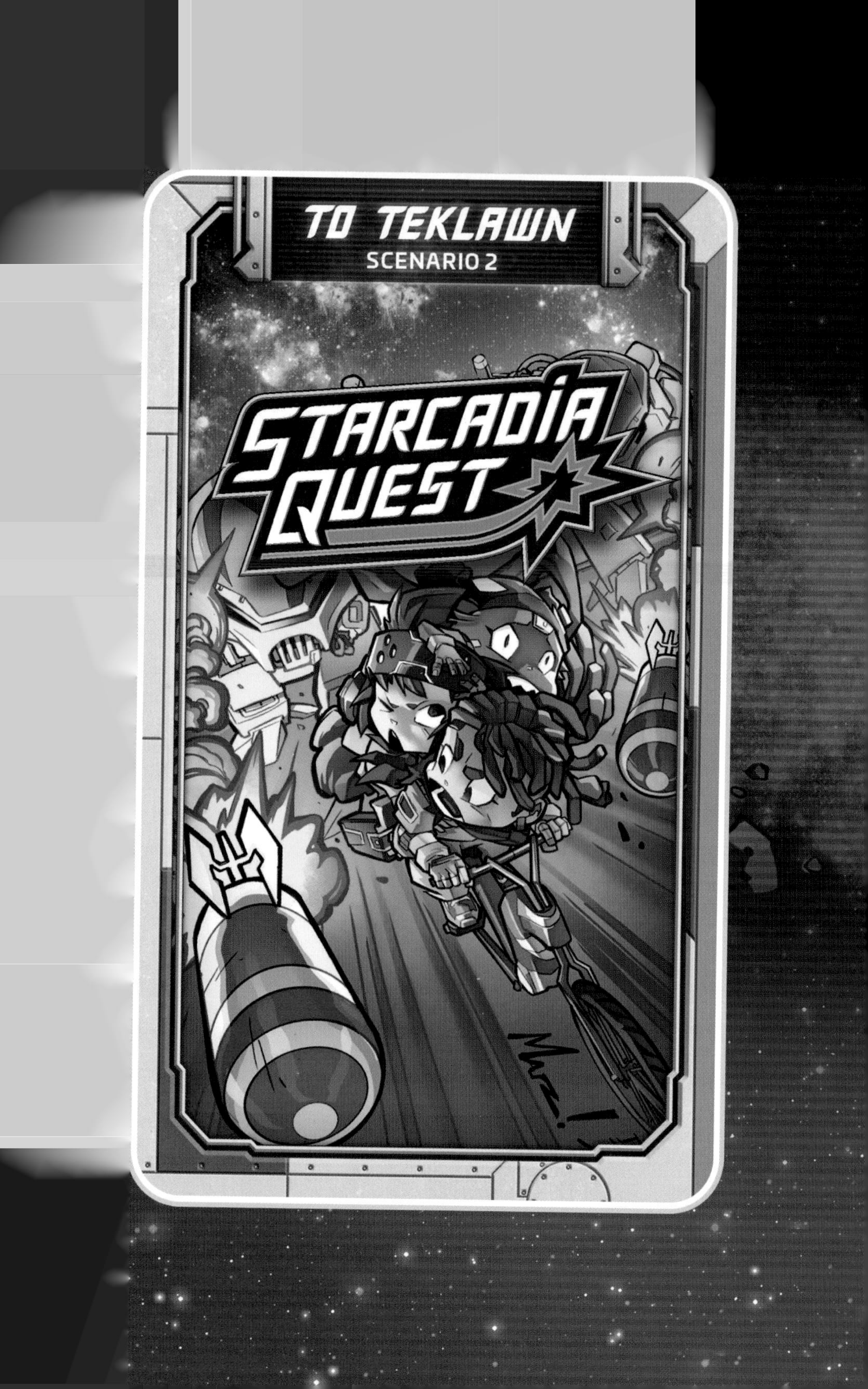
TO TEKLAWN
SCENARIO 2
STARCADIA QUEST

THE THORNE OFFENSIVE

SCENARIO 3 - SETUP

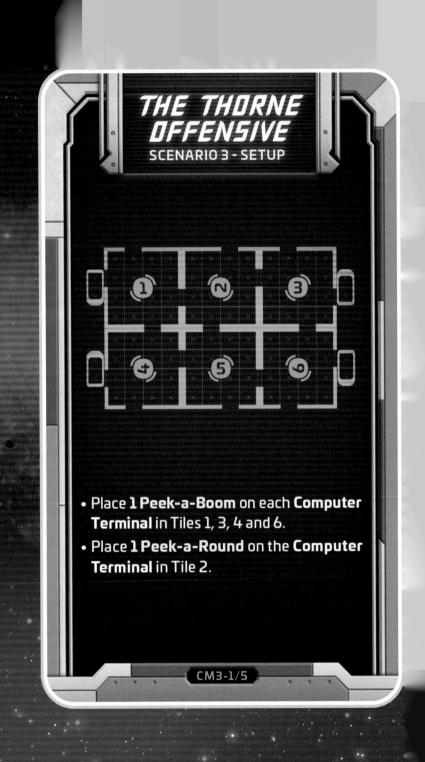

- Place **1 Peek-a-Boom** on each **Computer Terminal** in Tiles 1, 3, 4 and 6.
- Place **1 Peek-a-Round** on the **Computer Terminal** in Tile 2.

CM3-1/5

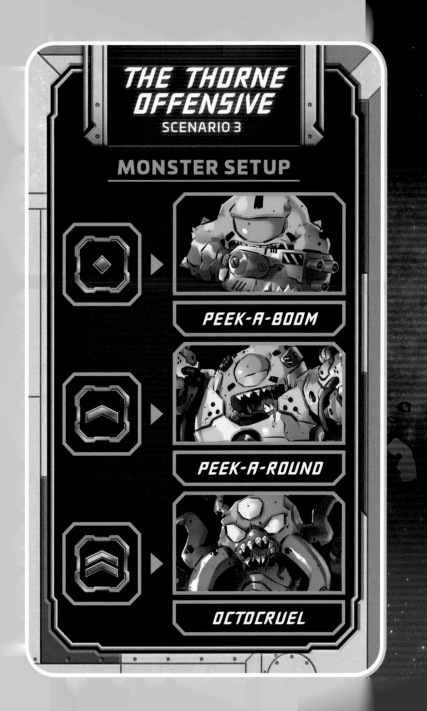

THE THORNE OFFENSIVE
SCENARIO 3

MONSTER SETUP

PEEK-A-BOOM

PEEK-A-ROUND

OCTOCRUEL

THE THORNE OFFENSIVE
SCENARIO 3

- QUEST 1 -
KEEP PEEKS AT BAY

PVE QUEST

- The first player to kill any combination of **3 Peek-a-Booms and Peek-a-Rounds** completes this Quest. Keep track of your kills with **any Quest tokens** .

REWARD

▶ 4 ✦

CM3-2/5

THE THORNE OFFENSIVE

SCENARIO 3

- QUEST 2 -
DE-AGE THE PEEKS

PVE QUEST

- The first player to end the activation of a Hero on the **Computer Terminal** without any Close enemies in Tile 2 completes this Quest.

REWARD

► 5

THE THORNE OFFENSIVE

SCENARIO 3

- SETUP -

- Remove all **Peek-a-Booms and Peek-a-Rounds** from the map.
- Place **1 Octocruel** on the **Computer Terminal** in Tile 5.

- QUEST 3 -
STOP OCTOCRUEL

PVE QUEST

- The first player to kill **1 Octocruel** completes this Quest.

REWARD

▶ 4 ✦

CM3-4/5

THE THORNE OFFENSIVE
SCENARIO 3

- QUEST 4 -
HOLOGRAM ARMY BLUFF

PVE QUEST

- The first player to end the activation of both their Heroes on the **Computer Terminal** in Tile 5 completes this Quest.

REWARD

▶ 6 ✦

CM3-5/5

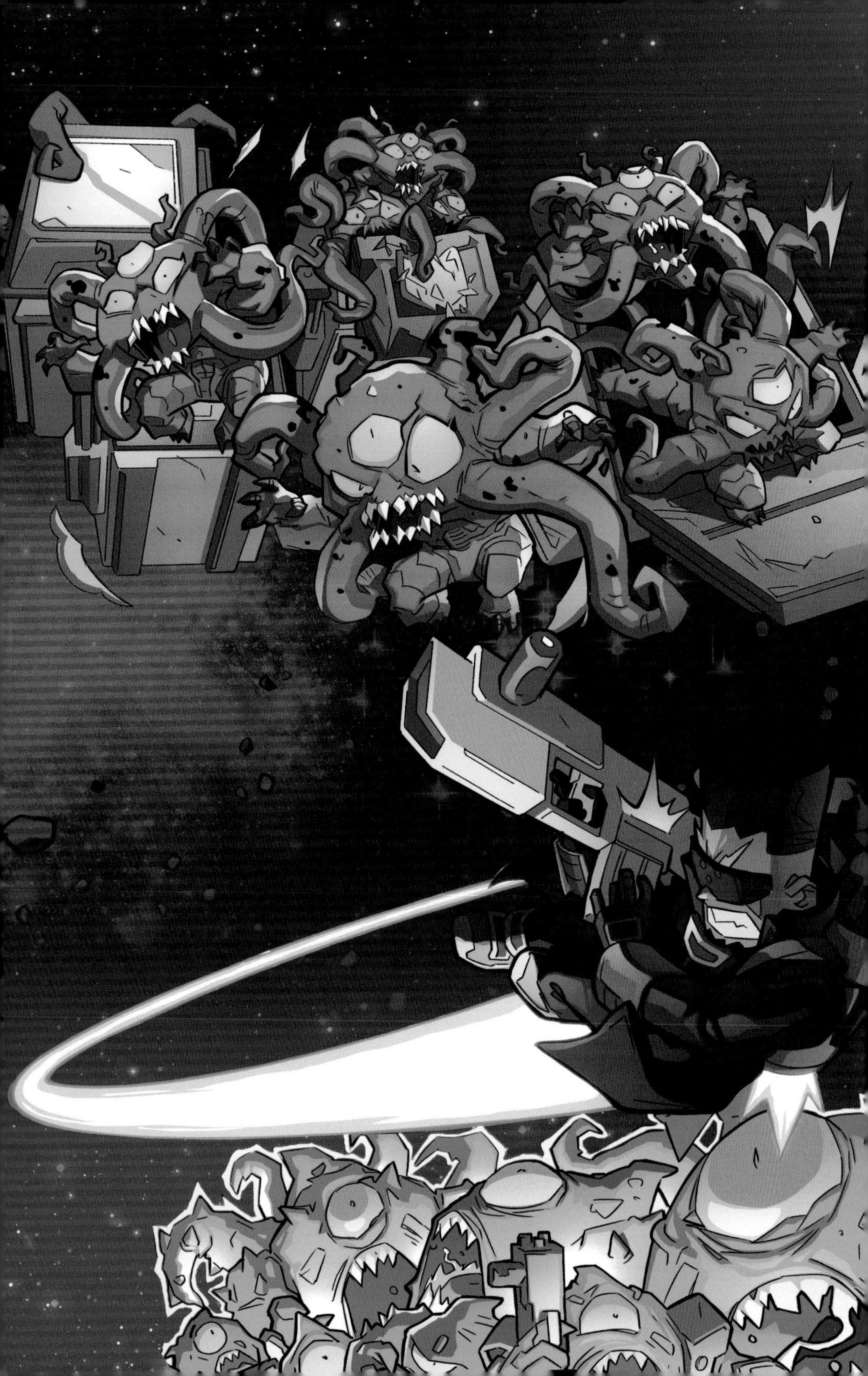